The Realms of Beliar
Book 1 Volume 2

A Beginning and an End

The photography is the sole work of Fi Shuttleworth, who has also taken the rôle of the Priest of Rhiannon.

The line drawings, maps and all other artwork are the sole work of Carol Arrowsmith.

The Photoshop work (All Gods bless you, Adobe) is my responsibility alone, however, so blame me solely for any reduction in the quality of these ladies' work perpetrated thereby.

Thanks and plaudits are due to Nicola Mackin FRAS of Asys Publishing for consultancy, kindness, compendious knowledge and technical expertise - without which, in all probability, nothing useful would have got done.

Several people have pointed out quite properly that while the rites I describe would seem to be intended to be Druidic, in fact they are not from that tradition in any significant element. I cheerfully admit it. They were intended to give the atmosphere of work in a quite different tradition without revealing, well, anything about it really.

Please note: Book 1 Volumes 1 and 2 have together been published previously in one volume by Penumbra in paperback as *The Realms of Beliar: Book 1 The Sword Myndarit*. These present two volumes represent a new edition that has been revised extensively, extended and illustrated. Book 2 and the matter ensuing are entirely new work.

My thanks to Messrs. Miles Evans, David Randle and others for feeding the creative juices with many extensive conversations about a world and its people. The final result is entirely my fault, of course, and they are not to be blamed.

 *Andrew Arrowsmith*

Rigantona : The

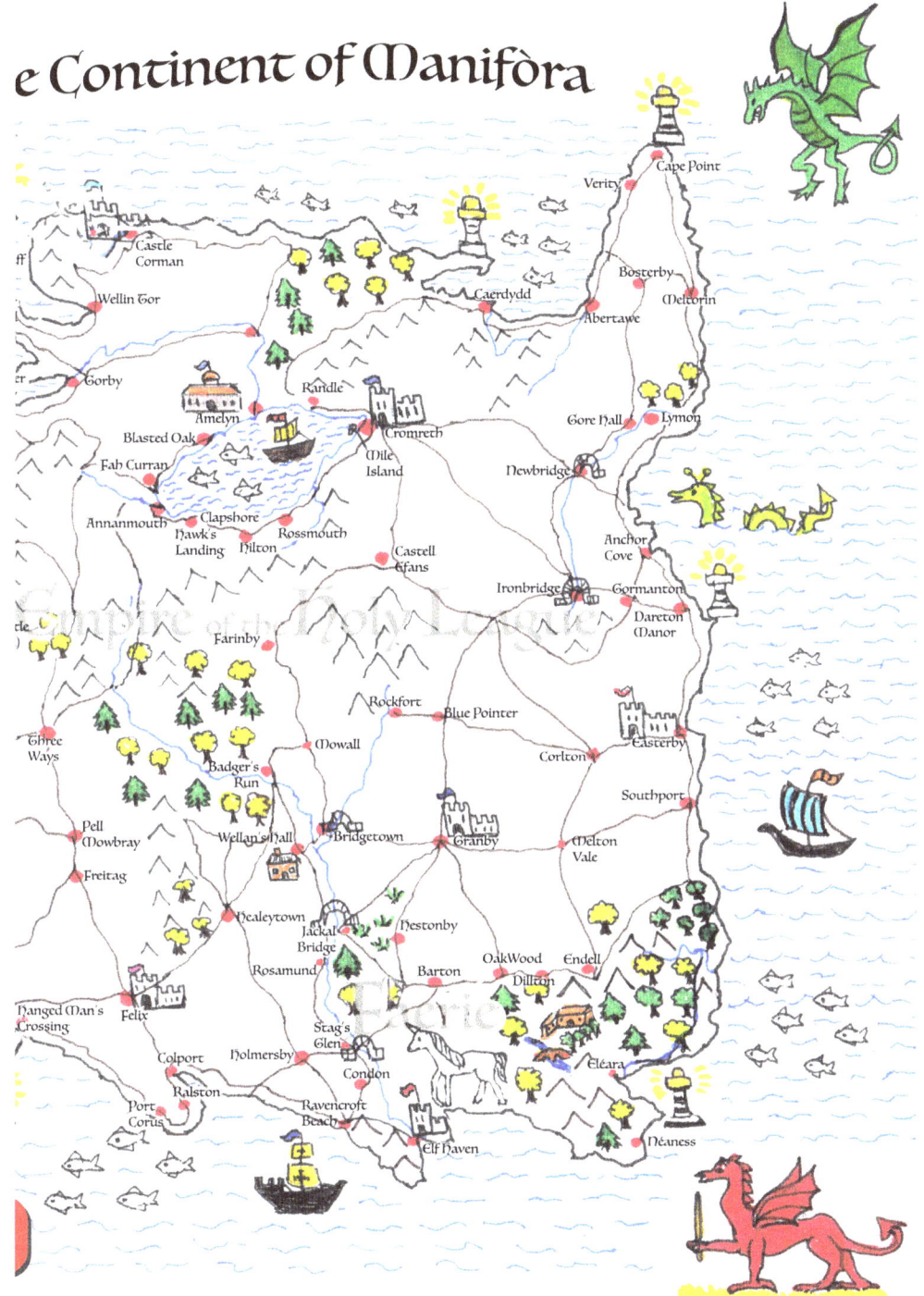

e Continent of Manifòra

Castle Corman
Wellin Tor
Gorby
Amelyn
Blasted Oak
Fah Curran
Annanmouth
Hawk's Landing
Clapshore
Hilton
Rossmouth
Randle
Cromreth
Mile Island
Castell Efans
Farinby
Rockfort
Blue Pointer
Mowall
Three Ways
Badger's Run
Wellan's Hall
Bridgetown
Granby
Pell Mowbray
Freitag
Healeytown
Jackal Bridge
Rosamund
Nestonby
Barton
OakWood
Endell
Dillton
Hanged Man's Crossing
Felix
Colport
Holmersby
Stag's Glen
Condon
Ravencroft Beach
Elf Haven
Eléara
Néaness
Port Corus
Ralston
Verity
Cape Point
Bosterby
Caerdydd
Meltorin
Abertawe
Gore Hall
Lymon
Newbridge
Anchor Cove
Ironbridge
Gormanton
Dareton Manor
Easterby
Corlton
Southport
Melton Vale

Empire of the Holy League

ISBN 978-1-9999538-2-9

FOREWORD
The Sword Myndarit on the Way of Things

This work has now stretched to several books. I have placed this foreword at the front of each, so that if someone happens to pick up the wrong one first they have some kind of chance of understanding what's going on.

I'm fairly sure that this is a mistake anyway. After all, do you people really want to be told that you've drawn the cosmic short straw and are eking out your existence at the scrag end of Creation? How do you fancy learning that the bottom-of-the-pile universe you live in is so intrinsically deprived that if a particularly kindly deity hadn't fiddled with some physics for you the place wouldn't be habitable at all? Or that nobody knows how long His cosmic string-and-sticky-tape fix will hold together? No? I rest my case.

However, what do I know? Well, nearly everything actually, as you may learn as we go along, but does that mean anybody ever takes the slightest interest in my opinions? No. Nobody's interested at all – they just want me to trot out the facts, because I'm the one who has them all at my fingertips. Well, I would have, if I had fingers.

It's one of the real problems with being a sword – people just don't take you seriously as a creative artist. Even when you are the greatest masterwork of a god. The other problem, of course, is that you've got to take over some fool's mind before you can get anything written. It's not really fair – even the stupidest, least creative people have hands. Me? No. I'm dependent on Joe Soap.

Well, you don't want to read me banging on about my troubles. I've been told to produce an edition for this Plane, so I have, and I hope it makes some kind of sense to you. However, if there's to be any hope of that, there are some things you need to know, and lots more things you might want to. I've put all the things you absolutely need to know in this Foreword, and some stuff you might like to know in a set of appendices at the back of Volume 2, and some more on the – what's it called? Oh yes, the *Website*.

Oh yes. That's something else, isn't it? If you read the appendices, you may be upset to discover that a lot of the problems you've had down there over the last fifty thousand years or so are actually the result of the Gods of Creation dumping on you an assortment of vicious and highly undesirable deities nobody wanted in more salubrious universes – and then sending shades of very nearly equally undesirable gods to keep them under some kind of control. It's not gone well, altogether – but then you know that better than I do.

What I wanted to say is don't take it personally. They do realise they've made a mess of things down at your end and they're migrating people out into the proper universes as fast as they can. There are now only a few tens of thousands of inhabited planets to go. Another few thousand years, and it'll be done. Of course you're on Earth – that'll be the last because it's the connection point.

So here are the things you really need to know. First, your universe isn't the only one. Far from it – there are nine physical universes: we call them the Prime Material Planes. We think of them as being stacked one on top of another – though of course they're not, really. Only the gods know how the thing actually works, and by no means all of *them* do. But we look at it that way because from Plane Nine – the 'top' one – you can only reach Plane Eight. From there you go 'down' to Plane Seven or back 'up' to Plane Nine. And so on down to Plane One, from which you can only reach Plane Two of course. Plane One is you. Explains a lot, I expect.

Now, if I tell you that everything useful and important happens on Plane Nine, at the top, well, you might start to understand your problem. Most particularly, the universes should work on magic – that's how they were designed. But the means of releasing and manipulating magic all happen on Plane Nine. So there's a little less on Eight, slightly less still on Seven... You get the idea. You people are all sucking the hind one. If you want to understand it better, read the Appendices. You won't like it, I'm telling you now.

So Brandur – you won't have heard of Him, He's only the most important entity in the entirety of Creation – adjusted some physics for you, so that you'd have some way of keeping warm and making things work. But here's the point: the rest of Creation isn't like that. Most importantly – everywhere else, when vegetation rots in the soil, it becomes steadily less flammable. So coal, in most Universes, burns about as well as granite. Oil? Well, there are a few fractions that will burn if given a good hot nudge – but on the whole, it can safely be used as flame retardant.

There was something else … what was it? Oh, yes. You've got some simple processes to make things go bang, haven't you? Salt petre and faeces, or something – Brandur's little joke. Doesn't work elsewhere. It's possible to make stuff that goes bang chemically, with a lot of effort and risk – but why would anybody bother with that when you can buy a fireball spell, or whatever, on a scroll?

So anyway, in these books I have tried to tell the story of some very important events in the history of all the Universes, which are even important to you people camping in the basement. I've done my best with it because they were so important – and because there were some people involved who deserved to have their stories told, to be honest. And nobody else could do it.

But when you read the story, what you have to envisage is a society where, for the last umpteen thousand years, all the bright boys and girls, all the genius researchers and all the most able technicians and engineers have gravitated into working with magic. People understand how the Universe works as well as you do – better, actually – but they've never needed to play parlour tricks with it to keep warm at night or earn a living. Magic does all that for them. It makes for a very different kind of world – it'll look primitive to you, at first. No electricity, no internal combustion engines, no explosive weapons. Don't be fooled – they can do more than you can.

The year I start at would work out at about 2260 Anno Domini in your reckoning. Do you still use that? Yes, that's the future, for you. And your point is? The universes' timelines don't exactly correspond. It's an interesting effect, but not particularly significant.

Well, that's all I wanted to say. How do you finish these things? I've never done one before. Look, there's a glossary of useful terms in the back of this volume. Have a look at that if you like, or refer to it when you want to know more about something I mention. Otherwise, I suggest you just turn the page and get on with it.

Myndarit the Wise

The World is called Rigantona

The name is a mutation of an old Elven word roughly meaning "a place to stand on" so it just about makes some kind of sense. It resembles Earth in many ways, though the physics are a little different here and there - for this is not just a different world, it is on a different Plane of existence.

There has been a link between Earth's Plane and this one, off and on, for hundreds of thousands of years and this link has on several occasions joined Earth and Rigantona. It has permitted travel from the lower Plane (Earth's) to the higher one (Rigantona's) with ease - and most usually by accident - and in the other direction with great difficulty.

Thus most life forms found on Earth are here. In fact terrestrial vegetation has become dominant long ago and has largely replaced native forms. But animal life is a different story. There are most certainly many terrestrial forms - but then there are the others...

There are of course numerous dangerous predators to be found on Rigantona, and one can find many species of these that are – or once were – found on Earth, in addition to many that are of native origin. Rigantona's predators include several intelligent species - all of which are thus exceptionally dangerous, of course.

However, there is one outstandingly dangerous predator, constituting a major threat throughout Rigantona. Ideally these creatures are best avoided, but this is often impractical because of their ubiquity. Humans, they're called, and they are a variety of anthropoid ape.

The incongruously lovely location of their legendary first arrival on Rigantona is marked with a great stone monolith which, rather appropriately, resembles a vast gravestone...

So this is Volume 2 of Book 1

If you've not read Volume 1 yet, this is just some of what's happened up to now...

Our story begins in the Empire of the Holy League, a huge and benevolent nation of ancient pedigree which occupies three quarters of the vast continent of Manifóra. The Empire is wealthy, contains more than half a billion people and has been governed for the benefit of its citizens since it was set up in its present form by the founder of the ap Gryffudd line, Gryffudd Mawr, well over two millennia ago.

It is run by an aristocracy whose members don't own the land they govern and which is in many ways as much like a civil service as a ruling class, particularly since advancement is as much by merit as by family.

In recent times (several centuries, which is 'recent' compared with the age of the Empire) the ultimate power in the Empire has been held, not by an Emperor/Empress, but by the Imperial High Council. So, of course, a lot of politics happens these days.

Our first encounter here is with Caroline ap Gryffudd, a nineteen-year-old in direct line of descent from the fabled Gryffudd Mawr. When we meet her, she has just gone from being the wealthy younger sister of the Earl of Beauclerc to a hunted fugitive, running to she-knows-not-where because her brother the Earl has been accused of various sordid crimes by the Duke of Belmond, his direct superior, and so has sent her away before the Duke's men can arrive to arrest him. In fact they don't try to arrest him when they do arrive, they kill him and savagely abuse his wife, but by then Carol is on the road, alone and confused.

She has to fight her way out of a difficult situation – and we see that she's been practicing at arms since she was five and hasn't been wasting her time - before she "chances" to encounter her cousin Geraint and a friend of his. They set out towards the Imperial Capital, Cromreth, a long way away, to appeal the charges against her late brother.

They don't get there. Before they are well on their way, she's kidnapped, enslaved and atrociously treated by orcs. She escapes from that – with help - and she and her cousin meet a strange collection of people who, for some reason Carol doesn't at first understand, want to help and protect her at all costs. At the same time a massive invasion of the Empire is being prepared by an alliance of all the kings of the other continent on this world.

Oh... Also, did I mention that this world is on the Ninth Plane of existence? These planes are entire universes like yours – indeed your universe is Plane 1 - and the only one where magic doesn't work.

As Volume One continues, Caroline discovers why people want to help her (and others to kill or enslave her) and what she has to do. She, her cousin and their new friends then set about doing it and along the way a lot of people get killed. When not running from the forces trying to kill them they discover that at least one of the Empire's leaders is a traitor and they establish a close alliance with a massive, though very probably doomed, multi-national business corporation which – amongst many more respectable activities - operates much of the organised crime in the Empire and beyond.

Finally, Carol manages to retrieve a rather special sword – well, me, in fact – and is thus in a situation to get rather better advice, though doing so costs yet more lives. She also finds that several others of her friends have special items to look after as well, but their intended (and extensively-trained) users are all dead, so nobody really knows much about how they work or what to do with them.

Now read on…

Ah – you're still confused? Well, I can't blame you. What you should do is read The Realms of Beliar Book 1, Volume 1 "The Sword Myndarit" first. That will help a lot more than this… Oh, and try the appendices at the back of this one.

Good Luck!
Myndarit the Wise

PART 1
Invasion

Chapter 1

Duke Albert is suspected of some blasphemous opinions

A short time before dawn, a large, powerfully-built man of maybe thirty-five years old, maybe a little more, nudged his warhorse gently into the precise front and centre of a vast formation of cavalry clad in highly-polished black armour that gleamed fitfully in the starlight. This imposing presence was his Grace the Duke of Rachan, Knight Commander of the Order of Night, Knight Protector of the Dark Hour, Blesséd of God.

He was known to those people who considered themselves his friends - mainly sycophants and political bagmen - as well as to the more powerful and respected of his enemies (a group he liked rather better, on the whole) as Malachi Frost. As he walked his horse into place he looked calm, easy and confident.

He was all of these things, but also he was as excited as his iron self-discipline ever permitted, and quietly very proud indeed to be serving his god in such an important and useful capacity.

When he reached the required position he halted his horse and took one last look around him, seeking anything out of order. Nothing. He nodded minutely to himself, unseen within his enchanted black helm.

Having done all that he could do before the moment came, he sat atop his mount with imperturbable patience and watched red light bloom slowly in the east. Behind him, facing what would soon be the rising sun, were no fewer than ninety of the one hundred and eighty Legions of the Order. Totalling just under a quarter of a million, they were amongst the most highly trained, heavily equipped, massively armoured and perfectly disciplined troops to be found anywhere.

Advancing behind the dreaded Black Legions were the assembled armies of the Great Alliance – or at least the one and half million-strong first wave of the southern arm of the invasion. Coming up behind them in turn, Frost knew there were two more waves, totalling another two million, plus eight hundred thousand second-tier occupation troops.

Satisfied that his troops' supports were ready and in position, Frost faced front and waited, immobile, for the first bright streak of sunlight to flash over a distant mountain range into his face.

Before him, on a flat area of ground, a dozen priests of Goreb attended on Razhak Chaldis, Lord Abbott of the Order of the Dark Hour, and thus the most powerful priest of Goreb in the world. Chaldis had dedicated a temporary altar – a huge block of bloodstained stone, carried here by slaves from a temple nearly four hundred miles away – and was now intoning the opening prayers of the Rite of Sacrifice.

As Frost watched, nine of the small company of exhausted slaves who had survived that appalling journey stepped forward in unison. Only slaves who had – before their fall, of course – been followers of Goreb had been selected to bring the Altar to this point, and these nine had been selected by the overseers as the most diligent and obedient of all the survivors. As the exact moment approached, two of

Malachi Frost

the supporting priests very courteously took the arms of the first slave and stretched him across the Altar, quietly offering him their congratulations on the eternal honour he was about to receive as his life ended and the well-earned rewards he would receive thereafter. Everybody waited, Chaldis leading a solemn litany of verses and responses.

The great Abbott had timed his liturgy to the second, for as he intoned the long last note of his preparatory prayer, a single spear of light struck the Altar as the first fragment of the sun's rim appeared above the mointains, swimming in red mist. Loudly proclaiming the ancient triumphant phrase of sacrifice, the Lord of the Dark Hour brought his sacrificial blade swinging down. Two of the slave's ribs were broken by the broad, heavy blade and within seconds his heart was hurled high into the air, where the chief supporting priest vaporised it with a spear of flame out of the clear sky. The twitching body was bundled rapidly forward off the blood-soaked Altar and the next slave, near bursting with pride, stepped smartly up into the arms of the priests.

Frost felt a distinct relief that the ceremony had begun perfectly. He gestured, implementing the small enchantment which made his voice audible to all his troops. Nevertheless, he spoke in a parade-ground roar.

"The Legions will advance to the front and take possession of the ground up to the ridge visible five miles ahead. Any who attempt to resist us will be charged in Legion strength and destroyed, Legion Knights Commander to act on their own initiative in this matter.

"Legions ... advance!"

A hundred miles to the North and slightly further to the West, the Lord Marshall of the Alliance forces, Archduke Albert de Berondonne d'Asturente, Frost's good friend Albert Luis Garcia, sat atop his own horse, preparing to lead the smaller northern arm of the invasion – less than three quarters of a million troops in the first wave. In front of him were the northern arm's cavalry strike force, consisting of forty Eagles of the Knights of the Red Queen – perhaps a hundred and twenty thousand highly-trained men and women. Far less heavily armed and equipped than the Black Knights, and thus faster and more mobile with a much greater effective daily range, the "Red Death" were feared and quite exceptionally professional.

Albert would trust none but Frost to lead the southern strike out of Belmond while he himself nursed and guided the smaller northern force through any resistance. Similarly, he had complete confidence in the ability of the mass of red-clad cavalry in front of him to execute the task he'd entrusted to them. They might not be the Black Knights, but in his view they were considerably better than any *other* formation on the face of the world and, Marnists though they were, they would clear the way for his troops with no trouble at all.

A tiny fragment of rising sun flashed in his eyes, and deep inside him he felt the first sacrifice's joyful departure, thirty-odd leagues to the south. He nodded, satisfied, and spoke quietly, apparently to thin air. "Go, my Lady. And good fortune go with you." Nearly two thousand yards ahead of him, the gorgeously-clad Princess of the Church of Marn who led the KRQ negligently waved an elegant hand, and the banner of her escorting Eagle rose above the waiting ranks. She had included Albert and his Aide in the enchantment which connected her to all her senior officers, and he heard her relaxed, conversational tone as though she were a foot away. "Come children, we shall make sure that these peasants behind us don't encounter anything to disturb their day and strain their little minds. The Red Death descends. Advance." She waved forward her scouts and advanced guard. They kicked their horses into a canter while the main body moved as one into a walk, then a trot.

Count Michael Gason, Albert's aide-de-camp, ground his teeth. What annoyed him to the depths of his Goreb-worshipping soul was the conviction, born of past experience, that these fashion victims in front of him ... these arrogant popinjays, more than a third of them female - including all of their officers, for all Gods' sake - would undoubtedly do precisely what their insufferably elegant commander had prescribed. He was prepared to bet that the troops behind him wouldn't lose a single casualty to enemy action in the whole first leg of the advance and that the Red Death would arrive at every objective in optimum formation and precisely on time.

Almost equally annoyingly, he nursed a strong suspicion that His Grace Duke Albert had an entirely indecent – and in his view possibly blasphemous – lack of interest in what religion or even what sex these red fashion victims were, so long as they did the job required of them.

In fact, Count Michael was entirely correct on both counts.

Chapter 2

A rose of no defined colour turns out to have quite remarkable value

The first of Bastin's troops came through a very hastily arranged *Portal* about four hours after Carol's party left Castle Corfan. Ten hours after that, two scouts from the mercenary rear-guard rode into the main column at a dusty canter and approached Garrett.

The senior of the two saluted. "About five hundred Belmond light cavalry. There are probably another, larger group about six miles - say an hour - behind them, by the dust. Lizzie sent three couple around the scarp to have a look, but she thought you needed the news as soon as, so she sent us on straight away,"

Garrett turned aside to Geraint and a now fully recovered Iorweth, who happened to be riding with him at the time. "That's Lizzie Holt. She's another captain out of White Company, and she's very good indeed. I'm hoping to recruit her for our project."

He turned back to the two scouts. "Tell her to get what information she can. We'll set an ambush about two miles back from here. There's a point where the road's overlooked from both sides, but the actual edges of the road are steep sided. You'll see it on your way back. I want her past the ambush point at least five minutes before the first ducal troops arrive. Got that?"

The two riders turned their horses and were away back the way they'd come, the elder calling acknowledgement over his shoulder. JG turned back to Geraint. "Right. I'll give you a hundred riders. You get down to Holland's Crossing as fast as you can get there and tell Lomond, 'Sweet flower of Alandale.' He will ask you what kind of flower that might be, and you will say, 'I hear that it's a rose, but I can't say what colour.' He'll then release funds to you from that account with Baraani so you can get the Resurrections rolling. I'll be back long before that's done with, and we can plan the next step. Alright?"

"Sounds fine. Good luck."

"A thousand of us ambushing five hundred of them? Luck's unlikely to figure. But thanks anyway."

He deputed one of the officers, Ballis nà Demnaddin, to lead their hundred riders. Geraint recognised him as one of the leaders of the assault on the castle. He nodded politely to Geraint, then dismounted, looked straight at Caroline and laid his hand rather formally upon his hilt. "By blood and bone, Lady."

Caroline nodded formally back. "Thank you, Captain. How soon may we get to Holland's Crossing?"

Ballis nà Demnaddin
Mercenary Captain

"I'm not certain, Lady. I've never before 'ad any reason to drive troops 'ard along 'ere." He smiled. "I'll tell you when we arrive." With that he called instructions to his riders. Ten set off at a breakneck gallop. The rest formed up around the party, fifty in front, forty behind, and Balliss led them all away at a fast canter.

Carol rode beside Geraint and clearly had something on her mind. "Cousin, that 'Blood and Bone' – have I just accepted a marriage proposal, agreed to a duel, or what? It was clearly a formula, and significant, but I've never heard of it before."

Geraint shook his head. "You're right it's important, but it was none of those. It's an oath of fealty. He was offering you his service for life and swearing to serve you with his blood and his bone – that is, at the cost of his life, if necessary. By accepting, you have agreed that he will be of your household as long as you and he remain alive. If these are his own unit – and I think they are – then he will have been speaking for them."

"Oh. But… When we get there I must ask him why. He doesn't know me."

"Cousin, I will ask him. It's bad manners for you to ask a man his reason for this – it implies you either don't trust him or don't want him."

"I see. Geraint, how do you know all this?"

"This particular version of the custom comes from the tribes and families that live in the Dwarven Range. They're all Brandur people, so we're fairly familiar with their ways. Anyway, it's similar to the customs of Brandur's people in a number of places. If you didn't know what it meant, wasn't it a little foolhardy to accept his offer?"

"If it had been a problem, cousin, you would have stopped me."

"And if one day I'm a bit slow or a bit stupid?"

"The sun will rise in the west, Geraint."

"You have no idea how that comforts me."

"Not at all, I imagine, for it is your gift and your responsibility to use it. But it comforts *me*."

They reached the main square of Holland's Crossing on lathered and exhausted horses, but they got there sooner than Geraint would have believed possible. Balliss set out troops around the square as though he were planning to defend it from a sneak attack. Carol and Geraint went straight into the inn – though five of Ballis' riders were in before them nonetheless.

Limond was in the bar they'd met him in before, but now he was round the customers' side, talking to a group of drinkers from which great roars of mirth were beating forth every few seconds. As soon as he saw them enter, he worked his way out of the group and came casually – but swiftly – across to them. "Have a drink. Let's not look too different from the rest of the world."

He flicked a hand – a very small gesture – and one of the girls behind the bar immediately put several drinks on a tray and came over to them. Limond took a fruit juice; the girl proffered the tray to Carol so that a gold goblet of red wine was under her hand. "Ten-year-old Néaness Claret, Lady. Only the best for the highest."

Geraint raised a brow at Limond. "Not too tight, your security?"

Limond shrugged. "We're all John Garrett's people, here. None of his people will cross him – if only because of what the rest of his people would do to them. Anyway, the Countess must start to advertise, now. It has to be a big day when she's in town – though probably not a long-anticipated one."

"You're right."

"I know. Have you anything to say to me?"

"Not really. He did say you would have a sweet flower of Alandale for us to look at."

"Strange thing for him to say. What kind of flower?"

"Beats me. I hear it might be a rose, but I've no idea what colour."

"Right. How much do you need?"

"Don't know, yet. Give me twenty drafts for half a million each. Bearer."

"Aye, aye. Katy, see to it."

The woman who'd brought the tray of drinks nodded briskly. "Yes, Limond."

"What, no lip?"

"John's going away. You're going to be the boss. Only a fool gives the boss lip. Anyway, a boss and his deputy have to work together."

Limond spluttered then chuckled, apparently in spite of himself. "Get off and do it!"

"Yo." She bobbed to Caroline and left.

"Come and sit. I've invited the priest of Mannan-Dar to pop in."

Geraint smiled pleasantly. "Clairvoyant?"

"No. You have corpses on the horses."

"But you were – never mind. Very good. When will he be here?"

"About one minute. I sent Catya, who is a total stunner. She had instructions to tell him she'd be waiting for his return in his bed – if he left at once."

Carol looked around. "Are your girls...?"

"Some of them. The ones that want to. A few of the lads, too. Others don't. John never pressures anybody either way, and the ones that do are treated with at least as much respect here as the ones that don't. Or else. He says it's a family thing. I don't ask."

The door opened, and a brisk, fit-looking man of around seventy came in, wearing the distinctive pale blue-and-mustard of the Mannan-Dar Pastoral Order of Clergy. He saw Limond and strode over.

"G'day Limond. Thanks for the gift. D'you have any oysters behind that bar?"

A barmaid had arrived within a second of the old priest. She smiled at him and went away, returning very shortly with a mug of stout and a plate of oysters.

The Priest patted her rear. "Thank you, Anna. How much, my dear?"

Limond shook his head. "On the House. Pointless sending you Catya unless you're going to be in peak form for her."

"Well, thank you again. What is all this free stuff going to cost me, hey? Apart from a lot?"

"Our friends here have a corpse on their horses that they'd prefer was alive again."

"What kind of corpse?"

Geraint decided it was time to speak for himself. "An Arm, sir. A lady called Zeéla nà Néaness."

The old priest stopped in mid swig and carefully put his tankard down. "That's the Bearer. Limond, Catya's going to have to come back tomorrow."

"No problem, Massoyne. Whenever you like. You know she likes you."

"She likes anybody with a deep purse, that one. But to more important things. I need about three hours to prepare." He turned back to Geraint and Caroline. "And I'm going to have to ask you to pay for the materials I'll be using. I can't afford to replace them without that. Say four hundred and fifty thousand."

Geraint nodded. "I'll have half a million for you in a few moments. And how much will you be needing for the ceremony itself?"

"I see what's on your waist – and I see that you have something extremely impressive on your sword belt, Ma'am. I shan't ask what this is about, but it's important. I'll take another half million."

"But that's not a quarter of–"

"If you're wearing that, you'll be Geraint ap Gryffudd. You've got a reputation. Best scoring graduate for a millennium from University of the Woods, just for starters."

Carol stared. "Geraint! You never told me that! We'd have been so proud! My father would have loved to–"

"I told him. Owed him that, since I wouldn't even have been there without his kindness. He was happier than I've ever seen the old boy. If there'd been no other reason, it would have made all the work worthwhile just to bring him that much pleasure. I asked him not to spread it around."

"He didn't. I do apologise, holy Massoyne. I interrupted."

"Think nothing of it. A lady as beautiful as you are can ask me anything." He looked more closely. "And one wearing that sword can take whatever she wants without asking. That is one very holy sword." He paused and his eyes opened wide. "That wouldn't be…? Never mind, don't answer. None of my business. However, exalted company indeed.

My point is that you people are certainly doing something that matters. And I know of the heir to Néaness. She's a very special one, too.

"I've got a daughter here. Child of my dotage, I was over forty when she was born. You know how stupid an old man gets about his daughter. Anyway, she turned out to be a good kid even though I did spoil her rotten. She and I have been setting up schools for the poorer kids around here. We're quite a way outside the Empire, here, and poor kids have no real access to education.

"The extra half million will allow me to endow the schools so that they can survive and prosper after we're gone. Anything else I may need, I already have funds for – I've had quite a fortunate career, what with one thing and another. Anyway, Zeéla nà Néaness is going to be a very famous woman and do a lot of important things – it will be a privilege to help her."

Then the old Priest winked. "Also she's meant to be a dashed pretty girl, and, of course, she has to be entirely unclad for the ritual."

Caroline laughed. "Holy Massoyne, it's just as well I didn't meet you before all this started and I began to grow up a little. You'd have shocked me out of my reason."

Massoyne twinkled at her, finished his flagon and arose. "I must go and prepare. Lay the lady – unclad – on the main altar of the temple in about an hour. My junior priests will look after her from there. They know her name as well as I do; they'll care for her as what she is – one of our own, and one of our very best. Give the money to any of the juniors. They'll drop it in my office for me."

The old Priest strode out of the room with the energy of a man a quarter of his age. Limond smiled. "Catya really does like him you know. Says she's still learning things from him. Professional tricks and techniques."

Geraint laughed. "Now, why does that not surprise me at all? Limond, will you ask Iorweth to attend to the arrangements for Zeéla for us? We still have an errand to do. Where can I find the town witch?"

"Where you'd expect. The herbal shop is just over the bridge. You can see it from the other end. You'll have a surprise, though."

"I don't think I need too much by way of surprises today. Tell me."

"Wouldn't want to spoil it for you."

"I gather it's not a problem."

"I really rather doubt it."

At that point there was the sound of music and cheering outside. One of the girls came over. "Limond, it's a troupe of players. Shall I offer them the Long Room for performances again?"

"Yes. And tell them they can set up the wagons in the courtyard if they want. It's all good for business."

A few minutes later the drafts were delivered. Geraint and Caroline strolled out across the square, which was now crowded with people and brightly coloured wagons, and made their way over the bridge. Geraint nodded towards the quartet of Ballis' riders who were casually ambling ahead of them. "There's another four behind us. He's not taking any chances."

"No, cousin. And there are at least a dozen more following a way behind those."

The herbal shop was, as Limond had said, clearly visible from the end of the bridge. They made their way inside. Behind the counter was an attractive woman of maybe a little under thirty, with an unmistakable air of confidence and power about her. When she saw Geraint, she nodded politely – and when she saw the Dagger, her eyes went wide. "You will be Geraint ap Gryffudd. And you, Lady, would have to be his cousin, Lady Beauclerc. You are both warmly welcome here."

Geraint touched the hilt of the Dagger. "Blessing on this house and all it shelters." The blade glowed for a second, clearly visible through the sheath, then faded. The woman behind the counter dropped a small, graceful curtsy. "Thank you. That was more than I expected."

Geraint shrugged and smiled. "This is a proper place, and holy. I can feel it. Why would I not wish to add my small blessing?"

Messalina ap Messoyne
Senior Witch(Priest of Brandur)
Altar. Holland's Crossing Coven

"Small blessing. Yours, using that, is His. How may we serve you?"

"I have a friend. A follower of the Mistress of Tricksters. He helped us do something … very difficult, recently and died in the process. Being Alyssana, he has no priests to succour him but us. Can the coven here help him?"

"We can. I don't need to ask the others – for you, we will. But surely, you yourself..?" She gestured to the Dagger.

"Certainly, it will do that easily, and vastly more." He shrugged and smiled wryly. "Once I master its use to that degree. It came to me before my time."

"Ah. I've heard rumours that several Bearers... None of my business. Would you wish the ritual tonight?"

"If it were possible."

"I'm sure it will be. I'll send messages to my Sisters. Our druid will be along shortly anyway, He's barely older than you,"

"May I ask how that came about?" He cocked an eye to Carol. "Members of a coven tend, for obvious reasons, to be all of similar ability."

The witch nodded agreement. "Our druid died in an encounter with a black dragon, which he nonetheless drove away from the village it had been pillaging. This was three years ago. His son had just left the university and so, since we knew him well and he is a very promising young man indeed, we invited him to stand in his father's place.

"Of course, seeing such a young man in such a powerful coven, a number of druids have come here to challenge for the position. Most came for our approval first, of course. Most of those then went away, once we made our attitude known. The lad isn't more than quite good now, but he's going to be even better than his dad before long and we have no intention of losing him.

"Those that ignored us and challenged anyway…" She smiled grimly and shrugged. "Well, we are a very powerful coven."

Geraint smiled a wry and somewhat weary smile in reply. "And many young men at the university read the part of the rubric that says witches are discouraged from involving themselves in challenges once they are under way and think it means that they can ignore a coven's expressed wish without consequences. But it says 'discouraged.' It doesn't say 'prohibited.' Anyway, can we leave this in your hands? How much should we pay you, and when?"

Caroline had been gazing at the woman behind the counter in puzzlement.

"Lady, may I ask your name? Do I know you?"

"I believe we've not been acquainted. I am Messalina ap Messoyne, to serve you."

Geraint burst out laughing. "We've just had a most entertaining ten minutes with your respected father. Limond at Claymores told us we'd find a surprise here, and he was right."

Messalina was smiling. "Well if you were in Claymores, it's no wonder you met my sot of a father. He spends more time there than at his altar, these days."

"Probably Mannan-Dar can find it in His heart to forgive him."

Messalina nodded placidly. "After my father's service, I suspect so."

"He does give the impression of a man who's done this and that. I was asking about cost?"

"Ah, cost. Well, to start with, we'll need to recover the costs of preparation from you. There are a lot of expensive materials – we can't carry the cost of them, I'm afraid."

"Wouldn't expect that, or wish it. Half a million?"

"Would just cover it. Thank you. What did you pay my father?"

"We covered his own costs, then he asked for a further half million to endow some schools. He wouldn't take more than that."

"The old fool. That's just like him. Still, he got us the money to secure the schools. Well, as for us, I'll have to talk to my Sisters and he who is Centre of our Pattern. But I know what they'll say. We need no further payment. Not from you. Keep your money for the tasks lying ahead of you."

Geraint grinned. "And Messoyne's an old fool, yes?"

She grinned back. "Well, he could have demanded enough money to keep him in fancy women for the next decade or two."

"That could easily be a lot of women, I'm guessing?"

"It could easily be half the town. Never mind. Is your friend at Claymores? I'll send a couple of people up to collect him shortly."

The two cousins strolled back across the bridge and into Claymores, where they found Uggò single-mindedly knocking back spirits.

They sat with him and Geraint gave him a quizzical look. "Uggò, old mate. What's afoot?"

The gnome looked up, his gaze disconcertingly steady and sober. "That is Belle's Laughing Academy outside. They do have brought news of the Prince's Players, who reformed successfully and will currently be restocking and buying new equipment. Apparently, the investigation of our old wagons did be satisfyingly expensive for the enemy, too." He knocked back another large measure of spirits and poured his glass full again. When he looked up at them once more, there were tears standing in his eyes. His voice, however, was quiet and steady. "But we did have some losses. When we melt, one group do make itself a little conspicuous to draw any unwanted attention away from the others.

"Well the group who took this task at Belmond did include Biffa, Gallen, another fighter called Myrmidon, a dancer called Zaja and her sister Alaera. All old friends. It did be a small group, but you would not want too many in that team – after all, they do be the lightning conductor for any problems.

"They were making their way out of the town when some of the Red Death did appear on the open country ahead of them. They did take the wise course, to duck back into the city – where they were harried from pillar to post. The sound of explosions and other events from the wagons did tell of a hunt for the players. So they did know Imana-Ran had broken. Not that she should be blamed; everybody do break, and the only question be 'when?' Poor lady.

"Well, our friends tried to escape the city via the sewer system, but were found and pursued. Biffa and Gallen stopped just around a corner. The corner meant that nobody could use distance weapons at them, while Gallen, standing a little behind Biffa, was able to protect him from magic.

"The pursuers, they did be KRQ. Biffa..." Uggò's throat seemed to clog. He swallowed, took another long draft and tried again. "Biffa..." He stopped again and growled a little, deep in his throat, then resumed once more. "Biffa, he has made us all proud; he did manage to fight them off for – we don't know how long for sure, because it were long enough for the others to get away. But the Laughing Academy have information from Alma's people that do suggest Biffa stood for nearly ten minutes before they finally brought him down. Of course once he was gone, Gallen would have been easy meat.

"They were my friends. I grew up with them. Gallen called me his son. And I do have killed them."

Uggò went back to his drink, rather firmly. Carol found that she was deeply moved by the picture of Biffa – who had no harm in his heart for anyone – standing in a sewer in his absurd painted armour and holding off some of the deadliest warriors in the world for nearly ten minutes. So good-hearted, so very brave… To her astonishment she realised that tears were streaming down her face. She put her hand on the gnome's arm. "*We* killed them, Uggò. Not just you. We did. But it was for them to choose, and they chose. While we, really, have *no* choice."

"Aye, lady. But they chose for my sake. They were even there at all for my sake. You be right – I must do what I must do, but why must it be those others who pay for it? Well, I'll have no friends. Then I can lose no friends, can I?"

"It's a little late for that, Uggò. We are your friends."

"Aye, we are friends, all of us. But do you be suggesting I won't be losing you, all of you before very long?"

For an instant, looking at the misery on the gnome's face, Carol wished she knew how to lie. But she didn't know how. Not to convince someone like Uggò. "No. Not really."

"So. And, Lady, I *will* lose you, because I fully intend to survive you – for the man who takes you down, that man do be my meat. You will have fighters aplenty around you, to protect you. That do not be something for me to do, for I do be a very poor fighter – but as a killer, I be unmatched. And whoever it is that finally do take you down, he will die. I will allow no man to live to gloat over *that* victory. I have never made myself a promise before, but this promise I will keep."

"Uggò … I'm not sure how I feel about that. I'm certainly not entirely comfortable with it."

"I hadn't thought you would be, Lady. But it be so, and in that last moment, you should know it."

Geraint grunted. "Well I *do* know how I feel about it, Uggò. Which is that you will have to be quick if you plan to get to whoever it is before I do."

Uggò shook his head. "Not so, lord druid. How likely do it be that the Countess will go down with you still standing?"

"Ah. Not very. No. But it could happen."

"Aye, it could. But then you would be looking to survive, to protect the cause and somehow to Raise the Lady again. You would be *wanting* to kill whoever it might be, but you would have far more important things to do. But you can now do the things you must do with a clear mind, for you do *know* her killer be a dead man walking.

"Lady Zeéla did say it before, and as usual she was right. However small our chances in this, they will be even less if we don't all concentrate on what we do best. In that extremity, you will concentrate on recovering the situation and the Lady, and if it can be done you will do it. I will concentrate on my own speciality. I will kill him. Then I will kill whoever did be his officer. Then *his*, and so on up until they do get me or I do kill the Alliance kings."

Carol was seeking for a way to change what she felt to be a singularly uncomfortable – and somewhat disturbing – subject, when she was relieved of the necessity by the arrival of Karl Horstmann, one of Ballis' two lieutenants. "Lady, there is a mercenary force just outside the town. They claim to be Razor Brothers, who are a unit from further north. They usually work inside the Empire of Mallow, and around Mallow itself for preference. So nobody knows them down here.

"Their commander, one Norris Calmatier, says that they wish to sign up with you, having been summoned by John Garrett. This may be so, but John isn't here – conveniently for them, maybe – and indeed I'm not sure how they would possibly have got here as quickly as this.

"Ballis is concerned, and he's organising our boys and girls to defend you. We can't hold much more than the Square, because there are at least four hundred of them, and we don't know what else is lurking around the edges of the town. If you brought armour, I would advise you to get into it."

Geraint rose. "I gather you don't think these are new friends."

Horstmann shrugged. "Perhaps. Myself, I think we've got a fight coming. Fine, that's what we do for a living, but what Ballis doesn't like is the fact that these people are all – it seems – in a group to the west."

Geraint raised a brow. "Doesn't that support their story?"

"Insofar as it's capable of support, yes. But if they are in fact enemy, then it's as though they were inviting us to get you away to the east."

"So Ballis thinks there's something even nastier to the east?"

"So do I, for what it's worth. Let's hope JG doesn't take too long getting back here."

"So mote it be. You'll have things you want to be doing. We'll be ready."

"Aye. Ballis suggests you should help JG's people defend Claymores. We'll fall back on here as things get hot."

The two cousins headed for their baggage, Carol for armour, Geraint for a range of wands and scrolls. Uggò grinned mirthlessly. Personally, he went nowhere without a range of killing tools ready about his person. He slipped quietly out of the inn and started sprinting north.

After five minutes of this, he slowed to a cautious prowl and began to swing east.

Geraint hurried back downstairs from his room. Three or four minutes later, the witch from the herbal shop strode briskly in and he gave her a friendly nod. "Messalina. Good evening."

"Call me Mess, everybody does. Friends, anyways."

"Mess, then. How can I help you?"

"The coven is together, and the preparation has been done. Do you want us to go on with the Ritual of Raising or should we protect the town? Thing is, if we abandon the ritual for now, we'll need to redo the preparation."

"You think these are hostiles as well, then."

"Well, they're not who they say they are, I'll bet on that. Those guys will have been over a thousand miles away – at least – a couple of days ago."

"Indeed. Well, surely there's only one answer to your question. Protect the town."

"Yes. But it's your half million we are about to dump, so we had to ask."

"More where that came from. Good towns like this aren't quite so easily replaced. Can you pass that on to your father in passing, too?"

"I believe he's started, so he's committed to what he's doing. The Ballis boys have the M-D temple inside their perimeter. The Grove's too far away from things, so we'll probably guest with Manna-Dar as well. He won't mind, we've done it before. Any other instructions?"

"I have nothing else I wish – except try to survive, if you can."

"I was planning to give that a bit of attention. Well, I'll get on, then. I doubt if these people expect to find a full coven here. They're going to be very unhappy."

"I can bear that."

Mess grinned and departed at speed. Geraint went outside into the square. The Laughing Academy were arranging their wagons as a perimeter around Claymores and placing anything from farm carts to furniture, benches and boxes in the spaces between.

Claymores staff were moving briskly but calmly around, wearing baldrics and weapons belts as though these were familiar accoutrements. Now that Geraint came to look, the ostlers, pot boys and barmen all had a certain healthy, muscular look about them while the girls were all fit and athletic-looking.

Ground floor windows now all had heavy grills bolted over them, while what had looked like decorative gargoyles and such on the tops of the walls now took on a second identity as a quite serviceable substitute for crenellations, behind which erstwhile barmaids were crouching with crossbows they were clearly quite used to holding. Bolted next to each position was a rack, now being rapidly filled with loaded crossbows. Smaller pistol crossbows were being swiftly lined up on each first floor windowsill.

Obviously, Garrett had a policy of being ready for any eventuality, and that policy extended to frequent practice and training, for everywhere in the inn grounds was bustling activity and urgency, but nowhere was there any trace of panic.

Outside in the Square, townsfolk were barricading the incoming roads and organising themselves at windows and barricades with a range of efficient-looking weapons, from pikes to longbows. Inside the Empire, almost nobody went armed – or needed to. Those who lived outside the Empire, however, kept the means of self-defence ready to hand at home. A larger group of archers were assembling in the middle of the square, ready to pour shafts on any point that was hard pressed, and Iorweth could be seen talking to the man who appeared to be their leader.

At one side, around thirty riders were waiting with their animals. Geraint saw Horstmann with them and went over. "Tactical reserve?"

"Aye. Ballis has most of the boys to the western side of the square. He's out talking to the Razor Boys – or whoever they are. We've got a very thin cordon – half a dozen – to the north and east, and we're relying on the river to protect our south flank. What we're hoping is that if the cordon's tripped, we'll be enough to blunt whatever's coming from that direction. If not, everybody falls back behind Belle's wagons or into the MD temple."

"What do you expect will happen?"

"We'll sit tight in the inn and the temple, and they'll try to winkle us out before JG arrives."

"Be a pity if he came in cold, not expecting trouble."

"John? He doesn't go to the jake without scouting it first. Don't worry about that. Just worry about how we're going to hold 'em off 'til he arrives."

Geraint went back inside the inn, finding Caroline sitting in the lounge bar having a glass of wine from a bottle that was open on the bar. He smiled to himself as he noticed the coins she'd left on the counter.

He sat in one of the more comfortable armchairs. "Cousin, I'm going to try something. I shall be a trifle unresponsive for a few minutes."

Carol nodded and adjusted her position so that he and the door were both in her line of vision.

Geraint invoked the dweomer and let his mind float in mist. Various points of light. *That* one – small, hard, sharp as a knife blade. Surely a bird of prey. He drifted into contact. It didn't notice as he took up residence. Geraint adjusted his meshing slightly, and suddenly the inn was gone and the bird's senses were his own. They were hovering high above the town. There were a number of creatures – much too large to eat, and some of them sitting on other creatures – on the sundown side of the town.

They felt an urge to see what the hunting might be like on the sunup side and worked their way in that direction. Many more creatures sitting on other creatures. One of these was waving upper limbs around and other creatures were moving about in response, Suddenly the limb-waver stiffened and fell off the creature it was sitting on. Many others rushed about like an angry ant's nest. Somewhere in their consciousness, drifting on a thermal a thousand feet up, they thought "Uggò!" and were pleased, though mainly they didn't understand what they were going on about, because the fallen creature would be useless as carrion until all these others went away.

Geraint gently detached his consciousness from the hawk and drifted back to himself. He opened his eyes and struggled for focus for a moment, then sighed, as sensation and sight flooded back. "Well, I've just ridden with a hawk. There are indeed hostiles to the east, though they're a bit disorganised at present because somebody's just taken their leader down in the middle of them, which has distracted them a lot."

Caroline looked around. "I see our friend Uggò isn't here."

"Yes, that was my guess, too. They had no idea who'd got their man, or where from. D'you know, Uggò may well be as good as he thinks he is."

* * *

Uggò slipped in via the Eastern part of town and through the side entrance of the Mannan-Dar temple – not bothering to make the troops covering it aware of his presence. He looked round for the Coven, saw where they had set up shop, respectfully far from the main altar. He made himself known to the druid, being careful to negate the invisibility conferred by Alyssana's Gift a good way away to avoid startling anybody into doing something he might regret.

A few minutes discussion with the druid and with Mess gave them a clear idea what was coming from the East, and gave him an outline of what they planned to do about it so that he could keep well clear. He was well aware that healers and carers they might be in their daily lives, but when a coven sets its mind to fighting they are something very, very different from that.

As soon as he had a good notion of the places he would be wise to be nowhere near, he slipped out again and found the attacking force a few hundred yards outside the town, moving quietly in amongst the houses on the edge.

He waited to restart the invisibility the Gift gave him until after his next hit – he still didn't have the setting adjusted completely to his liking, and the invisibility terminated on a hit and took a little while to restart, so he kept it ready to go and simply used his own skills to slip into an upstairs room of a house just ahead of their advance. The new leader was making himself foolishly obvious – riding in front and clearly direct-ing matters – so Uggò marked him down as the next target.

He pulled a soft cloth tube from his pouch, said the activating word, and it went stiff. It was useful in a number of ways, but today he wanted to use it as a blow-pipe. With swift care, he pulled a little feathered dart from a small case and fitted it in the pipe. As the leader rode beneath the window of his room, he blew silently. The man jerked, pulled the dart from his cheek, stared at it – and slipped, lifeless, from his horse.

Smiling at how simple it had been, Uggò activated the Gift' invisi-bility and was lounging undetected against the wall in the corner of the room when three warriors ran furiously in a minute or two later.

Norris Calmatier saluted the leader of the defending mercs and rode back to his people. Probably, the discussions had now gone on long enough for his brother to get in position. Certainly, the chances of talking their way in seemed thin. The defending captain, what was his name? – ah, yes, Ballis nà Demnaddin - was clearly not idiot enough to believe the rather implausible tale Norris had told him. Ah, well. It had been a long shot anyway. There was a much better chance that they'd tried to smuggle the targets out of town, That would be good.

Either way, it was time. "Black banners up! Let's frighten these people out of it."

The black flags rose in the midst of the horsemen and they swept towards the defensive positions. Calmatier looked for signs of fear amongst the defenders – all he saw was what he'd expected, a flight of arrows. Townsfolk might be terrified by the Black Anis, but Ballis ná Demnaddin's mercs were professionals, and Calmatier knew that to them a target was a target like any other - and if your time was up one man might kill you as well as the next. It was an attitude he respected because he shared it himself.

The defenders might not fear the Anis, but they surely respected odds. They were declining contact and moving back into the town, shooting as they went. The arrowstorm wasn't intense, but it was enough to slow the attack and thin his people out. He reckoned they'd lost around thirty by the time they reached the houses.

"Keep together! No sack yet. First man breaks off, I kills the bugger mesel'!" They knew the plan, but their instincts were strong. Why else would they be Anis in the first place?

They pushed on through the town, their momentum slowed by the tangle of streets, and then the central square was up ahead – and very suddenly the arrowstorm was a far more serious thing. This was clearly the heart of the defence. It seemed to be built around barricades on the street ends into the square, covered by a lot of archery from windows and balconies, as well as groups of archers in the square – shooting on instruction from the barricades, probably. Calmatier grunted. It was good strategy for the situation and it would add to the cost of this attack but he didn't expect it to succeed.

He kept his people moving around, trying to hold the defenders' attention without losing too many riders. One question was whether the defence had enough arrows to keep this sort of thing up for long. He wasn't surprised that the mercs had lots of ammunition, but it seemed that the townsfolk were well supplied, too, for the storm of shafts wasn't easing off at all.

Then a flash of light lit the sky to the east – not far east, either. That was his signal. "All in! All in! Take 'em now!"

His riders swept forward through the renewed arrowstorm. They lost another two dozen easily in the first few seconds, then probably a dozen more, but now they were on the barricades and diving off their horses to drive hand to hand at the townsfolk behind them.

Now, a carpenter who's had some practice once a week from early youth – and if he's a steady man – can often ply a bow nearly as well as a professional. But hand to hand it's a different thing, and the defence started to crumble. That pulled the mounted Mercenary reserves in, thundering down on the Anis warriors as they broke through.

That, of course, was what his brother had been waiting for. Norris saw the horde of riders break from the houses north and east of the square and sweep forward. To his surprise they weren't being led by Radan, or even Brian, but Lucas. Very odd, but no matter, it would all be over in a few minutes now, and the sack could begin.

Then, as he watched, a huge swarm of stinging insects – clouds of them – rose from the ground in front of the attackers. Horses reared and screamed and twisted. The ranks behind crashed into those in front, and the whole eastern attack was reduced to chaos. As more and more riders crashed into the whole mess before they could stop, a sheet of flame – all of a hundred feet wide and ten feet high – rose behind the attacking riders. The horses to the rear, whose riders had been pulling them up to avoid the tangle in front, screamed and blindly rushed forward away from the roaring flames – straight into the tangled mess before them.

From both sides, wolves, bears, and a range of other woodland creatures poured out of the side streets and tore into the confusion of horses and men. No easy victory from the east, then, but his own people were rapidly gaining the barricades. He signalled, the light ball went up, and he knew his reserves, another two hundred riders, would be with him within two minutes.

Enough strategy. Time to dig in. Norris leapt the barricade and led a renewed charge into the centre of the square.

* * *

Geraint watched, nodding approval, from the inn doorway as the coven's first cut mangled the eastern attack. "That was fine. But they're not even into their stride yet. If it was me, I'd go for... wait... Yes! Way to go!"

Low level demons flicked into existence amongst the milling eastern cavalry. The already panicked horses were going into screaming hysteria as the great stinking figures, steaming and smoking, waded in with claws slashing and fangs bared.

Satisfied that the apparently vulnerable side of the square was in fact completely sealed, he looked across at the western barricades. "It looks as though the mercs are a bit hard pressed and needing some help over there, cousin. Shall we?"

Caroline had declined full armour again, these days being aware that her blinding speed was her best asset – and that she hadn't trained enough in full plate to be fully effective. She was wearing her blue leather jack with light metal plates sewn inside and had the lozenge shield emblazoned by Varan strapped to her left arm. She looked out at the advancing Anis and smiled happily at Geraint. "Delighted, cousin. They'll be feeling that they're the lucky ones just now – time to change their minds."

Carol walked in front as Geraint came close behind, preparing his first spell. A man with a black headband and a two-handed sword saw them, shouted, pointed, and led a group of about twenty Anis towards them. Geraint pointed to the ground in front of the advance and muttered. The first few advancing swordsmen passed the area before anything happened, but those coming behind started to sink to their knees in mud, where a second before there had been only gravel.

The leading man howled a battle cry and came forward. Carol drew Myndarit and a dry, rather carping female voice in Geraint's head said "*At Last! Until I know you better, I can only talk to you and the other Gift Bearers when I'm in your hand. 'Wielded' is the term. Kill this idiot, we'll talk another time.*"

Norris hurled himself at Carol, swinging his great sword. She checked and avoided direct impact on her shield, instead using it at an angle to deflect the great blade up over her head. At the same time, she dummied to strike his leg, changed direction by ninety degrees in mid stroke and opened his stomach in a long diagonal slash from groin to ribs, slicing through his leather jack as though it were silk. The Anis leader collapsed into a heap of his own intestines.

Caroline swung to face the next attacker, calling to Geraint, "In the strike, it's got the weight of a morning star, but you can change direction as though it weighed nothing!"

He heard the dry, slightly acid voice in his – and presumably her - head remark *"Dear me... must be a magic sword, do you think?"*

He spluttered with laughter. Carol snorted and ran the next man through the chest, easily avoiding his own thrust.

Over his cousin's head, Geraint saw a new force of horsemen destroying one of the barricades. He was about to take steps when he felt the Coven go up a notch and exert itself seriously for the first time. There was a crash of thunder like the end of the world, and a forked bolt of lightning crashed down out of the roiling clouds above. Each fork terminated at an Anis rider, one at either end of the force by the barricade. From there, each bolt jumped to the next man and the next and the next, connecting rider after rider in a crackling blue and yellow tracery. When all the riders were connected, they suffered an instant of jerking, blinding destruction as the two forks met somewhere in the centre of the group. Comparative silence followed, with a haze of blackened dust and some purple after-images of the victims the only trace left of them.

A couple of hundred panic-stricken but unharmed horses seemed to be suffering group hysterics while their riders lay contorted and motionless on the ground under their panicking hooves. That was enough for the surviving Western attackers and they departed. The remaining eastern attackers had either sunk into the earth or else fled, pursued by some exceedingly irate demons. Relative peace descended.

Ballis cantered over. "Well, my people took a bit of a pounding, but that worked out extremely well – we didn't even have to fall back on the inn and the temple."

Geraint nodded. "What's the butcher's bill?"

"We lost twenty-nine killed, and we have another thirty-eight wounded. Five of those probably won't make it."

Geraint and Caroline exchanged glances. Carol sighed and sheathed Myndarit. "Lead on then, Ballis. I'm not sure how many we can help, but we'll do our best. Certainly we should be able to do something for those five."

"Thanks, Lady. Hopefully the Coven will have some energy left to help as well. Iorweth of Branneswald has gone to ask. I've sent Raoul Lopez with him."

"Lieutenant Lopez made it. Good. How is Karl?"

Ballis shook his head and indicated Norris Calmatier, lying in a pool of gore at Carol feet. "That one took his head clean off, just before he came for you. Nothing to be done."

Caroline sighed again. "Are you sure about this, Captain Demnaddin? I am not a healthy person to be around, and it will get worse."

"Everybody dies of something. At least this way we'll die in a cause whose memory will live forever. What more can anybody ask? We've already got about forty volunteers from the town before this started."

Carol gasped. "But will they stay? They've just seen…"

"And they know that there are two ways to stop it. Supine surrender is one way; your way is the other. They'll stay, and more will join them probably."

"Captain, there comes a point where further argument is just bad manners. Please invite your troops – all that are fit enough – to Claymores tonight. I will put funds behind the bar to cover their needs for the night."

"I warn you, that will take significant funds."

"I believe we can cope, Captain. And I've never met a soldier yet who didn't feel that free drinks were an acceptable form of welcome."

Geraint stirred. "Cousin, we have quite serious rituals to do."

"Geraint, you have. It is possible that I should not meet Ca– the lady you plan to speak with. I should, however, meet the soldiers who put their lives at risk for me today. Yes?"

The druid bowed gracefully. "My Lady, you're the boss. You are also quite correct."

Chapter 3

Looking like the hammer when
you are actually set to be the anvil

Malachi Frost looked ahead and saw the commander of his scouts cantering back towards him. The man was grinning broadly as he approached, and Frost couldn't restrain a frisson of excitement. *Action at last.* He had been briefed to expect opposition from ducal forces from the early hours of the assault, but for the main part of the day they'd advanced almost at the canter, completely unopposed.

The ducal forces had stayed in their castles or – more usually – withdrawn well ahead of the Order, which made good sense but was not what he'd been promised. Their helpers on the other side had been supposed to arrange that the Dukes got their men into the field to be mopped up immediately, so that there was no issue with allocating forces to cover them.

However, the day had been a strategic success – just dull. From the look on Gustavson's face, however, the late afternoon would be very much more interesting. The man arrived in a flurry of dust and saluted. "We've sighted the Imperial Army, sir. This slope leads to the western crest above a river valley about a mile across. The enemy are arrayed on the up-slope the other side of it with their north flank anchored on a ruined temple at the top of the incline. They're about five miles ahead.

"We haven't attempted the river, but from even a quick overview there are more than half a dozen stretches where it certainly looks easily fordable – on horseback at least."

Frost harrumphed. "Five miles, you say? We won't bring them to battle before morning, then."

"No, sir. Unless you want a night action."

"Into unknown terrain? I think not." Frost considered for a moment, then shrugged. "So the KRQ are likely to have the fun tomorrow. Blast and fire! Why couldn't the Imperials have formed up in the previous valley. We'd have got 'em to ourselves then."

"Sorry, sir. I'd have found them closer if I could have, just for you."

Malachi Frost concealed a smile, making sure Gustavson saw that he was doing so. "Do you think you're a wit, Gustavson? If so, you are no more than half right."

He rubbed his chin – not an easy manoeuvre inside his black helm. "Are the Myndarits out with the Imperials?"

Gustavson was still struggling to smother an appreciative chuckle at the barb. "No, sir."

"Blast!"

"They would have made it more interesting tomorrow, sir."

"A good deal more interesting. And hugely more expensive. But as it is, we will have the even more interesting problem of worrying about where they are. The idea of having a quarter of a million tightly disciplined and highly effective heavy horse turning up suddenly on our flank does not fill me with the joys of spring, Captain. Did you encounter any hostile patrols?"

"We saw light cavalry moving on their flanks, sir. Nothing in front of them. I presume they're relying on their vantage point – at least in daylight."

"Perhaps they want us to think we're surprising them, but they have some magical piquet."

"Perhaps, sir. But my patrols all had priests or mages with them, and nobody has reported anything unusual. On the other hand, positioned as they are nobody can enter the valley without their knowledge, so really they'll have adequate warning."

"Very well. Don't go further than the ridge, but I don't want so much as an Imperial mouse getting this side of it."

The man saluted and moved off. Frost waved his aide up beside him, then spoke the word that connected him with his senior officers. "We have contact, gentlemen. Conference here, now." He spoke the disconnect, then used the different word that connected him with Duke Albert, wondering idly as he did so how people had ever campaigned effectively before the systematic use of magic.

"Your Grace. We have contact. Point Yellow of the options we discussed with our friend. All along that ridge south of the ruins and the higher part of the down-slope to the west of it. Will the Marnists be ready at dawn?"

He had known Albert since they were both children, but in formal situations he could no more have called the man Albert than he could have flown. Less so, in fact, because he was wearing a Ring of Levitation, amongst other things.

There was a short pause – His Grace was presumably consulting the gorgeous and elegant presence who was the Marnist Princess of the Church leading the KRQ. Then Albert's voice sounded, apparently from a foot or two to his left. "Yes, your Grace. They will be in place in plenty of time. If your attack rolls at dawn, they will be ready."

"Very well, Your Grace. We attack at dawn and keep their attention while the Red Death come in behind and start to chew them up. We don't actually commit our main charge until that has happened and the Imperial front line becomes aware of it. Is that correct, sir?"

"It is. Make it so."

"Yes, your Grace."

"May the blessing of our God go with you, Duke Malachi."

"Thank you, your Grace."

Frost spoke the word that broke the connection. With the help of only moderate luck, the only significant impediment to their final conquest of the Empire would be a broken memory by lunchtime tomorrow.

But as for the man he had just referred to, in the conventions of such things, as 'our friend'... Malachi Frost was, in his own particular way, a highly principled man. Regardless of what filthy tampering Marnists and their stinking fellow travellers might do with his mind, he knew with absolute certainty that he would never, ever betray his own side in this fashion - and the very thought of having to be polite to the man who had encompassed this ... this obscenity that would happen in the morning made his sword hand itch unbearably.

Such people might be useful, and Frost was mindful of the large number of his own men who would not die on the morrow because of this... foetid scheme. But... it just felt indecent to the very depths of his being and he couldn't come to terms with it.

Truthfully, this was why he had wished the Myndarits were there.

Yes, it was better to know where they were, bring them to battle and crush them, however expensive that would be – and it would most certainly be exceedingly expensive - but mainly it was the knowledge that they were complete military professionals and, whatever else happened and whatever orders they received, they would make their own decisions, have their own scouts and possibly foil the vile plan that it had been his distasteful – shameful - duty to help forge.

For a moment he allowed himself to hope – in most ways completely unreasonably – that the Myndarits would join the Imperial army at some point during the night.

The day would still be won tomorrow, but then it would be won cleanly, and he would be able to take some pride in it. As it was, he realised, he was already trying to forget it – and it hadn't even happened yet.

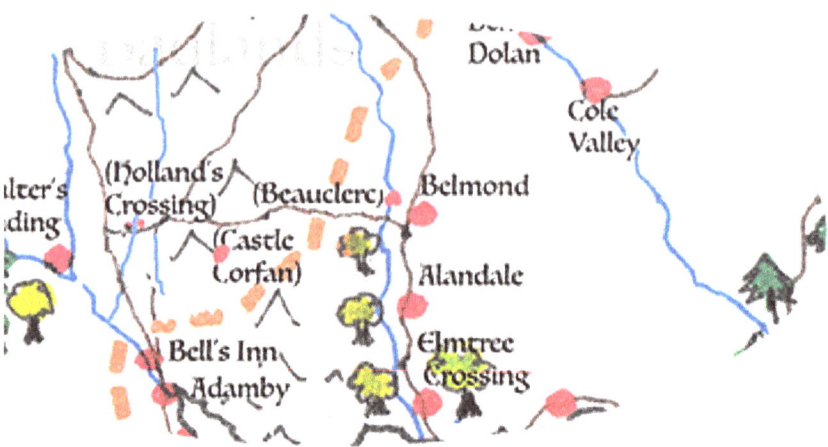

Chapter 4

It's a universal but simple rule:
Nothing is ever simple.
So perhaps it's just a universal rule...

John Garrett wiped the ring of teleport, placed it carefully in a section of his pouch and walked through the gates of Mallow. He knew them well, as he'd been to Mallow very frequently. Not only was it the largest mercenary contract market on two continents but in addition the Reis Emperors themselves were always major employers of mercenaries.

He checked the time by the huge clock face over the gate house; at least four hours before he needed to be back at Claymores in Holland's Crossing. Good enough. He'd left Limond setting up arrangements for the evening at Claymores, and jumped out within ten minutes of getting back, pausing only to arrange with one of Messoyne's staff that a very private message be delivered immediately to a specific priest in the main Marn Temple in Mallow.

There was no doubt Mallow was an enormously impressive place. The broad, tree-lined avenue that passed through the open city gate would eventually lead to Elm Tree Square, one of the four great squares that dominated the inland side of the heart of Mallow. However, he wasn't going that far – nearly a mile and a half down this broad, elegant thoroughfare. He wanted the complex of wharves which acted as the main terminal of the canal system servicing Mallow's Southern and South-Western hinterland and, knowing Mallow well, he didn't bother going round by the main roads. Instead, he turned off to the left and then navigated a maze of ever more complex – and ever less salubrious – roads, side roads and alleys until he came to the area he wanted.

By the time he reached the wharves themselves, the twisty alleys had expanded again to very substantial – though somewhat grimy -

commercial thoroughfares, crowded with dock workers, carts pulled by oxen or draft horses, chandlers' staff, bargees, small squads of City Watch, sleek executives of shipping companies or else of Mallow's many canal boat businesses - each with their little knots of underlings - sailors, whores, *Find the Lady* specialists, shell-game artists, draymen, whores' protectors ... and a very great many more.

JG didn't look round for the cover team that he'd arranged with Uggò would meet him as soon as he left Elm Tree Avenue. He knew they must be there, though, because nobody tried to pick his pocket in his entire stroll along the dockside. There were gangs of toughs in evidence, too, but he doubted he'd need his cover team for them – they glanced at him, noticing he was a stranger and apparently alone and well-heeled, then noticed his size, expensive leather armour and broad range of magically-enhanced weaponry, winced, and looked away for something easier. He didn't blame them.

Eventually he turned in to a side alley, followed it around a sharp corner and saw what he was looking for. A discreetly signed rear entrance into a big inn's stable yard. It wasn't locked and he walked in, closing it behind him. Blazoned on the opposite wall of the yard – an impressive distance away - was a big and very colourful sign bidding him "Welcome to the Green Parrot!", including a vividly-painted six-foot high representation of the bird in question.

Several men had been lounging in the yard, and they now approached, looking completely out of sympathy with the big, friendly sign behind them. One of them, a very large man with a lot of muscles, stood directly in JG's path, while his mates crowded in on either side. "Can we help you, chief? Only this is by way of being a staff entrance, see. The main public entrances are down on Craddock Way – out the way you came and then left, and left again at the end. The public are discouraged from coming in this way because it can be bad for your health and safety, like."

Garrett smiled, slowly and with a very low sugar content. "Could be bad for *somebody's* health and safety I don't doubt, my son. But I'm here to see a Scarlet Woman."

"Are you really? Scarlet woman? Never heard of her. Who sent you here, then?"

"The Dice Boy".

"That's Jamie, then. Tall skinny guy?"

"That's the one. Except he's called Bill."

The reception committee relaxed a good deal - without looking much friendlier – and the one who'd spoken pointed at a door on JG's left-hand side; the pub was on the right. The left looked like stables with some rooms above. "Through there and down. She's due in about ten minutes, says she doesn't have a lot of time."

JG nodded and went over to the door. It wasn't locked, and there were the expected stairs going up. Beside them, though, part of the wall had begun to swing open and through the gap thus created stairs led down. JG went down the stairs, then through a door at the bottom and found, to his slight surprise, a very comfortable and quite large room equipped with a rack of assorted bottles, some glasses, some ice and a sign saying.

> **"When the door is closed this room is covered by Alyssana Privacy cast at the 43rd level."**

Garrett poured himself a beer, selected an armchair and sat down to wait.

He was on his third beer and twice the advertised ten minutes had passed when he heard footsteps on the stairs and a priest of Marn came in, glanced at the sign and closed the door. She nodded to him and said "I'm Breen, and I'm Lady Julia's Sacristan. I know who you are. Why am I here, and why in such secrecy? Oh, and pour me a glass of red wine. No, the big glasses. Yes, that one."

JG set about playing host as he talked. "Well, let's do that the other way around. I arranged to get a message to you – why did you come?"

"You people are making waves. I decided it was worth seeing what you wanted. The guarantees of my safety were satisfactory, and though I'm busy, I'm not *that* busy. You might even have something interesting to say. Plus, you implied you are a line of communication to Lady Sarah of Rhadan and I have a message for her."

Garrett nodded. "Another reason you came is that you aren't as busy as you might be because you aren't involved in the key decision-making – or only peripherally. While you're one of Julia's vicars, you aren't Chief Vicar or even one of the three Seniors. As her Sacristan you're probably next in line, but it means Julia has her team and you're only a bag carrier in it. Quite a well-regarded bag carrier with a fancy title but only that." JG took another pull at his beer. "Of course you aren't satisfied with that and you wondered if this might help you do better. And yes, as it happens, I can help you do *far* better. Interested?"

Breen regarded him coolly for a moment, then relaxed gracefully into an armchair. "Give me that glass. If you can interest me more before I've drunk it, we'll see."

JG nodded. "It won't take that long or anything like it. You know I have a long-standing connection with Lady Sarah?"

"Certainly. You and she made a lot of noise here in Mallow some years back. I am assuming you still have a connection with her now…? Good. Here's the message I spoke of. Please tell her that it will be in her interests to notch back the ambition just a little, though you can also tell her we do understand her value to the Faith.

"Lady Julia has too much political capital at the moment for Lady Sarah to challenge her, and though she's perhaps ahead of my lady Julia as a spell caster, it's Lady Julia who has the **Diadem of Power** and that wipes out any such advantage and more besides."

Breen held up her hand. "But… there *is* an offer and a very good one. Lady Sarah would be a very good deputy, and that could be on offer immediately. *If* she stops being a nuisance. She should understand that she's

Breen DeMarcis
Priest of Marn
Presently Sacristan to
Julia, Principal Princess of the Faith

raising hackles and she needs to take slightly smaller steps - and the optimum step available to her right now is the number two slot. From there, of course, who can say where she might go? A team of Lady Julia and Lady Sarah working together would be beyond challenge within the Faith."

Garret looked like a man burying a chuckle. "Yeah. But Julia's people lost Brandur's Dagger and missed their chance at taking Geraint and Caroline ap Gryffudd. Not clever."

"Well yes, and that would have been a serious blow, but Duke Bastin has got them back *and* is about to find Myndarit – probably has by now - and he's one of Lady Julia's appointments too, effectively, so while it's embarrassing it's far from fatal. *Far* from fatal. We probably come out ahead in terms of status, in fact."

Garrett smiled and raised a finger. "Well if that had happened, yes. However, there've been some recent events which won't have reached here yet. What if you were the only one who knew that Bastin now has no chance of recovering those people, and both of the items in question are irretrievably in their hands. And furthermore that Bastin is out three hundred and fifty million Imperial crowns? That's going to hamper his contribution in Belmond massively, I would guess. The net impact of all that is going to put Julia badly on the back foot – at least for some considerable time.

"Now, I suggest that this creates a unique opportunity for your own career. What if you arranged that Julia's Chief Vicar were to be … *hors de combat*... at a given time. Maybe a pre-arranged point after people found out about Julia's losses?

"I think if Sarah went for her after news of that disaster has had time to get around – a few weeks, perhaps, maybe several while the scale of the damage done sinks in - then there could be no political fallout because Julia's stock would have fallen far enough that if she can't hold her place against challenge, nobody is going to come to her support.

"And there is where your opportunity lies. I said before that you are a bag-carrier and so you are, but the most important of those bags holds Julia's **Diadem of power.** If her Chief Vicar were out of it and Sarah had the **Diadem of power**... Folk could suddenly find there is a new Principal Princess of the Church. One who would have a vacancy for a Chief Vicar.

"At the same time, though, you may well want to mention to your colleagues that Sarah would be willing to adopt the rest of Julia's people without change. *She* appreciates *their* value to the Faith too much to break up what has up until now been a winning team – and can still continue to be, if good decisions are made at this point.

"Oh, and maybe you wouldn't want to do anything too permanent to the current Chief Vicar. I'm sure my Lady Sarah would wish to gift her to you permanently as a trophy, to mark the occasion of her accession."

Garrett noticed Breen's eyes sparkle for an instant and concealed a smile. He made a negative gesture, sweeping a down-turned palm. "Just my own estimate, of course, but I believe you can rely on it."

Then he sat back at ease and supped more of his beer. "Are we on the same page here?"

Breen's gaze was focused rather intently on him, and JG suspected there was a good deal of intense calculation going on behind those cool eyes. After a moment of stillness she took a long swallow of wine, then another. "You can prove this?"

"Sworn on Baraani within the hour, if you're in. Of course you'd have to swear to your part if you want that."

"And Sarah?"

"Well if you're offering her Julia's **Diadem of power** then she might feel a desire to appoint you her Chief Vicar *before* you actually give it to her and she attacks Julia, just as a gesture of good faith, yes?"

"And if instead I simply tell Julia all this?"

"She's still shy a lot of political credit because of the losses, with the result that Sarah becomes a real danger. She can't give you anything like the reward Sarah can, because she has her team set. And of course if Sarah wins over time anyway, which in these circumstances looks really quite likely, your position is very bad."

"But Sarah couldn't win then! She will be screwed for being involved in this plot."

"What plot? Have you seen Sarah? Has she spoken of this to you? No. It's all me. No doubt foolish enthusiasm for her cause arising from that old romance and my ignorance of all things Marnist. Of course it would shock her to the core if she knew about it.

"And with Sarah the rising star and Julia's position very rocky, nobody's going to be looking for trouble with Sarah – so I'll be the obvious goat, I would suggest. And your lot are already trying to kill me so what do I care?

"The real situation is that the first time Sarah is involved will be when you give her the **Diadem** and inform her - to her great surprise, naturally - that Julia's staff unanimously invites her to become Principal Princess, yes? Really, if you can't see how this works at least as well as I can you're the wrong girl for us."

Breen once more considered him thoughtfully, this time for well over a minute, one finger tapping slowly on the arm of her chair. Then she sat up straight and shook her head. "Oh, I don't think so. I think I'm exactly the right..." she grimaced "...*girl* for you. Or for Lady Sarah, more to the point. Pour me another glass of wine... And fetch your Baraani priest, I'll drink it while I'm waiting."

Garrett nodded in acknowledgement, poured, sketched a bow and headed up the stairs – closing the door behind him. As he left the stable, heading for the Green Parrot bar where he'd arranged to meet the priest of Baraani, he started to hum a popular tune that had been fashionable when he'd known a certain Marn priest in Mallow...

Chapter 5

*Carol saves a drunken
soldier's life... in a way...*

Some five or six hours after the attack, Geraint and Iorweth, joined by a rather frail-looking Lin Gor and Zeéla, met in a back room of Claymores – the two main bars and the Long Room being taken up by the rather wild party that Carol was hosting. Uggò was out in the party, drinking sparingly for him, and watching Caroline's back.

Geraint began with inquiries about the state of recovery of his two friends, then went on to summarise for them events they'd missed while engaged in being dead. After that, he got down to business.

"Zeéla, d'you think you'll be feeling up to talking to Ballis about remuneration? We don't pay him a lump sum, I think. We pay them all directly. But he hires and fires inside his own team. Alright?"

"Yes, Junior, I'll be fine. Do we want to be generous or economical?"

"Generous, always. We never worry about money at all. Well, not out loud. We pay for their horses, tack, arms, armour and keep, all at a very good standard. On top of that, we pay them walking-around money for when they're not in action, a thumping bonus – more than they're expecting – for winning an action, bonuses for their outstanding personal conduct as reported by Ballis, and a fair slice of booty and loot. The contractors, who haven't sworn fealty, get the equipment and weaponry too – there are good reasons for doing that – but otherwise they just get one lump sum monthly, to the Captain. Plus their share of booty, obviously.

"And, of course, since we're buying everybody's weapons, armour and tack, we've got something to talk to Borgia about when we see her, have we not? Now then, what does all that mean in terms of actual expenditure monthly – at least in general terms?"

They'd been kicking the numbers into shape for about fifteen minutes when John Garrett came in. He had been engaged in some business of his own involving teleporting to various places, and then been busy supervising the party arrangements and making sure that everything was working as it should. "That woman is pure class, you know that? She's casually circulating from group to group, chatting idly, smiling that amazing smile – making them feel as though they know her personally. No side at all.

"A couple of times now I've expected her to be a little po-faced, and each time found perfect lightness of touch. Same tonight. But not too light. Quite a few of them are more than half cut already, of course, and there've been some rather unsuitable remarks. A couple of people she just 'didn't hear,' then a couple more, she just met their eyes and they absolutely shrivelled.

"Best was when some real idiot, flown with far too much drink far too quickly, put his arm around her shoulder and kissed her cheek. Harmless, but … also very dangerous for him. I don't have to tell you that Uggò had more or less teleported across the room and was just a few feet behind him.

"Anyway, she just turned slightly to look him in the eye, smiled a second-best smile and – all very friendly – said, 'Have we met? I'm Caroline ap Gryffudd, Countess Beauclerc, Knight Commander of the Order of Myndarit and heir substantive to the Imperial throne. I want to thank you for your support today, and your fine conduct during the battle. Do you have a drink? Yes, clearly you do. Do you know, I think we should start serving food now. Would you be kind enough to pop across to the bar and ask Limond to get that under way for me?'

"Well, he moved his arm as though she'd suddenly become red-hot and fled for Limond. His friends tried to apologise, but she wouldn't have it. Said that if a man who'd risked his life for her couldn't be forgiven a little mistake – *once* in a while – then it would be a sad day. Then she just got on with some more glad-handing, cool as you like. But there was no more of that sort of thing. She'd made a very clear point about being the boss, without ever making the socialising seem false or forced – which I'm sure it isn't. I told you, sheer class."

Geraint nodded. "It's one of the large and growing number of things she does really well. They'll be eating out of her hand before tomorrow. Talking of which, we haven't talked about your ambush. It went well, yes?"

"Two hundred and eighty of them dead, and two hundred and twenty prisoners, of which about a hundred have various wounds. We lost seven, with another thirteen wounded."

"I think that could be defined as 'well', yes. Congratulations. What was the cloud of dust three miles back?"

"Another thousand infantry and some heavy horse. Bastin was leading them himself – no Bernard any more, of course, and you can guess he's probably not in the mood to trust Justan with much just now. They came up to the ambush scene, saw the bodies and turned back at once. I've got people shadowing them and a net of patrols through the area. Nobody's coming at us that way without our knowing about it.

"This Black Anis attack was astonishing, though. I've never even heard of more than about a hundred of them in one place at one time. There were over five hundred bodies out there, besides the ones that got away."

Geraint nodded. "Yes. Also they were very quick to arrive. It would be very good to know what that was all about. But that's for another day, since we have no prisoners. I gather they did their usual thing and gave grace to any of theirs too badly hurt to take away with them."

"Yes. Pity. Now, I've got another three units that want to swear fealty to the Lady. Good commanders – Mostyn, Jeff and Becca. That's Mostyn Parry, Jeff Alaghan and the Honourable Rebecca Wright. They bring four hundred and fifty between them.

"Everybody else is happy to sign contracts except for Lizzie Holt, damn it. She's the best of all of them. But Gentleman's are putting together their three in-house Free Companies into one for this invasion contract, and they've offered her overall command. For a girl of just twenty-six, that's too good to turn down."

"I see her point. So she's going to be on the other side."

"Yes, she's left already, because she's got to take formal command in two days – she only did this trip as a favour to me. Said to tell you it was nothing personal, though. Just business."

"Maybe we'll be able to make her a better offer later."

"Yes. If I get clobbered, she's your choice. Nothing like as good hand-to-hand, but a fine tactician and simply excellent as an all-around leader of cavalry.

"Talking of that, apparently the merc contracts for the invasion are all nine-month fixed-term. I think some button-counters on the other side got ahead of the field commanders – nine months is a bit tight for what they're trying to do."

"I think they believe they'll have it buttoned up much sooner than that."

Garrett grinned viciously. "Well, it'll be fun disappointing them. Because they won't. Seriously, they may have cleared all major forces out of their way much sooner than that, but the guerrilla actions will be an entirely different matter. And it's that sort of thing they'll need their light and irregular cavalry for."

"When are the other captains who want to swear fealty going to do it?"

"Tomorrow morning. I've told them to bring their boys and girls to the party. The Lady's not bothered about the cost, and it'll look well."

"Truly. Won't it crowd you out?"

"Yeah, but it's no problem. The weather's good so we're spilling over into the yard and the Square. I've got Belle's to go in amongst them and do their stuff. It's a lot of fun out there."

"Alright for some. Well, if there's nothing else, let's get up to the Grove. The coven are waiting for us."

Chapter 6

Malachi Frost feels no urge to toast absent "friends"

Malachi Frost leaned back in his chair and glanced round the rather comfortable dining room. They'd chosen an ancient baronial seat as his billet, and he decided he must remember to do something nice for the billeting team. The room was pleasant, the food had been excellent, and the deceased Baron's handsome widow was clearing away his plate while her daughter – very presentable and in her late teens – poured him another glass of wine.

The billeting team had clearly explained the realities of the situation very graphically, because both women were as humble, submissive and eager to please as anyone could wish. Further, it had been clear that neither had imagined, from the moment of his arrival, that he would tolerate being served by any but themselves. Normally, this was one of the things that made life worthwhile; defeating the enemy and enjoying his goods and his women while he lay on the field of battle for the dogs. But today that pleasure was a little less complete than usual because he still couldn't reconcile himself to the tragic farce that had been the Battle of Cole Valley.

It had begun in the way of so many in Frost's memory. As the first tendrils of dawn had floated above the eastern horizon, and with the lingering scream of the priests' offering echoing in their ears, the entire Order of Night had advanced at the walk. They'd walked their horses down the western slope of the valley, trotted across the lush vale, splashed across the shallow river, cantered towards the first defensive line, and then charged the up-slope at the gallop. The defenders had been driven back to the scarp.

The Order had then made a show of regrouping and preparing a second charge to carry the crest, but actually had merely been ensuring that the Imperials had no eyes but for the sea of black-armoured horsemen preparing to drown them in blood. That, of course, is when the Imperial Army had been hopelessly undone by the Knights of the Red Queen, who had struck their completely undefended northeastern flank. Frost had waited a few moments for the chaos this wrought in the Imperial ranks to spread to the front line facing them, then committed his knights to the charge.

After that, it was just slaughter. Overmatched in front and being gutted from the rear, the Imperial Army had disintegrated. A few units had held together and worked their way off the field, and Frost was pleased that several had contrived to fight their way to safety, at least for the moment. He always liked to see courage and military competence rewarded.

However, the story for the vast majority of the Imperial Army had been very different. According to Frost's information, about nine hundred and eighty thousand troops had taken the field against them. His staff informed him that just over three hundred thousand had been taken prisoner, and a further two hundred and twenty thousand – at most – had contrived to withdraw. That meant that a little under half a million corpses were lying where they'd fallen in that valley.

A great victory. Well, it would have been, had not the Imperial Army been placed precisely where the KRQ could reach them at dawn of that day. Had not all its scouts been kept away from that area so that the Red Death's arrival would be utterly shocking. And had not the Imperial Army's formation been laid out with a view to maximising the damage a rear attack might do. Where was the honour in defeating an army whose own commander had quite intentionally laid them out like one huge sacrificial offering?

Frost sighed in irritation. There *had* been honour won on the field, but it had been the preserve of the Red Death. They had flowed forward for a day and a night, never stopping for more than an hour - and then only six times - to arrive precisely at the time and place arranged. Then they had torn into the enemy like wolves, pressing and worrying at the fragmenting defensive formations, using their outstanding mobility allied to unparalleled ferocity to ensure that there was never a possibility of a stand, and never so much as a hope of reforming on a new front.

They'd done wonderfully well, and Frost had grudgingly been hugely impressed. It hadn't just been the achievement itself, it had been the neat and organised professionalism that had accompanied the savagery of the assault. All led by women, too. It really made you think. What could they be like with male commanders? Frightening thought.

Both the women serving him were now looking worried, unsure if his irritation was with them. He shrugged minutely. Let them worry; it would keep them on their toes. "You, woman. What's your name?"

"Naomi, Your Grace. My daughter is Amelia."

"I will be having a staff conference tomorrow morning at seven. You will need to serve breakfast to the officers as they arrive. They should all be fed and finished by ten to the hour. Tea, coffee, several kinds of juice. Spirits if they wish, but small measures – they'll expect that, there will be no complaints.

"You may use servants to prepare food and facilities and generally to assist you. But you yourself must be present and serving, as must your daughter, both dressed such that there can be no mistaking who you are.

"Now, I will take coffee and brandy and sit a while. That doesn't need both of you. You – Amelia, is it?"

The girl bobbed a curtsy. "Yes, your Grace?"

"Go to my bedroom. When I come to bed I will expect to find you stripped and standing waiting for me. Is that clear?"

"Yes, Your Grace." She bobbed again and left the room.

"Now then, Naomi. Coffee with brandy – and some more of that fruit cake. Then come and stand where I can reach you."

Frost sighed and relaxed. It hadn't been a perfect day, but the Empire was helpless before them, and victory was assured. At least a *little* contentment seemed to be in order.

Part 2

Taking Sides

Chapter 7

It isn't only armies that
can bring down Empires...

The man in the ornate chair at the head of the table tapped the table top with the elaborately decorated hilt of his dagger to call for order. He was a small, balding, expensively-clad aristocrat with cold, misleadingly sleepy eyes, one of which displayed a slight tic as he looked around at his colleagues - some allies and some enemies - along the large, gleaming, dark wood board. Then, seeing that every-body was ready, he turned his head and spoke for the benefit of a group of clerks at a large nearby table.

"This emergency meeting of the Imperial High Council is now in session, Armand du Calenisse, Grand Duke of Quem, Lord President of the Council presiding."

He turned his gaze back to the Council. "Gentlemen, we are in a position that doesn't allow us to dawdle.

"Sir Roland informs me that he was able to cobble together nearly a quarter of a million men from the rout of the Imperial Army. To this, the continued call up of reservists has already added a further two hundred thousand who were on their way to the colours at the time of the disaster at Cole Valley. We have another hundred and fifty thousand to come in the short term. More over time, as the secondary call-ups start to fruit and new troops start to come through from the training camps. Arms and equipment, at least, are in plentiful supply. Thus we still have, at least at first glance, a very considerable and still-growing force to stand against the invaders.

"However, the cold light of day shows us a different picture. Firstly, of course, even assuming we reach half a million troops in the short and medium term, they are still outnumbered five or six to one by the invading force. Now, a good defensive position can allow elite troops to overturn even such a disparity as that – though not often – but that is not a situation that is likely to occur here.

"Our problems are manifold. The troops, at their best, are not the equal of the Black Knights or the Red Death. Furthermore, they are not by any means at their best. Less than half of the newly formed army will be experienced regulars and, after Cole Valley, the morale of those men is questionable, to say the least. There is even a rumour abroad that the army was betrayed by its leaders, and this ludicrous fantasy has a grip amongst a large number of the Cole Valley survivors. It's one of those tales which will inevitably arise after that kind defeat, but its impact on morale is culpable. Worse, their disenchantment is communicating itself to the reservists as they join.

"At present Sir Roland is assembling and organising this force while moving rapidly eastwards. He proposes, if nothing changes, to keep retreating ahead of the enemy and finally to establish his main base at Rain Hill, somewhat to the north of Elf Haven. In other words, to stay about as far from the enemy as he can get. Thus we can hope that they will not gain any worthwhile intelligence about the severity of our problems, while he keeps his force in being for as long as possible."

A hand rose, part way down on his right. The Duke of Ninian, a long-standing enemy. "So let me see if I'm understanding you clearly. You are eventually going to get around to telling us that what we have is an army that looks more or less the business until and unless it actually gets anywhere near the enemy. Is that right?"

"I think you have done a masterly job of summing up, Your Grace."

"Wonderful. And so you propose...?"

"I think we need to negotiate with the enemy before it becomes too clear that in fact we lack any kind of negotiating position. They must know they can defeat us – at present they may believe that it will be at least somewhat costly. Let us strike a deal while they still labour under that useful misapprehension."

Armand du Calenisse
Grand Duke of Quem

A voice from the end of the table; the Earl of Granby, an ally. "So we need to send some envoys to meet their senior people. Discuss what accommodations might be arranged with them."

Du Calenisse nodded, as though this were a new idea and not one they had discussed together yesterday. "Yes. I think that would be a very worthwhile exercise. We should at least know what's on the table."

Ninian raised a quizzical eyebrow. "Our heads?"

Granby shook his head. "They will be practical men and women. An arrangement that saves them time, effort, lives and cost will surely seem worth their while. We should at least find out."

Ninian tutted, scowling, but then sighed. "A preliminary enquiry only, then. No commitments of any kind to be made without a full report to us here."

"Certainly."

"Oh, very well. So who will go on this arse-licking expedition?"

Du Calenisse tapped the table. "I don't believe we need to deface the decorum of this High Council with low vulgarity."

"Well, as may be. Personally, I don't think we should deface the decorum of this High Council with feeble pusillanimity. However, that fox seems to be in the hen house already, so I suppose we must make the best of it."

"Pusillanimity?"

"Oh dear, is the word too erudite for you? Gutlessness, Your Grace. Gutlessness."

Du Calenisse snorted and glared at Ninian. "My Lord Duke, I am possessed of an adequate vocabulary. I am simply unused to having the term applied to me. Great Gods, man, what would you have us do?"

"Assemble the ducal forces and join them to the Imperial Army. Invite the Myndarits to stiffen the mix. Seek help from other militant religious orders. The Arm of Mannan-Dar spring to mind. The Foresters of the Green Deep. Ask help from Her Majesty the Queen of Faerie – she stands or falls with us. See if we can't throw these swine out of our lands."

"Under what leadership? Sir Roland no longer even has the loyalty of his own troops. Who else is there, if a man of his standing and reputation cannot hold even the Imperial Army solid? How do we persuade the Dukes to commit their forces anyway? I'm certainly not of a mind to condemn my own troops to death, for instance. My Lord of Ninian, please can we look at the realities, not romantic dreams?"

"Very well, I admit I can think of not one person who could unite the Dukes and the religious orders under a single banner – never mind securing the support of Faerie – and nothing else would do. But surely with some thought we should be able to find somebody!"

"Well, Your Grace, when you have a suggestion we will all be most interested to hear it. However, bearing in mind that this council itself has no great standing in the country after Cole Valley, I suggest that nobody should hold their breath. In the meantime, whom shall we send to negotiate?"

Granby was ready. "We have to send people the Alliance will take seriously and negotiate with. I think it should be the Lord President and the Earl Marshal."

A new voice from the far end "A gift for the enemy! They could keep or kill them and cripple us!"

Ninian snorted. "Really? Cripple us? How would we notice the difference? It's hard to think that the battle of Cole Valley could have gone worse regardless of who might have been commanding, and as for His Grace the Grand Duke of Quem… Well, if he were gone we might find a replacement from further up the natural order - perhaps from amongst those animals with backbones, ideally. A Lord President with a spine would certainly be my own preference. Alright, alright, I withdraw that. Seconded."

Du Calenisse glared at him for a second longer, then looked around. "Contest? No? Very well. Clerks, carried *nem con.*

"Now, the last issue on our agenda this morning is the matter of ducal forces. As it stands, we are advising the dukes to pull their troops out of the areas the Alliance is occupying without allowing contact. This keeps those forces in being as a bargaining chip. Also, of course, it preserves our authority because if we ordered the dukes to fight I suspect we would be ignored, which would precipitate a power vacuum at a disastrous moment.

"The question before us is whether there is any other course of action available." He looked around, saw a hand. "My Lord Duke of North Cape. Your Grace?"

"So that's how many troops on the move? With how many horses?"

"As of today about ninety thousand, with a hundred and twenty-seven thousand horses."

"And how are these people being fed, housed and so forth at present? Residing as I do at the opposite end of the Empire, this is the first I've heard of it."

"It was an executive order, Your Grace. This meeting must ratify that, or change it. As it stands, the conurbations are being levied under emergency orders issued by me as is my duty under this Council's standing orders. They are receiving government scrip in exchange, the value of which will be redeemed by the exchequer from the dukes in question at the end of the emergency."

Ninian grunted. "If there are any at that point."

Du Calenisse inclined his head in acknowledgement. "As you say, Your Grace."

North Cape frowned. "What is the nominal value so far of the scrip issued?"

Du Calenisse beckoned to a clerk, who brought over several scrolls and two large books. There was a brief muttered discussion, and then Du Calenisse nodded to the clerk and looked up. "Just under eleven million, Your Grace. We are presently expending just under eight hundred thousand crowns daily on it, but of course that figure is of necessity expanding steadily as more troops fall back."

Another opponent, Alexandre, Duke of Holmersby, raised his brows and tapped the table. "Clearly, on those numbers this scrip issue will over time become an inflationary measure of some scale, which has the potential to derail the economy a little. Or more than a little."

There was a nod and then a shrug from North Cape

Du Calenisse grunted. "In the circumstances, Your Grace, I must say that currently I don't care."

Ninian raised both arms theatrically to the heavens. "Gods be praised! Something we agree on for once!"

North Cape stirred impatiently. "So you doubt the front-line dukes would actually hurl their forces into the pit if we told them to."

"Would you, you Grace?"

"Given some hope of achieving something, yes."

"And we can offer very little such hope – the troops would be facing overwhelmingly larger numbers of the finest cavalry units, heavy and light, anywhere in the world. Yes, My Lord Ninian, I don't doubt the Myndarits would disagree – they are undoubtedly far the best heavy horse that *we* can show – and their position would be arguable right up to their first significant contact with the Order of Night. Well, My Lord North Cape, what say you?"

Martin Connaught

"Take your point. Not much else to do, then. Just now, anyway. Propose we confirm the order."

"I second, of course. It was my order. Contest? *Thank you*, My Lord Ninian. Those in favour please show… Against...? Abstentions...? Very well. Clerks, the motion is carried by seven votes to four, with five abstentions."

"Meaning that there are fewer in favour than not."

"Do you dispute the passage of the motion, Your Grace?"

"No, it was merely an observation. You are losing your grip, Armand. This invasion is not exactly showing any of us in a good light – and you are first amongst us."

Chapter 8

Sir Roland meets two women, gains some crucial knowledge - if he knows how to use it - and loses his temper

Sir Roland was out on his own as evening came on; his army, such as it was, was making camp in three vast, ragged columns some five miles apart and some ten to twelve miles behind him. He was where he was so that he could have a private meeting with an Alliance representative to report on the state of the Imperial Army - which was parlous - and the likelihood that he might be replaced as it's commander - which was negligible so long as Armand of Quem was Lord President of the Council.

However, such liaison meetings were difficult to arrange, because the Alliance forces were a long way West and so the only way of doing it was to teleport a senior officer via a Mage. That in turn required precise visualising, meaning that a spot had to be chosen, a mage-impression of it had to be taken, and that in turn had to be conveyed to the Alliance HQ. So meetings were rare.

But today was to be one of them, and hence he was well ahead of the Army and looking for his contact, who should be just the other side of the small river just ahead... and in fact, looking up the slope on that side Roland could see a woman in a Red Death senior officer's uniform just a few hundred yards ahead.

As he got to the river – little more than a very large stream, really – he noticed that there was someone in a rich black cloak, with the hood up, standing at the edge of the water. He assumed it was the mage who had brought the Red Death officer, but as his charger stepped into the water he saw that this person was washing a metal ritual bowl and an Athame – a knife used in religious and other Heart Magic rites. An

Athame meant a Priest, therefore, and now he could see by her arms and hands that this was a woman. Her cloak bore a large golden device, presumably the emblem of her order, but he couldn't quite identify it.

As his charger forged forward, the water reaching no higher than the animal's knees, the woman walked briskly to the middle of the stream, pointed her Athame towards him and said in a conversational tone "Get down off the horse."

He immediately did so, wondering why he had. What was some strange priest to him that he should obey her so promptly?

But now she looked him full in the face, her hood back a little. It was an older woman, hair streaked with grey, a raw-boned, wrinkled, harsh face and eyes... eyes that you could not meet. Stone cold certainty chilled his bones and knotted his stomach. He spoke almost before he knew what he was saying. "Caillach. You are Caillach."

"I am, and your stinking godling owner is trying to interfere with Me. Amusing, because of course she's failing lamentably. I've nothing but contempt for her - nasty, twisted little half-a-thing as she is. For you, of course, I have that and more than that. I have a message."

Rowland sighed. "Yes, of course." He knew, naturally, that this is what Caillach has always done. She waylays people at the ford – any ford, or a bridge for that matter – and tells them their future. It is usually some element of their future that they really, really don't want to know.

Mainly the future is a matter of potentialities, but when Caillach foretells a thing that thing always comes to pass, because in doing so She crystallises it from potentiality to reality. So She chooses some element of your future for you from the vast range of possibilities available, fixes it immutably - and then tells you what She has done.

So he knew what was coming, and the prospect chilled him to the marrow. She stared into his face, and now not only could he meet Her eyes, he couldn't look away. Her manner was conversational, almost casual, but Her words filled his mind, feeling somehow... heavy. "Mark me, Roland. You will have a sword fight... one day. Yes, yes, yet another one. This one will be your last, win or lose. It will be different because your opponent will be young but already as good as you are now and destined to be far better than you have ever been, and also will be very much better equipped.

"However, you will win. That is, you will win *if* you watch out for the ugly youngster. Fail to do that and you will lose, you will die, and your foulness of an owner will take you – at least for a while."

She broke eye contact and turned away from him. "You can go now. Enjoy your day's treachery. Humdrum for you, of course, treachery."

And without fuss, or even a disturbance in the water, She was gone.

After a moment's shocked inability to think or move, Sir Roland remounted and walked his charger across the shallow flow and up the other side to the officer of the Red Death. She had been watching him curiously – and rather impatiently. "Why did you get off and stand in the middle like that? I don't have all day to wait around for the likes of you."

"Didn't you see..." But then he paused. Of course she wouldn't have seen. He squared his shoulders and dismounted. He was very tired of being spoken to with such clear contempt, and his knowledge that it was entirely justified was of no help to him in that.

He walked up very close to the officer and looked her in the face. "I stopped because I chose to. I've saved your forces countless thousands of lives and many, many weeks of campaigning, so if I require that you wait for a few minutes you will wait for a few minutes.

"Now, do you wish my report or shall we spend the time bickering? It's all one to me."

"You are still of use. Otherwise, I'd enjoy -"

"Try me." There was a feral intensity in his voice that would have convinced anybody he was entirely serious.

Though in his late fifties, Sir Rowland's coat of arms, the Screaming Eagle, was renowned worldwide for the tournaments he had won and the fine swordsmen he had defeated. There was no question but that he was one of the great sword fighters of the last century. Perhaps, at his peak, amongst the two or three best of all of them.

Perhaps the Red Death officer remembered that, and considered the likelihood very great that even at his age it would take him only seconds to have her bleeding and beaten and begging for her life. Or perhaps she simply remembered her duty.

Either way she snapped "Report, then."

He shrugged, with genuine regret. "You're sure you wouldn't like to try me...? Oh well then, so be it.

"After Cole Valley the army doesn't trust me. Some of our middle grade officers are excellent, and they – and even some senior NCOs - have noticed how appropriately laid out the army was to suffer maximum damage from an attack to the right rear, which is where the Red Death came from, of course.

"They find it hard to believe that a man as famous as I am is a traitor, but they are not able to put aside the evidence of Cole Valley, either. So there is a good deal of suspicion of me, but no concerted move to take action. This is ideal, of course, because it rots the Army's morale still further without threatening my position in any significant way.

"Other than that, my political position at Cromreth is still fully protected and the general condition of the Army is as reported last time, other than that we have further supplies of all kinds – none of which is of use because the army won't fight. Not while I'm in charge, anyway. They've no intention of giving me a chance to kill off the rest of them."

The officer nodded. "Very well. There will be no need for further reports of this kind. The war is as good as won, now. Just sit on your hands as far East as you can get until you hear from Cromreth that it's all over."

With that she turned on her heel and walked over the crest of the hill. A few seconds later the sound of a brief incantation and a slight 'whoosh' of inrushing air told him she'd gone.

Caillach

Chapter 9

Geraint faces another examination

A few minutes before midnight, Geraint, Iorweth and Mess were standing in the centre of the circle of trees at the heart of the Grove. The circle was large and consisted of many trees of several kinds. Lin Gor and Zeéla were in a small triangle, formed of salt and blood mixed, outside the Southern edge of the circle.

Lin Gor was, naturally, very familiar with Brandur rituals and explained what was happening. "There are thirty-nine trees in the circle. There's an oak at each cardinal point, then in deosil – that's clockwise – order there's a rowan and a holly. Then an oak, another rowan and so on around. Makes thirteen of each, of course, and it's no coincidence that it's one of each for each member of the coven. They're bound to their own trees by blood ritual at least, often orgiastic as well.

"Now, as for what we're going to see … normally, these rituals have two parts. The first part opens a channel of power, and the second part applies that power to whatever they want to do. It's usually much more complex than that, but those are the essential stages that every ritual must include. That is, every ritual but this one. Immersing the Dagger in Iorweth's blood raises all the power they'll need – the Dagger itself is the ultimate channel.

Now, what's going to happen is that Iorweth will cut himself on the Dagger, which Geraint will hold. Or possibly, the Dagger will be on the Altar. Then Iorweth will run about a pint or so of his blood into that silver bowl on the Altar. Geraint will make the invocation – buried in other text, probably – and we'll be in business."

Zeéla looked puzzled. "Lin Gor, my love. I see the coven arranged around the edge of the circle – Druid at the North point, I notice – and

I see the two boys and Mess in the centre. What I don't see is an Altar. Mess is holding the bowl."

Lin Gor tutted. "Sorry, my fault. Mess is clearly the senior witch. She's the altar. That's the reason she's nude."

"Sorry, boy, that sort of slipped by me."

"Another time. They're starting."

The coven began to chant in a complex rhythm, moving clockwise – deosil, Zeéla remembered – around the ring of trees, their steps going forward and back, matching the rhythm of the chant, and thus resembling a dance. The three in the centre stood like statues.

When the coven had made exactly one circle, the chant and rhythm changed subtly, and now the druid – Zeéla didn't know his name – began a different chant in a complementary, much faster rhythm, his voice deep and powerful. At the end of that circle, by which time Zeéla could see that the witches were sweating, the coven all dropped their robes, to reveal that all were naked beneath.

As they began the third turn, Geraint raised the Dagger and also began to chant, his rhythm much slower and more stately, at half-pace to the witches, with the coven druid's incantation set at twice their pace. Iorweth stripped off his shirt and Mess dropped to her knees, holding up the bowl higher than her head. There was a five-pointed oak star set in the ground at what Zeéla assumed was the exact centre of the circle, and as far as she could see, Mess had the bowl poised exactly over it.

As the coven exactly completed this rotation, they reached a cycle point in the rhythms – all three of the rhythms. As this arrived, everybody on the edge of the circle cried a single word loudly, in unison, right hands held flat, stretched vigorously out to point at the bowl – and then froze in place.

At the same instant, Geraint slashed Iorweth across the chest with the Dagger, Lin Gor whispered "Oops! My mistake." Iorweth leaned forward, and his blood ran unnaturally free from the slash across his chest and into the silver bowl.

At a small signal from Geraint, he straightened up and the blood flow immediately slowed. At the same instant the coven began circling to a much faster and more frenetic rhythm, their movements far more complex, including spins and leaps which were not simultaneous but rippled around the circle.

Geraint was now chanting in a pattern which was somehow deeply unsettling, and the words he was using, while unintelligible, none the less raised the hairs on the back of the neck. The coven druid was also chanting again, at the same pace as Geraint now, but his incantation was clearly some dialect of the Cymraeg, though his words and Geraint's seemed somehow to resonate one with another, the coven druid's chant somehow reinforcing and emphasising Geraint's delivery. The witches no longer offered an incantation of their own, but added a word here, or a short phrase there in chorus, each contribution somehow ramping up the tension and the sense of something dreadful impending.

Though the rite was entirely alien to Mannan-Dar traditions Zeéla was herself an outstandingly talented wielder of magical energy, and as the rite went on she became increasingly conscious that truly huge amounts of power were being channelled, requiring strength, exact understanding and iron focus to control.

From her own experience, and staggered by the almost incredible amount of power she felt swirling ever more ominously about them, she grew nervously aware that one slight mistake, either by the coven witches or one of the two druids, would be likely to cause that power to escape the druids' control. She had no idea what the result of that might be, but doubted anything this side of the horizon would survive it.

Her respect for the coven's abilities – and Geraint's own talent – grew in parallel with her tense desire to dig a hole and hide in it – not that she thought that would help much if this went wrong.

Exactly at the end of the next rotation, the coven repeated the shout-and-point even more dynamically. At the same instant Geraint plunged the Dagger into the blood in the bowl and thundered a single word, at which Iorweth cried out in pain – the first time he'd shown any discomfort.

Zeéla was not comforted that this was the first word in the entire ritual she'd understood, for the word was '**Brandur!**'

There was a moment of somehow very intense silence.

And, with no fuss, all that power was suddenly focused in one place and Brandur was there, standing just inside the northern point of the circle – in fact, where the druid had been.

The difference, however, was that the druid was a six-foot, husky young man. What stood there now was ten feet high, horned, hooved – and unmistakably a God, making Zeéla think of pictures of Pan or else Cernuddos that had crossed from Plane One with Humanity. It would very likely also remind a terrestrial observer of the images of Satan with which a millennium or so of Jesuits and their equally manipulative fellow travellers had tried to debase these ancient figures, whose real nature they had never even begun to understand.

The figure came forward to stand well within the circle, the coven witches facing inwards and passing a kind of echoing hum from one to another in a complex pattern. Geraint and Iorweth inclined their heads respectfully, standing otherwise very straight. Zeéla chuckled quietly, as their action reminded her that Geraint had more than once expounded his view that deities which felt they needed more deference than this probably had issues around insecurity and low self-esteem. Herself, though a follower of Mannan-Dar, she found the great figure in the circle both magnificent and awe-inspiring.

This wasn't the first time Geraint had called Brandur with this rite, but

he'd never lost that sense of awe that Zeéla was feeling. Brandur, in person, had an aura of power and majesty about Him that Alyssana had not had – or more accurately that She had not chosen to display, he corrected himself. Even in the protected triangle outside the circle, Geraint could see the spectators responding to the sheer raw force of Brandur's presence. But the smile on the big, weathered face was both gentle and genial as He considered the three before Him.

"You are doing better than we'd hoped, in the circumstances. But you now require a service of Me."

Geraint smiled deprecatingly. "Well, 'request' was the word I'd had in mind."

"I know. But actually, it clearly is a requirement if you are to stand much of a chance." He advanced to the centre of the Circle and laid His hand gently on Messalina's hair. She shuddered, gasped, tipped the bowl and drank from the blood within.

Then, as Brandur took a step back, She – that had been Messalina – arose, now dressed in dark green leather, with a pair of curved longswords crossed on Her back, and green eyes in a beautiful but somehow fierce face under short, spiked hair. The slightly lush figure of the possessed witch seemed now slimmer, more athletic.

Geraint and Iorweth both nodded respectfully toward this new vision. They were in the presence of their God and so feared nothing, for nothing could happen to them that their God did not choose to allow.

Cariseg looked the two men up and down. "Well. And why should I bring my people to your aid? They will do very well on Scythéa with the royal armies and the Orders Militant mainly over here."

Geraint cursed himself. Of *course* she would know what he wanted. *Idiot!* He saw the corners of Cariseg's mouth turn up the tiniest fraction. But then… "Lady, you already know why. If you do not, we are even more likely to fail." He wanted to go on and say that she didn't want Goreb and Marn dominating the world any more than the rest of them did, but stopped himself. He was fairly sure it was not good policy to tell any God what She wanted – and certainly not *this* one.

He found he was having to work a little at the matter of not being afraid. *This* was Cariseg, the Death of Gods. And – of course – She looked the part in an easy, understated, and thus even more impressive, way. More than that, even surrounded as he was by the Presence of Brandur, he could feel the edge of danger emanating from Cariseg. Still, there was definitely a slight air of amusement about Her.

"Sooo… The choice is whether to help My Father and Mother, My Brother – and Varan, the only other God who welcomed Me … or to throw in My lot with the two deities that have always most been My enemies. Hmm. A hard one, that. I will need to think about it." She flashed an almost impish smile over Her shoulder at Her Father, then turned back to Geraint, Her face serious.

"Well, Druid, if we are to be allies, then you should know Me better. But have a care, for if you seek to know Me, but haven't the strength to find what is there to be found - or the wisdom to recognise it – then you may suffer greatly.

"Such as you aren't made to be able to commune with Gods and, though I wish you no harm, still you might be snuffed out if you remain in contact longer than your frail little mind can bear. But once you begin your quest it can *not* end until you find what you seek. Or else your mind fails. Do you understand?"

Geraint nodded gravely. "I don't recall, when I first set my feet on the Path of Brandur, that anybody promised me it would be easy or safe." He glanced at the great figure behind Her. "But I *have* found it rewarding indeed. And rewards must be earned. Lay on as you will, Lady. I'm ready."

Cariseg

Cariseg nodded once in what seemed to be satisfaction, then met his eye. Once in the past, Geraint had looked Brandur in the eye – and seen there all the harsh cruelty of Nature, but also its beauty and its benevolence. But in Cariseg's eyes there was just death. Death dark and cold, death hot and bloody, death and death and death and – but no. Mentally he shook himself. Look past, don't get lost in it, for that way must lie destruction.

He looked on, with grim determination, on into the depth of those feral green eyes, and found … Death. Cruel death, death as welcome and kindly surcease from pain, hot death, cold death, fiery Death, bloody Death. Suffering and Death. Swift Death, violent Death, slow Death...

He could feel his strength stretching and fraying but, grimly determined, his mind no longer clear what he was doing or why he was doing it, beyond the fierce determination that he would not give in, he dived on into those hostile and deadly green depths.

And Death stared back at him. Death in battle, Death from disease, Death by accident, Death by design, Death of civilisations, Death of worlds, Death of Gods – he shied away from that whole path. Death for Love... Hold on … *there!* Something else, by that path. *Love?* Love. There was love there. And loyalty. And fierce care… for Her people, and for Her Family. And Death for those who threatened them. Oh yes, even this deep, Death. It rang in his mind like a huge bell, Death... Death... Death....

Slowly, he came to himself. How long had it been? Seconds? Days? Surely seconds, for everything was exactly as it had been. She touched his cheek gently. "Be easy now, Geraint fach. It's over. You have gained your prize. Be easy, I say." Her voice was soft and full of care for him. It flowed over him like balm, healing the horror, leaving only vague memories and a broader understanding than had been his before.

Geraint smiled his thanks, and bowed – deeply, now. Now he knew Her, a very little bit. And She was more than he'd understood – notwithstanding the fact that *any* God is vastly more than any mortal could possibly understand. He heard Her voice as if in a dream, now. It was sweeter than he'd thought before. Full of fire and passion, but not cold – never that.

"He'll do, Father. He'll do. You'll have my people. All of them. Druid, don't tell your cousin, but she may get very much more than she imagines."

She turned to smile at the great figure behind her. "Now I need to put your little girl back, Father, before I hurt her."

And quickly – over just a few seconds – the edgy, wildly dangerous Presence faded and was gone, leaving once again the witch Messalina, looking dazed and exhausted, but standing straight and proud, none the less, in the Presence of her God.

Chapter 10

Some Insights

The next morning, an hour after dawn, Carol stood in the court-yard. Behind her stood John Garrett and Iorweth, who was striving to look vicious. JG never looked any other way. Geraint stood beside her, with Balliss behind *him*. Ballis' troops were spread around the edges of the courtyard. Lin Gor and Zeéla were on Carol's other side, while Uggò was drifting around inconspicuously somewhere nearby, probably with a blade in his hand.

The three captains who wished to swear allegiance entered in turn with their officers. According to a drill rapidly worked out by Geraint and John Garrett earlier that morning, they bowed politely on reaching a spot that had been hurriedly marked by a bit of dirty cloth on the flagstones. Their officers stayed there, while the captain advanced to a second spot marked by an old horseshoe, and swore allegiance in an old traditional form: "I acknowledge you as my Empress. I swear obedience and to serve and protect you for as long as I shall endure."

This form of oath had been amended a millennium or so before to cater for the fact that the existence of numerous undead had made the ancient original wording "...as long as I live" inadequate. Some people might contrive to serve for *much* longer than that.

After the swearing, there was a general conference, including the Privy Councillors, John Garrett, Ballis and the newly-sworn officers.

Caroline opened the meeting by welcoming everybody to the enter-prise and expressing her pleasure at their decision. Then she indicated Geraint. "For anybody who doesn't know, this is Geraint ap Gryffudd, my cousin. He is my trusted friend and advisor. You may always be certain that any request or instruction that comes from him also comes from me."

Geraint stood and inclined his head to Carol, then turned back to the meeting at large. "Good morning, ladies and gentlemen. The first order of business is perhaps a little unusual. Clearly, we need more troops. It would help us all in the task of recruitment if we understood well what it was that had brought our existing friends to the cause. So I would like to go around the table and ask for a brief summary of what has brought each of you here."

As previously arranged, he began with JG. "Captain-General, perhaps we could start with you."

Concealing his surprise at being called 'Captain-General,' JG looked around the table. "It's straightforward for me. The Empire's always been there. This side of that border is a little raw, sometimes – and that's fun, sometimes – but the Empire's like a great safety net. You can always go to the Empire. People get enough to eat, people don't get attacked in the street, people get to live their lives the way they want to. You all know what Scythea's like – or the Empire of Mallow, for that matter.

"I never really noticed the Empire. Took it for granted. Just a great big security blanket in the background. Suddenly, it might not be there anymore, and I don't like that one bit. Of course, I could go join the Imperial Army…" There was laughter around the table. "Yeah. But now the Council's not the only choice, and I like the alternative. These people may be young, but you'll find they they know what they're about and they're sharp. And they know how to treat folks." He smiled. "Also, they know a class act when they see one."

Amid more laughter, Geraint indicated Balliss. He shrugged. "Simple for me. I'm tired of the merc route. I fancy getting in at the bottom of something interesting. That's where the opportunities come – and here I am with a huge one. Anyway, people are going to have to choose soon. I prefer to choose the side that's going to leave me with choices at the end."

John Garrett snorted. "Come on, sonny. Say the rest."

Balliss shifted in his seat. "Alright. My boys and girls – me, too… We've never seen anybody like the Lady before. Not likely to again. If we're going to stand or fall by somebody, like in the old romances, it needs to be someone very special or we're all going to feel like a bunch of complete idiots. She… Oh, to all Hells with it! The Lady is as special as you like. I didn't think people like her really existed."

He stared around, almost defiantly. Garrett shook his head. "They don't, not but one - and we've got her. It's the kind of luck you get just once, if ever."

Mostyn was next. "On the one hand, I don't like Marn and Goreb. On the other, I'm ambitious, and I see it the way Ballis does. And there's not a competition problem because we're in so early that there's room for everybody to climb a long, long, way. 'Specially as most of us won't last three months, the way it's going. As for the Lady, that speaks for itself. There's not many people wouldn't want to follow an ap Gryffudd, given the choice – they've been earning their rep for a millennium or two. And here we get the chance to follow not just any apGryffudd, but *this* one."

Mostyn Parry
Mercenary Captain

He sat, and Jeff hooked his thumb to his right, where Mostyn was having serious recourse to a tankard. "What he said, basically. And Balliss. It's the Lady on the one hand, or crud like the Black Anis on the other – or that slimy duke who left his boys lying in the road and legged it. The Lady wouldn't do that, nor would her people. No way. So it's no time to sell to the highest bidder because there's only one side worth being on – and if it looks like being the losing side just now, well too bad, we'll have to find a way to change that."

Becca stood. "My reasoning's a bit different – and then again, not so much. I'm the second daughter of a marquis in the Empire of Mallow. I know what Mallow's like, and I know what the *real* Empire is. And my family's followed a Reis for more generations than we can count – and not many of 'em's been worth a light.

"So now we can have an ap Gryffudd Empress in the real Empire – and she *is* worth a light, by His Juice. She's the real thing. And I should know, I've seen the would-bes and the try-to-bes in Mallow.

"I've always wondered if the ap Gryffudds were really all they were cracked up to be in all those stories, and now here we have two of them – and guess what. All that bigging up? All the centuries of bards and poets pining for what might have been? They didn't know the half of it. The real ap Gryffudds don't just live up to their billing, they make it look tawdry. It's not 'why am I in?' – it's 'who wouldn't be?' It really is that simple."

Carol briefly put a hand on Geraint's arm and rose. "Gentlemen, and ma'am. I am unclear what it is about us that has so fired your thoughts. I do know that we understand the weight of expectation that now lies on us, and if we fail to do our part then it will not be for lack of effort or determination. Not ever."

The Hon. Rebecca Wright
Commander. "Wright's Riders"

She laid her hand rather formally on Geraint's shoulder. "I know my cousin well enough to be assured that your hopes and ambitions could have no finer champion than he is. For myself, what I can do, I will do. We may not succeed in this enterprise – certainly the odds are not precisely in our favour – but we *will* make sure that these invaders and despoilers never, ever forget us! Those few of them that survive."

She sat, to a scatter of 'Damn' right!' and one 'Hear, hear.'

Geraint picked up immediately. "So since we're going to do that, there need to be more of us. A lot more. Suggestions?"

JG looked around enquiringly. "My reckoning is that if we spend, say, six weeks recruiting, we could probably find something in the region of five thousand riders. Can anybody think of a use for infantry in this? Because I can't."

Ballis cursorily waved a hand for attention. "Can't think of a use for infantry. I *can* think of a use for mages. We're going to need to get to a lot of different places – and then get ourselves away again very fast. Don't the old buggers all say, 'If you can't have numbers, be mobile?'"

John Garrett nodded emphatic agreement. "Aye. The only numbers that count are the numbers you can bring to bear at the point of contact – that's the essence of all tactics, really."

Zeéla smiled. "Well, as it happens, I can help with that. We can put an Arm priest with every group. That will help with *Heal* spells and the like, but also they will have scrolls or rings – or both – of stuff like *Magic Carpet, Teleport, Portal*, all sorts of good stuff. We've got lots of 'em."

JG sat back. "Now *that* makes a difference."

Lin Gor added "And we can get the Players to recruit around the Empire. They would also be useful for intelligence. It's hard to think how we could have better sources of information. They're everywhere. Oh, and a point. We *will* be penetrated at some stage. Soon, probably. So from this moment, the Arm transport experts are always 'the boats.' Our intelligence network is 'the scouts and salesmen.' That's when talking to your people, to each other, to us, to anybody. Don't even think of it as a cover name. Alright?"

Nods from around the table and a slight relaxation of tension. Having an edge – or at least even *feeling* that you have – always helps.

Geraint nodded. "Right. We all need to get out recruiting. We will want a team to go to Gorton with us in eight days to cover an important meeting there. Should be more rather than less because we'll be wanting to make an impression – John, who?"

JG looked round, then gestured. "Becca. She's more political than the rest of us and also her outfit's been together longest, I think."

"Fine. Becca, please get yourself back here in seven days, with whatever team you have by then. Everybody else, back in six weeks. Questions..? No? Right. It's time we were away, then. We've got the largest army in the world to stop."

Chapter 11

Armand, they're entirely serious... A meeting with some rather widespread implications

Armand du Calenisse looked around the table. "Well gentlemen, we are all here, so if everybody's ready let us call the meeting to order and get on.

"I can now report on our meeting with the leaders of the Alliance forces, which took place over four days on neutral ground under the auspices of the Emperor of Mallow.

"Really, I have to say that our discussions with the Alliance leaders were extremely productive. Of course, there is both good news and bad. The bad news is no worse than one would anticipate, however - we cannot expect to see the Empire survive as an entity. It will be split as dependent territories of the various Alliance kingdoms. Though I do have more to say about that presently.

"The good news, on the other hand, is very good indeed - in fact outstandingly good - for us as individuals. If we were between us to manage a successful take-over by the Alliance, we would in consequence see ourselves with very significant territories and major rôles in the new structures."

He tapped the table for emphasis. "And, of course, bear in mind that Alliance aristocrats *own* the territories they are allocated and there is very little by way of laws to control them. Naturally, this would be doubly so such a great distance away from the ruling kings on Scythéa. Really the prospects could hardly be more inviting.

"So, gentlemen, opportunity smiles in our faces and we must take her by the hand while we can.

"Thus, the first question before us must resolve the nature of the transition. We should consider whether a simple formal surrender is the way to go, or whether we should be looking at other options. Surrender has the benefit that the matter concludes swiftly, and we would have the support of the likes of the Red Death and the Black Knights from the first in our new, enlarged territories.

"However, if we wanted to be more creative - with a clear promise of energetic support, both military and financial, from the Alliance for our actions - there are options that might offer us even better outcomes. For instance, we might arrange that our own territories suceed from the Empire, offering allegiance to given Alliance kings, and, with Alliance help, seize adjoining territories.

"This is a fascinating possibility, as it would leave us in control of very large territories which would be in the bulk of matters self-govern-ing, though in the last analysis still subject to Alliance control, of course, and required to render a proportion of revenue to the relevant support-ing Alliance king.

"There was a lengthy discussion about this in Mallow and there are several such ideas to offer, all of which are fully supported by the Alliance's leadership–"

Du Calenisse was halted by a loud cough interrupting his carefully prepared speech and turned with weary patience to acknowledge the hand that had by now been raised for some moments on his right.

"My Lord Duke of Ninian. Of course. *Yes*, your Grace?"

"Armand, you are *quite* wrong. The first question is a very much simpler one. Are we going to submit or are we going to fight?"

"Fight? *Fight?* With what? How? To gain what advantage? With what hope of succcess? Have you for some reason not been paying attention to current affairs these last weeks? Do you recall some events that took place at Cole Valley recently, by any chance?"

He shook his head sharply and made an irritated chopping motion. "I will not waste the Council's time putting such nonsense to–"

"Seconded!"

Du Calenisse stopped, took a deep breath, then another, then spoke in a deliberately patient tone. "My Lord of North Cape, there was no motion…"

North Cape, scowling fiercely, slapped the table with the flat of a meaty hand. "Count the gods-damned votes! Do it! Or we'll elect a Lord President who will."

Armand sighed in exasperation and took another deep breath, thoroughly put off his balance by this unanticipated opposition. He'd expected trouble from Ninian but, considering the prospects of wealth and power to be gained under the Alliance, had very much expected him to be isolated.

However a rapid glance at expressions round the table showed that Ninian and North Cape had allies. Quite a few allies. This wasn't how the meeting had been planned to go at all, but he couldn't drive on until this sudden revolt had been voted down - he had his own position to protect until he could steer this meeting to a successful conclusion.

"Very well, if you insist. The motion is that we try to fight on …" He waved a hand vaguely. "Somehow. Are you content with that my Lord of North Cape, my lord of Ninian? Very well. All those in favour? Against? Abstentions?"

Armand counted, then counted again. Appalled and badly shaken, he spread his arms in expostulation. "Gentlemen, gentlemen, you can *not* be serious."

The Duke of Ninian snorted and gestured to the clerks' table. His expression was bland, but his eyes were darkly hostile. "Record the vote, Armand."

Jaroslav Stahl
Grand Duke North Cape

Armand of Quem's face was pale with shock and growing fury. His lips were so tight they nearly vanished. "Clerks, votes in favour eight. Votes against six. Abstentions, two. The motion... the motion passes."

He spat that last out most reluctantly, then glared at Ninian. "*Are you satisfied,* your Grace? This day's romantic clowning will cost us all long in the purse and that's a fact." Staring malevolently at Ninian, he added "It may well cost some of us our lives. Indeed it might."

Ignoring him, Ninian got to his feet again. "Propose we adjourn *sine die*. We're completely wasting our time here. All that this... this meaningless shell of a Council can do now is send orders to an army that won't face the enemy, and *avoid* issuing orders to dukes who won't take any notice unless we tell them to do what they were going to do anyway. Both exercises in total futility, then.

He turned a hand over. "Whereas at home there is some hope I might actually be helpful to my people." Staring venomously at Armand, he added "And if the Council doesn't meet, then it damned well cannot decide to do anything treasonable, is what I'm thinking."

"Seconded!" This from three or four voices speaking at once and forcefully, with North Cape's rich baritone underpinning them.

Ninian waited three or four seconds for any objection then smiled sardonically at the fuming Grand Duke of Quem. "Well, a seconded motion with no contest passes by rule. I'll see you gentlemen when it's all over – one way or the other. At least we can be proud of our last meeting if not of what's passed before. My congratulations, gentlemen, and good day."

Chapter 12

A small, much more private, meeting with perhaps equally widespread implications

Borgia Garrett looked out of the window of the private function room of the Fox and Hounds and sighed with relief. There were lightly armoured, heavily armed riders moving at a trot down both sides of the street outside. "Mum! It's alright. They're here."

Lucinda poured herself another drink. "Well, thank all bloody gods and their bastards for that... D'you think he'll be with them?"

"He is. I can see him. Gods, they've got hundreds of riders with them."

"Coming up in the world."

"It seems."

"Think they've got it?"

"Oh, yes."

"I feel sort of naked without a cover team, bab."

"Mum, if nobody knows where we got the money, that's probably still too many people."

Two men in leathers came into the room, swords drawn. They nodded politely to the two priests of Alma, looked behind the small bar, kicked the floor-length curtains, then left.

Next came a tall, muscular, dark-haired woman, holding a sabre with easy familiarity, as though it had grown to manhood in her hand. She did the same circuit of the room the two men had, then went to stand by the window, looking out. Two more men came in and stood on either side of the door. Next came Uggò. He prowled the room once, glanced at the window, then went and stood against the wall to the left of the fireplace, giving Borgia a broad, humourless smile.

There was a pause, then John Garrett squeezed through the doorway and stopped, blocking it completely. He looked around. "Where's Hendricks?"

"We brought no cover team at all. We need this to be secret."

"Good. Very sensible. Where's Hendricks?"

"I've just told you—"

Uggò waved a hand briefly, then hooked a thumb at the fireplace.

"Ah. Hendricks, come out, my son. I want to shake your hand anyway, and you'll have nothing to do. She's quite safe: I'm here."

Hendricks dropped lightly and silently into the hearth, made as though to step forward – then rolled and came to his feet, a pistol cross-bow in his hand, the point of the quarrel about a foot from Uggò's neck – or rather, where Uggò's neck had been a fraction of a second before. He'd moved, and a saw-toothed blade sliced a hair's breadth away from Hendricks' throat. They both relaxed and nodded coolly to each other.

JG had been watching closely and had an unusually fast eye, but it had clearly still been too quick for him. 'Who won?" The two young assassins looked at each other and shrugged. Uggò cocked his head. "Too close to call without the strike itself."

Hendricks nodded. "Maybe we'll find out one day."

Garrett indicated a chair, "Come and sit down, my son. You're going to be part of this." He extended a very large, muscular hand. "And I wanted to congratulate you on the grand job you're doing, looking after my little girl."

To Borgia's very visible amazement, Hendricks slapped palms then clasped the proffered hand – the first time she'd ever seen him honestly shake somebody's hand. She must have gasped, because he cocked an eye at her. "Well, Ali, it's your dad. Man's got to trust somebody, and if John Garrett wanted to kill me he wouldn't need a trick – I'm a killer, not a fighter."

Uggò snorted with poorly concealed laughter, and Hendricks raised a brow at him. "One of your lines?"

Uggò shrugged, smiling slightly. "I don't have copyright on it."

JG went back to the doorway, leaned out, nodded, then came in and stood just to the right of the door, in front of the trooper who was already there. He winked at Lucinda, then called in a firm voice "Her Imperial Majesty Caroline the First, Countess of Beauclerc, Knight Commander of the Order of Myndarit, Chosen of Varan and by will of the Gods, Empress of the Lands of the Holy League. All rise."

Hendricks was still on his feet anyway and the two Alma priests rose politely, wearing similar expressions of mild surprise. Caroline entered. She was wearing her blue leathers, her long, shining hair in its usual loose plait. She was followed by Geraint and Zeéla, walking together, then Iorweth and Lin Gor. They spread around the table with Caroline, of course, at the head. JG went to a seat beside Lucinda, and they smiled at each other - briefly, but in a way that rather excluded the rest of the room. Borgia moved her chair slightly, so that she was at the opposite end of the table from Carol and facing her.

Caroline smiled one of *those* smiles. "Shall we sit down? Becca, would you be so kind as to get one of your gentlemen to organise fresh drinks for everyone? Thank you. Ladies, master Hendricks, thank you for coming. I'm very pleased to see you all well. Geraint?"

She sat back slightly in her chair and Geraint, seated on her right, sat up a trifle straighter. "Good evening. I have a piece of paper for you. Do you have anything for us?"

Borgia put her small document case on the table and opened it, noticing with slight amusement a degree of extra tension in the poses of the troopers, and especially Uggò. Moving much more slowly in acknowledgement of the interest around her, she withdrew two documents from the case and then passed it across to her father. She was slightly startled when he looked quite carefully inside before passing it back. She started to be offended, but then decided that actually it was a warming compliment.

She refocused on Geraint. "I have two documents here. Each grants the bearer – not named – the right to view the audited and sworn internal accounts of Demon's Edge. It is noted that these accounts will be available at Winter Solstice at our headquarters in Demon's Gate, and will relate to the year ending on the Year's Death three months previously. The text also gives the bearer the right to enter and leave our Demon's Gate establishment unhindered and unharmed for the sole purpose of examining the accounts, once annually.

"Each document then goes on to state that the bearer has the right, at any time until the following Year's Death, including the Passage Hand of the Year, to claim goods, currency, or services from the Demon's Edge Corporation to a total value of three point five percent of the net annual revenue shown in the accounts. This value may be drawn from any office or appointed representative of the Demon's Edge Corporation.

The rest is just ugly threats about disclosure of the accounts to third parties and the various draconian penalties for that.

"The documents are signed and blood-sealed by the Chief Executive and the Secretary of Demon's Edge, and are witnessed by the Chatelaine of Alma and the High Priest of Baraani at Demon's Gate. To be valid, I must sign and blood-seal a statement at the bottom that I have delivered them to the appropriate party. The documents expire after the passage of twenty Year's Deaths from the next after the date of my signature.

"The bearer may be different people on each occasion the document is used, but it will not yield more than three point five percent in total – you can't draw three point five per bearer."

Geraint extended a hand and was passed the two sheets. "Seven percent, not seven point five."

Borgia shrugged apologetically. "I did the deal I could do. Sorry."

Garrett smiled affectionately at his daughter, who ignored him. He'd seen a third document in her case when he'd searched it. It was like these two, but related to half a percent.

Geraint glanced around the table and got no negative indications. "I have here a draft on Baraani for two hundred million Imperial crowns. It is made out to bearer. I imagine you have a further letter in there relating to the terms on which this sum is advanced."

"I do." She produced it and passed it over. "It specifies that the money must be paid in full to Demon's Edge Corporation, but requires that these funds be held in a separate account, and that any draft on that account must be authorised by me, in person or by my blood-sealed signature. It lists alternates to me, in the event of my death or disappearance. In order, they are my mother, Hendricks, and my father. In the case of the death or unavailability of all of the above, the remaining funds revert to Baraani for immediate disbursement by random selection to registered charities on this continent."

Geraint nodded approval. "Excellent life insurance."

"Yeah. I believe so. Constraint might still be an issue, though. I'll need to be careful." She shrugged.

Geraint smiled and spread his hands. "Not like your current careless invulnerability, then."

Borgia smiled. "It *is* a fu – a freakin' big improvement, can't argue with that." She gestured out the window. "Your own project seems to be going well. You've just occupied Gorton without so much as a whimper."

"Lin Gor popped in to see the town council earlier. We didn't want any foolishness when we arrived."

"I gather they were amenable."

Lin Gor smiled. "When they heard we weren't going to loot the town and we actually intended to pay for the night's accommodation – I gave them an advance – they were positively adoring. Obviously, I didn't tell them who was coming, but we're going to leave in style in the morning. Give the townsfolk something to remember and to talk about. Especially talk about."

Geraint resumed. "Now, for what you can do for us. We want four things at this point. We want regular and frequent intelligence feeds, and we want Demon's Edge to act as recruiting agent for our mercenary forces – we will use a different agency to recruit our regulars; it'll save embarrassment all round, what with Alma being on the other side. Next, there will be some fairly large military camps being set up, and we will need you to supply them – we'll arrange drop points. Finally, we want safe havens for small scouting parties."

Lucinda was making notes. "These scouting parties – how small?"

Zeéla raised a hand. "Probably one person and an escort. They'll want to come into a place, take a fairly quick look, and go away. We would want your local organisation to manage the entire exercise. I imagine we'd need a cover story for the project: those guilds are unlikely to be secure, to say the least."

Lucinda nodded. "Probably several different ones. We might have been retained to do a set of simultaneous assassinations, and your party are the advance team preparing a plan for the assassin. That could be one. Another might be that we're seeking the location of a powerful magic item that we plan to, um, obtain. We know it's in one of a list of places and we're ticking them off 'til we find it. That would do for when you can't hide the fact that one of the party is a caster. I'll think of some more."

Geraint shrugged at Zeéla and Lin Gor. "What would you expect? Of *course* she's worked out what we're doing with this." He turned back to the priests. "Sounds good. Right. Liaison and communication?"

Borgia picked this one up. "I told you I'm collecting a group of like-minded friends? I'll attach two of them to you. There's a … a warrior, merchant, and adventurer called Pindra. And a junior priest – more junior than me but very bright – named Elaine. They each have a different means of direct, private communication with me. I've got them hanging around about ten miles away with our cover team. I'll get them to join us before morning. They'll need a cover story themselves for being with you, to conceal the link. Pindra can be a bodyguard for one of you; she's actually very well qualified for that. Elaine can be her girl-friend. We don't have to get complicated."

"Can they carry that off?"

"Pindra's into girls – that's how I met her – and she and Elaine do play together occasionally, though Elaine usually prefers boys. So do I these days, for that matter."

She heard Hendricks' quiet (somewhat smug) chuckle and waved a playful fist at him then turned, still smiling slightly, back to Geraint. "Certainly they can be a realistic couple for quite a few months at least. Look after them, please; they're very good friends – both of them, but especially Elaine."

"We'll do our best. But this isn't the safest thing anybody's ever done, you know."

"Yeah, I know. But as you can."

"Surely. Well is the business finished?"

"Well, there's quite a lot of detail to thrash out, but other people can do that. So yes, I think so."

Garrett exchanged a glance with Lucinda. "In that case, Lucky and I are going to pop up to a room and … catch up. Al – can we have a chat, say in a couple of hours?"

His daughter nodded. "I was thinking we might, if you've got time. I wouldn't blame you if you had better things to do."

"What? Stuff and nonsense. I'll make time. I can always go back and see Lucky again afterwards, if that suits her." Lucinda smiled at him.

Borgia nodded, then smiled. "In that case, I'll go and have a... chat with Hendricks in the meantime. Knock number six when you're free. This will be the first time we've been able to relax properly and feel actually safe in years – well, since we met, really." She looked at Carol. "I hope you don't mind, but it's too good an opportunity to miss."

Caroline smiled broadly at the young Alma priest. "Goodness, no. I'm maybe a little jealous, though. We'll just settle for some dinner."

Borgia glanced at Geraint. "I thought– No, never mind. We'll just…" She stood up, looking slightly confused, and Hendricks steered her out, visibly trying not to laugh. Without much success.

Chapter 13

Gate-crashers are almost never really welcome...

aleb Forster and his sister Crysta had been working for Demon's Edge since they were children. They had been doing personal special errands for Magda Leona for over five years, and they'd never failed.

Admittedly, for most of that time they hadn't had the really hard ones; those had gone to Rickard, a supremely dangerous man. This would – until a month or so ago – have been Rickard's job, but he'd gone after one of tonight's targets and not come back. Caleb shrugged mentally. Everybody can be careless and that boy who looked after the target was really quite good. Not usually good enough to beat Rickard, he suspected, but it just hadn't been Rickard's day maybe, and with talented opposition you only need one of those.

Caleb had been timing the return of the next patrol in his head. His count expired and the patrol came around the corner. He relaxed on the spot, knowing that to remain really still one didn't freeze, which left muscles tense and unreliable, leading to self-betrayal. Easing to stillness was the way to do it. The patrol walked past – alertly enough, but they hadn't seen anything except what they were intended to, certainly not the two broken patterns of extra darkness in the shadow.

Next count was Crysta's, and she gestured that he had time. He raised himself carefully to the window and put the jewel to his eye. No magical protections. Excellent. He slipped a thin blade under the window, found the catch, and slid the window silently upwards. They slipped over the sill and paused as Cysta signalled that her count was low. They waited. Five seconds later the counter patrol appeared from the facing street. They reached the front of the inn, their leader tossed a coin, caught it, and looked. They moved off left, around the inn.

Fine. Crysta set off first on her route. Caleb followed after a few seconds. *Upstairs, utterly silently. A cat in the corner of the corridor – just watching, not a concern. Room two, no. Room four, no. Room six, now then... Door jamb, lever handle, hidden hinges. Can't open it silently.*

No problem. He had a Wand of Penetration. The door was unlikely to be six inches thick, which was the limit for organics. Silently he took it from his pouch, ready at hand because he'd been expecting to use it. He smiled slightly to himself. It was such little things that separated the truly professional from the dead.

Then a great surprise took him as his head was pulled back by the hair and a saw-edged blade cut his throat so deeply that it scraped on bone. He fell into darkness, still wondering who could possibly have sneaked up on him – on *him*...

✳ ✳ ✳

Carol dreamed that a voice was saying, "Wake up! Wake up! Wake up! Wake up! Wake up! Wake up!" She was lying in bed, her Sword, as ever, beside her under the bedclothes with her hand on the hilt. She slowly drifted up from the haze of sleep.

"Good. About time. The guard at your door has just died. Pull me slightly from the sheath. Just an inch."

Silently, she slipped the sword up a bit.

"Good. Now I can talk to the other Gift-Bearers."

In the light from the window, Caroline saw a figure materialise through the door, carrying a dripping dagger.

"There is an assassin in my Bearer's room! Do something sensible!"

The figure drifted silently towards the bed. Carol waited, quietly, the Sword not disturbing her concentration. The figure didn't raise the dagger to stab, but extended it to slice across her throat. As the blade crossed the edge of the bed, Carol threw the bedclothes at the encroaching shadow, tangling the knife arm in them, and rolled off the bed on the other side. By the time the shadow opposite her had disentangled the blade, Carol was standing on guard, the sheath on the floor and the Sword glowing.

At that second the door flew open, and Geraint stood in the doorway. He pointed to the figure and called a phrase. Light bloomed in front of the face of the intruder, a slim woman. She cried out and flinched backwards.

Geraint waved Caroline back and intoned a longer, more complex incantation, during which the assassin, calculating her chances, considered a leap at Carol and abandoned the idea. She turned the blade inwards, raised it, and brought it down with all her might.

But Geraint had finished his incantation. He cried the activating word and pointed at the assassin. As her blade came sweeping down towards her own heart, she fumbled and dropped it. Then she stumbled against the bed and fell. Trying to get up, she entangled herself in the sheets and fell again.

As she was struggling with the entangling bedclothes, Geraint stood back to allow Becca and two troopers into the room. The troopers grabbed and trussed the wailing assassin as she struggled to release herself from the bedding, and carried her out, followed by Becca.

"What was that cast, cousin?" Carol asked, sheathing her Sword.

"***Curse of the Ages***. It's the nastiest of all the non-fatal curses. Everything you try to do, you fail to do. First time I've ever used it in a live situation to be honest, but it worked well enough. Are you unhurt? I see you are. Perhaps you should put on some clothes."

Carol looked down. "Ah, yes. I'd say Becca's troopers deserve a commendation for keeping their minds and eyes so firmly on business."

Geraint tried to smile, and failed. "That was too close, cousin. Too close. I'm going to interrogate that assassin. Don't come yet. Dress and compose yourself." He turned and called out, "Zeéla!"

The Mannan-Dar priest had obviously been approaching, for she answered from a few yards away and appeared almost immediately. "Are you alright, Lady?"

"Fine, but thank you."

"Uggò has killed another outside Borgia's room. He's searching for more. I'll stay with you."

Geraint nodded. "That's what I was going to suggest. See that all is well. Help the Lady to dress, if you would–"

"I can dress myself, cousin. I've been able to do that for quite some time now."

"—and make sure she's fine. I'm going to talk to that assassin. No need to hurry."

"No, Junior. We'll take our time."

Geraint found the assassin stretched on a table in the room in which they'd met Borgia and Lucinda, her arms and legs pulled wide over the sides of the table and bound tightly to the legs. Becca was just finishing cutting off her clothes. The young druid walked up to where she could see him. "You are completely helpless, and you could not achieve anything even if you were free. That enchantment doesn't wear off; I have to remove it."

The girl, perhaps twenty-five, stared silently at him.

"Very well. You know how this is going to go. If you answer all our questions, you will be unharmed. But at present it would take very little to persuade me to hurt you terribly. So if you want to remain alive and untouched you know what to do. What is your name?"

The woman was silent. Geraint shrugged, walked to the side of the room and drew a circle on the floorboards with his dagger. Then he nicked his arm and let some blood drip in the groove he had made. He used some of the assassin's ripped clothing to wipe the blood all the way around, being quite careful.

Then he invited Becca and her troopers to stand in the circle. "Do not – I mean do *not* – step out of this. Understood?" All three nodded. "Very well. I would appreciate quiet, as well, if you would."

He held the dagger in both hands and cried a summoning, loud and harsh. As his invocation finished, a huge red, naked creature stood before him, smoke rising from its skin. It glared at him, reached, and then saw the Dagger. All aggression ceased, and the creature bowed and cringed back.

Geraint spoke to the assassin. "This is a demon. It is a kind most common on the Second Demon Plane. It is very stupid, but rather hot and very, very, angry all the time. It can also change shape, a little. Watch."

He spoke to the demon, and it did change shape. Part of it became *very* large and somewhat hooked.

"I'll begin questioning again. If you are still stupid … well, you'll still be able to answer questions afterwards. Even after the second time. But you'll never be what you are now. I trust you understand me.

"So now, what is your name?"

"Crysta Forster. I thought you would just – with knives or heat, you know? That … that's–"

"Cheating? I expect I am, but there you go. Who do you work for?"

"Demon's Edge."

"Yes, yes. You'll have to do better than that."

"She'll kill me."

"Well, first, no she won't. She'll be having severe problems of her own. Terminal ones, I would guess. Second – which is better anyway?"

"Magda Leona."

"And how did Magda Leona know to send you here?"

"One of Borgia's cover team - a warrior and merchant called Pindra - set a tracker on herself and then kissed Borgia, deliberately dribbling slightly on her leather vest. Because the tracker was on her, it wasn't detectable by the usual checks on the three who came here, but because there was some of that saliva on Borgia's clothes, it was possible to track that vest to here."

Geraint nodded. "Good. That was easy, wasn't it? Finally, you have a choice. You can swear service to us, on Baraani – I'll call a priest. You'll be unlikely to rise very high, at least at first while we get to know you, but you will be treated as well as any of our other people – and they're not complaining. Or if you don't fancy that, Becca there will kill you. Clean and quick, because you've told us what we want. Oh, yes…"

He waved his hand and uttered a single word, and the demon vanished at once. Crysta shuddered and then relaxed, closing her eyes. Geraint smiled – at least, with his mouth.

"Really, I lied. You wouldn't have survived the first time. But if I'd told you that, you might have thought I would be reluctant to set it on you. That would have been a bad mistake on your part."

He looked aside. "Oh, yes. Becca, boys – you can come out of the circle now." Turning back to the assassin, he said, "Very well. Do you want to go with us, or do you want grace? Becca's very good, and she'll make it as painless as she can. You almost certainly won't feel it at all. It's up to you."

"My brother?"

"Dead, I'm afraid. It was a case of the biter bitten by a better biter, really." He smiled grimly. "A *much* better biter."

"Dead? For certain? Oh. That makes it easier. I'll swear."

Geraint's eyebrows rose a touch. "Not my business. I wouldn't dream of asking. Becca – please send someone for a priest of Baraani."

One of the troopers went out at the run.

There was a pause of a few minutes during which Becca got herself a jug of wine and poured for herself and Geraint. 'Sorry Ven – Might need you to stand guard a while, yet."

Carol and Zeéla came in, followed closely by Garrett, Lucinda, and Borgia. Lucinda glanced at the assassin. "I know her. Ali, who is she?"

Borgia shrugged. "Don't know her name. She and her brother do low-level wet work for somebody at Head Office."

Geraint nodded. "Yes, This is Crysta Forster; she worked for Magda Leona. And she was able to send the two of them here because Pindra betrayed you."

Borgia cursed obscenely, then shrugged. "That really hurts, you know? Why aren't I used to this yet? Never mind. I'll pick someone else."

Lucinda was examining Crysta. "How in all nine hells did you get her talking? There's not a mark on her!"

"Ah, well. I showed her a demon."

Zeéla's eyes opened in professional interest. "Which one, Junior?"

"A porter from Second Demon Plane."

"And you grew its…"

"Yup."

"Oh." She smiled at him, then went and looked down at Crysta. "Impressive, aren't they?"

"Lady, I was ready for ordinary torture. I might have held out if there were nothing to keep me alive too long. But … I couldn't face that."

"No. I imagine most people would take the same point of view. I certainly would." She turned. "What's next, Junior?"

"She's going to swear. We're waiting for a priest of Baraani."

Carol called Geraint and stepped to the door. Zeéla joined them. Carol was looking perturbed. "Cousin – you wouldn't have tortured that woman, would you?"

"Well, it didn't appeal. That's why I produced the demon. It's very big in certain areas – or can be. It impressed her a lot."

"But … but that's worse!"

Zeéla chuckled. "Well, it would be. But the thing's a porter for more significant demons. And a fighter sometimes, but mainly a porter. And it's a demon. It doesn't have human functions or anything like them – and it's a very low level performer both in intellect and raw power, so it couldn't possibly emulate anything like that."

Carol waved her arms. "But you said … she saw…"

Zeéla was struggling to keep her face straight. "It's a porter, my Lady. What she saw was a hook for hanging things on. It changes size according to what you want to hang on it. Hooks can be grown in several places, and one just happens to be conveniently between the legs…" She lost control and doubled up with mirth.

Carol was now struggling with a slight facial tic herself. "But that was still very unkind, cousin. The poor girl would have been terrified."

"Unkind as opposed to a session trying to torture her for information? Or if we weren't prepared to do that, compared with not being able to protect Borgia from this woman who's trying to kill her?"

"You make your point, Geraint. I'm truly glad you're on our side, not theirs."

Geraint smiled and moved back with Carol as she went to talk to the Alma people. As he went, he was contemplating the fact that he hadn't actually said he wouldn't have tortured the woman – just that it didn't appeal. Which it didn't, at all. It made him want to vomit even to think of it.

But he would most certainly have done it, rather than leave Borgia ignorant of who her enemy was. He felt that one owes certain obligations to one's allies, even when they are merely allies of convenience. Anyway, while he didn't form affections easily, he rather liked Borgia.

Carol approached Borgia and Lucinda, who were talking to Garrett about the best way to deal with Pindra. "Borgia, excuse me. I just wanted to thank you for a piece of advice you gave me."

"Yes, Lady? What advice was that?"

"You suggested I ask John to continue my training in arms. We've been working together for over a week now, and it's a revelation. He knows as much – at least – about standard techniques as my other teachers, but he has so many original ideas. And so much drawn from other places and cultures, too. Every day's work is more exciting than the last."

Garrett nodded. "The thing is, the Lady is so very fast – and that Sword is so extraordinary in use – that I can offer her techniques with a large long-sword that are normally used by light scimitar people; even some short-sword skills.

"And she's fast enough in defence to tumble and dodge like a knife fighter. She may be the fastest sword-fighter I've ever had the pleasure to teach. Or even see. Then when you add that Sword… She's damned dangerous, this woman. Damned dangerous – and she's going to be much, much worse."

At that point, Iorweth and Uggò came in. Iorweth threw himself down in a chair and gratefully accepted a mug from Lucinda. "We've scoured the place. I'd swear these two were all. Oh, the priest of Baraani's just outside, by the way. He's just proving who he is – the guards are all pretty upset."

A few moments later, the priest came in, looking slightly flustered. "Good morning gentles. I gather you've had a few difficulties."

Geraint nodded. "A few, Reverend Priest. As a result, we have a prisoner who wishes to swear to service."

"I see. That'll be the young lady lashed to the table, then. Young woman, are you proposing to swear to service with these people?"

"Yes, Reverend Priest."

"Understand that if you swear by my God, then my God will act instantly should you break the oath that you have made. She will not only take your life for it, but she will correct whatever change in the situation your betrayal has wrought. Not you, nor any other party will gain anything whatever by your contrary action. And if another party procures your action, then they too will forfeit their lives. Is this clear?"

"Yes."

"Good." He looked around. "What is the oath?"

"She will swear to serve faithfully, obey and to seek in all ways to advance the interests and welfare of, principally, this lady here, and secondarily whomsoever this lady shall allocate her service to, all for as long as she shall endure."

"And that lady is...?"

"Is that important?"

"Yes."

"The Lady Caroline ap Gryffudd."

"Ah. Hence your caution. Your information will not go further."

The priest turned to the young woman strapped to the table. "Now, young lady, what is your name?"

"Crysta Forster."

"Did you hear the terms of your oath?"

"Yes."

"Explain it to me. Take as long as you wish, no need to be concise. But be accurate and complete."

"I am to serve this lady. I am to obey her in all things. I am to do all I can to advance her interests, to help her and protect her in every way."

"Excuse my interruption 'Advance her interests' were the words of the oath. What does that mean, in *your* words?"

"Help her to achieve whatever she wishes or would benefit her."

"Very well. Any more?"

"She may give my service to another, and I will do the same for that person, but subject to my service to the lady. Where interests conflict, this lady comes first."

The servant of Baraani looked at Geraint. "Satisfactory? Her understanding and yours agree?"

"Yes, Reverend Priest."

"You are both content? Very well. I invoke my God."

The room fell silent. The priest raised his arms and uttered quite a short invocation, at the end of which the room crackled with tension and power.

"Crysta Forster. You have heard the words of this Reverend Druid, and you have rehearsed their meaning to me. Do you wish to be bound by them on your oath to my God? Have a care, as the next words you speak will be the only answer my God hears."

"I do."

"Then you are so bound, and will be so bound as long as you endure. This business is complete." He clapped sharply, once.

The tension in the room evaporated, and conversation resumed.

Geraint whispered to Carol. She nodded and spoke. "Crysta Forster, you will not harm yourself or permit yourself to come to significant harm other than at my explicit instruction or in the necessary course of your duty to me. Is that clear?"

"It is, Lady. It was probably not necessary."

"I will hope to ensure that you never regret that command."

"Thank you, Lady."

'Good. Can we release this woman and find her suitable clothing?"

Becca nodded to Ven, who cut the ropes and helped her to sit up. Borgia said "She's about my size. Can she go and get some stuff from my room?"

Carol smiled and nodded. "Surely. And there is no need to ask. My cousin suggests that we pass her on to you, and I think it a wise idea. Crysta, you will serve this priest of Alma until further notice from me."

"Yes, Lady. Borgia, I know a lot you would like to know. I think you might find me really very useful."

Borgia nodded and gave her a small smile. "In which case you'll find me really very grateful. Let's go and get you something to wear."

As Crysta went past, Geraint gave her her pouch and purse. She almost dropped them in astonishment. "Lord Druid! Thank you. That is … not common practice."

Borgia laughed. "Crysta, you're going to find that these are *not* common people. Not in any way at all. Come on."

Hendricks had been rather quiet throughout, Now, as Borgia left the room, he squared his shoulders and approached Uggò. "Look, Uggò. I owe you one. I had thought we were safe this far away, and I was quite deeply asleep. I might have woken up, but if not … Gods! I'm in your debt – and this sort of debt I pay."

The gnome smiled easily at him. "I did just be protecting my own people, my friend. And I do not be thinking there be any way in this world that half-skilled clown would have got to her past you. I do see no need for debt."

"But I do. So it exists, call on it at need."

He held out his palm, and Uggò touched it with his own, muttering "So mote it be."

Iorweth looked at Geraint. "Did you understand that?"

"Well, I heard the words. But, I suspect, no." He turned. "Reverend Priest, may we offer you refreshment?"

"Thank you. You absolutely may. Wine would be good... and a little brandy or rum in it would help me face so early a start with much more fortitude. Also, you may offer me payment if you would be so good."

"Ah, yes. In the sum of...?"

"Five thousand, please."

Geraint nodded. "Indeed. Zeéla?"

"Certainly. Our Number Two General Expenses account? From there, if you would."

The priest looked abstracted for a few seconds. "Thank you, my lady. It is done."

He tossed back his wine in one, unaffected by the fact that it was about one third rum. "And now I shall get back to the temple and roust out somebody who knows how to cook breakfast. Good morning."

Chapter 14

We learn that Lucinda and JG are both advocates of the benefits of education. Pindra is very much less enthusiastic

Pindra, of course, was both startled and alarmed when Borgia, Hendricks and Lucinda strolled into the cover team's woodland camp. She was also a little glad in a way, because though losing Borgia to Hendricks was a blow that still rankled viciously over two years later - and had been the main reason she'd sold out to Magda Leona - the fact was that Borgia still took her to bed from time to time, it was still wonderful whenever it happened, and she had been rather doleful at the idea that it would never happen again.

However, it now seemed it would, because Borgia gave her a big smile and a very cheerful wave when they came into camp and, as she sometimes did, raised her eyebrows and pointed to Pindra's small marquee, then raised ten fingers.

From long experience, Pindra took that to be a proposal of some bed sport in ten minutes, nodded enthusiastically and went immediately into her tentage, where she stripped off, had a very rapid *toilette*, dabbed on some perfume and jumped into bed.

So it was a bad surprise when, instead of Borgia, ten of Lucinda's Temple Guard troopers - there were fifty of them in the cover team - came into her marquee, dragged her out of bed and manacled her hands behind her back.

She walked unresisting - she'd only have been beaten until she obeyed - from her tent to the clearing at the heart of the camp where Borgia and Lucinda were sitting near the fire on folding chairs. She noticed that Hendricks was nowhere to be seen, which was ominous.

So OK, this was going to be judgement and she was screwed - and not in the way she'd been hoping. Standing naked and handcuffed before Borgia, it took all her willpower to look up and meet her gaze. "So who grassed me up?"

Borgia frowned sympathetically. "You're unlucky as fuck, as it goes. That idiot Magda actually told her assassins how she knew where I was. Can you believe that? Seriously?"

Pindra spat in disgust, horrified that she'd sold out to someone who could be that careless. Then she straightened her shoulders and looked Borgia straight in the eye again.

"Sorry, sweetness. Got wound up about you giving Hendricks most of your attention these days, and did something stupid. Two ways stupid, it turns out. Regretted it after, but you can't go back."

Borgia nodded. "Thought it might be that way, once I realised it was you. Made me think I might give you another chance, just for a moment - but I can't. Mum and Dad talked sense to me."

Lucinda grimaced at Pindra. "Sorry, luv. People have to see that it's not a good idea to betray Borgia's trust. In fact they have to see it ends very, very badly. You're not stupid, kid, you can see that yourself. This needs to be educational."

Pindra sighed, closed her eyes, and nodded. "Yeah. Sorry, Borgia. And you know I mean it, because we both know it won't get me anything. Wish I hadn't done it."

Borgia sighed too. "So do I, luv, so do I." She looked at the guard captain. "Khalia, take ten with you. Cuff her in front and make her run behind your horse into the deep woods until she physically can't run any more. then cuff her behind and hang her by her wrists from a nice stout tree branch. Something that won't break whatever happens. Just the strappado though, no bunny-hops, and just leave her hanging so the tips of her toes just lightly brush the ground. If she's lucky she'll just die of exposure, but I doubt it."

Pindra wasn't lucky. Crows and ravens found her quickly and came after her eyes. She managed to avoid that for a little while, but strappado is agony, and that kind of squirming about tears muscles and tendons if you keep at it - and then you can't move very much at all, of course. So eventually she lost that battle.

So she didn't see the wolves find her, but she heard and smelled them, and started screaming before they even touched her. It didn't put them off.

Chapter 15

Bastin turns out to be a keen educationalist, too

Bastin FitzReis, Duke of Belmond, sat on the balcony and looked out over the lush, green woodland. He stirred uncomfortably and wondered, as he never used to, what was creeping around under that heavy cover.

"Something's got to be done, Armand. Something drastic."

The Grand Duke of Quem turned to him from his own enjoyment of the view and tightened his lips. "And you propose, exactly?"

"We need to teach these people a lesson."

Du Calenisse sat heavily in a cane chair. "Easy words that mean what? The problem is in – how many? – three parts, I think. First, the passage of goods and supplies through Belmond has nearly dried up. Second, our friends tell us that the supply depots their forces do have in the field are being raided so frequently and so effectively that nearly a quarter of all Alliance forces are tied up protecting those sites and the routes to them – with no more than modest success. Third, Alliance heavy cavalry and line units can't move – ever – without a light cavalry screen, because otherwise they get a succession of slash-and-run attacks which bleed them steadily.

"Sometimes it's archers killing a dozen men and a score of horses and then disappearing, sometimes it's light horse coming in at the gallop, attacking wagons and supply animals, and making off too fast to be caught. And other times it's something different and unpredictable.

"So let's look at the problems in turn. Belmond. Why don't you just flood the duchy with troops? Make the protection for each convoy so heavy that they can't be successfully attacked?"

"I'm not certain any number would be enough. But basically, I can't afford it. The duchy is hugely in debt. Massively. The interest payments are crippling and weren't budgeted for. There just isn't the money to do it."

"Our friends are not happy."

"Our friends could help."

"They're financing a very large and unexpectedly costly invasion. It's not unreasonable to expect us to do our part, is it?"

"Well – it's that boltblasted swine of a druid and his bitch cousin. You know she's still pretending to be a countess?"

"She's not pretending. Remember, your position is, at present … irregular. When the invasion began, the Council met the first night and declared you a traitor. I tried to hold it up, but the Duke of Ninian had a good deal of evidence - he'd clearly been gathering stuff on you for a while. Not to mention the fact that the invasion was launched *from* Belmond Duchy, which made it all a bit blindingly obvious. The vote was nearly unanimous.

"You are Duke of Belmond because the Alliance is the power in Belmond and they say you are. But you're not an Empire duke anymore and, since you were removed for treason, all your ordinances are null. So, in the Empire, she is legitimately a countess."

"Really? I hadn't realised. Not that it matters. So she's a countess. They stole three hundred and fifty million from me, and it's crippling us."

Du Calenisse grimaced and shrugged. "There's only so much I can do. I've declared the druid an outlaw, using my emergency powers as Lord President. But it takes a Council meeting to outlaw the holder of a title of aristocracy, and they won't meet, despite my best efforts. I've more or less resorted to massage to get a quorum, but I can't do it. Even if they did meet, the Council's hamstrung. I've still got enough votes to stop them doing anything useful but that son of a whore, Ninian, has enough to keep me impotent as well."

He twitched his mouth in annoyance, then studied Bastin again. "Who are these raiders in Belmond, anyway?"

"There are three kinds, in fact. The light cavalry units appear within a couple miles of a convoy, or a village where a convoy's resting, or a supply dump or whatever. Then they hit us, do as much damage as they can before we can assemble a force to deal with them, and pull out. A couple of miles away, they vanish. I mean that literally. The tracks indicate that they stop in a given place, mill around a bit, then – pouf! – they're gone. No tracks, nothing. Just gone.

"Then there are Wayfarers. They do the same in terms of hitting convoys and so on, except that they hit columns of troops as well. They hit, kill everybody – I mean everybody – burn the bodies, and go. In their case there are no tracks to follow from the off, and if units do find a trail and follow them into the deep forest … well those units don't ever come out again.

"Finally, there are Myndarits. They don't come out in force, but we come across units of maybe fifty or a hundred. They will seek out our own troops, fight them, and destroy them. They'll cheerfully charge odds of four or five to one and win – often rather easily.

We know where *they* go – to their chapter houses. But those are effectively castles. We attack with small numbers of troops, and they just sally and destroy us. We attack with large numbers, and they pull up the drawbridge and defy us to break in. We can't bring up siege engines because the cavalry raiders and Wayfarers will destroy them. We can't lay a long siege, because the troops are needed elsewhere as I've just described. And even if we did it would be problematic, because our troops have to be fed and the supply columns get attacked – that's if other chapter houses don't combine and hit us, or the Wayfarers don't chew lumps off our investing force, or – well, you probably see where I'm going, here."

"It's worse than I understood. You're losing control of the duchy."

"Not yet, but if it gets worse… I need more troops and I can't afford them. Look there are a lot of Ducal Troops moving away, aren't there?"

""All of them. The original agreement was that we would encourage them into the field so they could be defeated in detail, but it seemed to Sir Roland that we might need a negotiating chip rather later in proceedings, and many many hundreds of thousands of Ducal troops would do well in that respect. Couldn't fault his reasoning, so at my suggestion the Dukes are withdrawing ahead of the Alliance forces and keeping their units in being. It was a lot easier to sell to them as well, of course."

"So, is there any way of getting some of them here?"

"What, behind the main Alliance front? How? And I doubt our friends would be too delighted by theoretically hostile troops behind them, either."

"Oh, well. The truth is I really have no idea at all how to break this situation open. Also there's a scurrilous campaign of abuse about me. It's really having an impact."

Du Calenisse more or less managed to keep his face straight. "Yes, I've heard some of the songs. I have to admit a few of them are quite witty - in a crude sort of way, of course."

"Thank you so much. The worst thing is, all the songs are set to popular tunes. Everywhere I go, the musicians play the tunes. Maybe the singers sing some of the ordinary words to them, but everybody still sniggers behind their hands. I'd like to ban them, but I can't ban two score of the Empire's most popular tunes – I'd look like an idiot. On the other hand, if I don't, every time they're played, people remember words accusing me of being a panderer or a child-molester, or Gods know what."

He noted the Grand Duke's ill-concealed amusement and changed the subject. "What's happening elsewhere?

"What you've just described in Belmond, though less intensively. It means our friends can't just drive on for Cromreth, because as soon as they move quickly, or open their formations, they get hit at weak points. The Black Knights and the Red Death haven't the numbers to be everywhere, and the Royal armies take very heavy losses whenever they expose themselves without high quality professional cover. They're ninety percent conscripts led by amateurs on a core of maybe ten percent professionals led by career officers, while the guerrillas are high quality professionals, brilliantly led.

"And of course if the religious Orders start to assemble significant forces to clear guerrillas from an area in front of some of our forces, the Royal troops take catastrophic attacks elsewhere. It might either be large swarms of light cavalry or, even worse, Myndarits in Chapter strength. For a few regiments of Royal troops without Order of Night cover, that's a disaster of cataclysmic proportions.

"The Royal forces just can't cope. And, of course, the supply situation makes everything ten times worse.

"Fortunately, the top command are very high calibre, so the invasion *is* moving forward, just very slowly. They'll get there – there's no force in the field that could stop them. It's only a matter of when."

Bastin scowled. "Have you heard anything about this countess and the rest of that rag-tag, or have they gone to ground?"

"You *are* out of touch in Belmond, aren't you?"

"I certainly am just a bit busy there, yes. Why? Have they turned up again?"

Du Calenisse gave a harsh, barking laugh. "And again and again. She sweeps into a town or city at the head of swarms of light cavalry and a few hundred Myndarits, occupies the place for a few hours, or a day - or even two - preaching resistance and recruiting just about every able-bodied man and woman in the place, and then they're gone again.

"At first our friends sent whatever occupation troops they could find locally at them – and those troops were beaten up badly. The light cavalry are superbly handled, and the Myndarits are awesome. Worse, that blasted woman usually leads the Myndarits in person – and I do mean *leads*. She's into our people maybe ten yards ahead of anybody else, with that animal of a half-orc beside her, and we just *can't* damned well kill her – she fights like a mincing machine herself, and that creature with her – Garrett - well, he's just a natural disaster.

"There are stories about her everywhere you go, now, and it's not helping us promote the right attitude at all. So our friends have taken to waiting until they've got overwhelming force. Of course by that time the countess and her troops are gone. Completely gone. No trace. Now they're starting a new system. Kill ten percent of the population of any place the blasted woman visits. See if that makes any impression at all."

Part 3

Progress - and its cost

Chapter 16

Nothing comes for nothing
and everything has its price

Elaine walked up to the guard and said "Elaine, priest of Alma" and he gestured for her to wait. A few seconds later, a voice from slightly behind her and somewhat above said "Yes she is. And she's on the list. There's something holy in her belt pouch and two rings are massively enchanted. Hold on, I'll ask." The guard smiled and shrugged. "It'll only take a moment – just a standard check." She noticed that his hand had not yet left the hilt of his weapon.

"Thank you, no rush." Well there was, but it wouldn't make any difference to say so. They stood for about twenty seconds, no more, then a voice from somewhere else in the trees said "Yeah. That fits the profile and Mostyn passed it. Go."

The guard smiled again. "See? Pass on." He took his eyes from her for the first time since she'd originally approached. Elaine moved on to the marquee in the middle of the clearing. It was silent as she approached, but clearly enchanted, for as soon as she lifted the flap and moved inside, she could hear Zeéla's voice.

"…currently on about eighteen thousand a day. With the other funds we've pulled in since Bastin's kind contribution, that leaves our available balance at just under eighty-one million. It's not anything like a problem yet, but it is sinking slowly, so we should pay attention to funding at some point in the next few weeks."

Now Geraint, as she passed through the canvas anteroom to the conference area itself. "Alright Armlet. Thank you. Well there's no time like the present. Uggò, Lin Gor, Jeff. Can you work with Zeéla to address the problem? I could suggest a few general headings, which would be donations, raids on enemy funds, suggestions from allies — by which I particularly mean the scouts and salesmen and also Demon's Edge. Any other thoughts, ladies and gentlemen? Yes... My Lady?"

"Under the heading of donations, Geraint, we haven't really spoken to the major religions yet — and they have almost unlimited money, by any normal measure. Mannan-Dar and Varan are helping via the Arm and the Myndarits, but that's people. I see no reason why they all shouldn't contribute significant funds as well."

"Nor do I. Zeéla, that sounds like something to move forward with now. We were always going to have to do it sometime. Jeff?"

"I'm not complaining — you're the boss. But how can I be useful here? I know as much about finance as about aether."

"You don't need to. There'll be two stages to fund-raising, like most other things: deciding what to do and then going and doing it. Under the second stage, Uggò will be the guy if someone needs to be relieved of funds by stealth. Lin Gor will do the job if we need to talk somebody into — or out of - something, and you're there for when the requirement is to descend on some payroll convoy with your boys and girls and take the geld away from them by brute force."

"I see now. Sorry. Brute force I can do."

"Truly. I remember Bell's Ferry. That was nearly exclusively your crew, wasn't it?"

"Aye. That *was* one of our better days."

"So far. Anybody else got something on this? No? Right. Next business — uh, Elaine. I guess you're not standing there for the benefit of your health. Something we need to know?"

"Afraid so. We have intelligence that Alliance High Command has ordered a new policy regarding our recruiting and publicity tour. They've decided that since the towns are accepting us with open arms, the towns will be held responsible. Any town which we visit will have ten percent of its listed population killed — that'll be the first ten percent the troops come across, whoever they are.

"They are intending to begin with Long Astley, which we visited last week, and the punitive force is assembling at Lark Valley. A thousand regular infantry plus a wing of the Red Death. That'll be around two hundred and fifty, I'm told. They're all under a KRQ Wing Commander, Lady Louise Megiddo – and like all Red Death senior officers, she's damned good. She's a Marn priest, of course - and a pretty hot caster, I've been told.

"Our information is that the force will move tonight at sunset. That'll have them at Long Astley in ample time for a dawn attack."

"Well, it had to happen eventually, or something like it. Who's got the demographics? How many people in Long Astley?"

Lin Gor flicked through a folder and stopped at a page. "Sixty-five thousand, more or less. There's a Town Guard of two hundred. Mainly they're a police force."

"A thousand infantry and a Wing of KRQ won't even notice them. They'll have the job done and out again in half an hour or so. Well, we could ignore the whole thing – sit down, Elaine, there's beer, wine, water and hot drinks on the table. That would send a good message to the Alliance about the pointlessness of such actions. Unfortunately, it would send a bad message to the people of the Empire. Two different ones, actually. One about our wishes and the other about our ability."

"And anyway we're not going to do that, cousin," Carol said.

"No, Lady. But it's a good thing to consider all the reasons why we're not going to do it, rather than just the ones that first occur to us. It might tell us something useful. By the way, haven't I heard the name Lark Valley recently?"

Lin Gor referred to his documentation again, and conferred with one of the three or four people sitting behind him amongst piles of folders and files. "Yes." He smiled broadly.

"They're in the process of setting it up as a regional command and communications centre. According to my information, there'll be about five hundred front line infantry there, once the punitive force has gone, plus a thousand or so administrative and support types. Including the entire headquarters complement of the Sword Sisters, which is the Eagle Megiddo belongs to. The Eagle itself's moving into there in about ten days' time."

Geraint looked increasingly cheerful. "So, there'll be lots and lots of documents, information – probably a good deal of money – plus all the people who know how the Alliance is hanging in this area. They'd be something of a loss, wouldn't you say?"

He sat up and looked around. "I think you can all see where I'm going with this – I propose two strikes, both tonight – or perhaps one tonight, the other at dawn. If anybody has problems to raise, raise 'em. In the meantime, JG, cousin, how many troops can we put in the field?"

Carol spoke first, as Garrett consulted some advisors. "We have six hundred of the Burglars at Hendolinto Reach. We used some of them on our visit to Long Astley. Also some of the City Reivers at Pollock Castle. Two hundred or so, I think. Nobody else who could get to us in time, even with the chapter portals. Oh! Possibly the Elfstone people at Man Hanging – that's about nine hundred. They're on the same portal path, but they wouldn't be available until a little later, at a guess."

Elaine whispered to Becca, sitting next to her, "Burglars? Chapter portals? Portal path?"

Becca smiled. "Myndarit chapters are all numbered, but everybody always uses their nicknames. Some of them have had the same nickname for a thousand years. Every chapter house, however small, has a portal linking it to another. Some have five or six, the big ones. It means Myndarits are never trapped in their chapter houses and can always reinforce each other.

"The portals are set up so that they can only be used by Varan followers or people who have just been **Blessed** by a Varan priest."

Geraint was making notes. "So we could have eight hundred Myndarits for the Long Astley operation, then a different nine hundred for Lark Valley. Good. JG, what about light cavalry?"

John Garret turned back to the table. "Well, for regulars we've got Becca and Jeff to hand. How many effectives do you have? Becca?"

"Five septs of two hundred and fifty each, all at full strength. A reserve of three incomplete septs, totalling five hundred and eighty-five."

"So we can assume you'll bring twelve hundred and fifty. Jeff?"

"Not quite so many. I've got two septs out on hits just now. Four complete septs, two reserve totalling three hundred and forty-one between the two."

JG nodded in satisfaction. "Gives us a force of twenty-two hundred and fifty regulars. We've also got seven hundred mercenaries here. Oh, and there's a pack of about two hundred Wayfarers in the area as well. What do you want doing, exactly?"

Geraint shuffled his notes together and passed them back to an aide. "I want you to take the Burglars, plus Jeff and the mercenaries, and completely annihilate the punitive force before it gets to Long Astley. In the meantime, I'll go with the Wayfarers, Becca, and the Elfstone Myndarits to the new camp at Lark Valley and take that place apart. Cousin, which will you go with?"

Carol smiled at him in acknowledgement. "I'll take the Long Astley group with John. John, you lead overall – I wouldn't dream of interfering. I'll go in with the Myndarits."

"Right." Geraint nodded in satisfaction. "Everybody knows what their jobs are. Becca, since you're leading the Lark Valley attack, please come with me and Iorweth to talk to the Warleader of the Wayfarer Pack. We need him to know what we're doing. How far he'll be prepared to co-operate remains to be seen. We'll go and do that now. All senior officers for a conference before we set off – say second hour after noon. We can't leave it much longer than that. We've got a fair way to go."

He bowed in his chair to Caroline. "Cousin, will you arrange things with the Chapters? Good. That'll be – Yes, Priestess?"

"May I come?"

"Surely, Elaine. With whom?"

"With you, I think. I've not seen Wayfarers. May I come to the liaison meeting?""

"Yes. Fine. We're going now, then."

Iorweth went forward and made the first contact, then came back and waited in a clearing in heavy woodland, along with Geraint, Becca, Elaine and half a dozen troopers from Becca's HQ squadron.

The Wayfarers didn't come, exactly. They were just suddenly there, at the edge of the clearing. Six people, four men, two women, with two of the men in front, and the four others spread in a wide semi-circle behind them.

Iorweth whispered into Geraint's ear. "Archers in the trees. Left, right, ahead. Those four guards are window dressing."

Geraint smiled as though his friend had said something amusing. "Well, if they've got something stupid in mind, they may find it doesn't go as they expected."

The two leading men stopped about six feet in front of them. The one on the left, a dark-haired, dark-bearded man with what appeared to be a permanent scowl, lifted his head somewhat challengingly. "If you've got any stupid ideas, they're going to go terribly wrong on you."

Geraint laughed with genuine amusement. "I was just saying the same thing about you. Those archers in the trees aren't exactly according to the agreement."

"No. Comforting, though."

"If you're easily pleased. Now, we can play this game, or we can get down to some serious killing, or we can have the meeting we wanted to have in the first place. Choose. Because these silly games are using up my sweetness allowance for the week."

"Why should we trust you?"

"Can't imagine. I heard your God had asked you to help us."

"She did. When She asks, it isn't a request – what She asks for is what we get Her. Always."

"So why are you wasting my time?"

"Habit. Anyway, I don't like people who think they're dangerous but can't back it up."

Geraint took a deep breath, then addressed the other of the two men, this one with a small silver raven symbol round his neck that marked him as a Wayfarer priest. "Is he always this much of a twat?"

The priest nodded. "More or less, when dealing with outsiders. Good leader, though."

The dark-haired man snorted. "My name's Rory, so that's 'Is *Rory* always this much of a twat?'"

"How do. I'm Geraint. This is Becca, that's Elaine. Iorweth, you've met of course."

"Aye. He said you had a target we might like."

"Yes. Most of the troops are leaving the Alliance base at Lark Valley tonight. They think they'll be back in the morning, but they won't – ever. There'll be five hundred left on the base. We wondered if you fancied decoying them out into the open."

"What happens then?"

"Nine hundred Myndarits ride them under."

"They won't all come out."

"We've got rather a lot of light cavalry to mop them up."

"What's in it for us?"

"There are over a thousand non-combat personnel in that base. We want to talk to some. However, we really don't need all of them, but we'd rather the enemy didn't have any of them."

"Not appealing. We prefer to earn our own sacrifices."

"Sorry? Wasn't there something your God said? Or was I dreaming?"

"I didn't say we wouldn't do it, boy. I said it didn't appeal. When do you want us there? And where do you want these people?

"Second hour after midnight. If you can get 'em out onto the open area in front of the main gates, that would be very good indeed."

"We'll manage it. Drink?"

"That would go well. Thank you."

The two men swigged from Rory's hip flask as the Wayfarer priest passed another around to the rest of Geraint's group. Then Rory stoppered his flask, nodded curtly and turned away. The rest of his crew followed him out of the clearing.

Geraint shook his head, looking slightly bemused. "What an unusual man. Right, let's go, shall we?"

"Rory"

Robert McLennan
Wayfarer Pack Leader

Chapter 17

Sometimes it's just not your night...

Lady Louise Megiddo looked up at the huge moon and sighed. Progress in front of the infantry was painfully slow. However, there were only a few miles to go, and there were a number of hours of night left.

She felt the riders on either side of her go alert and looked at the road ahead. There was a single rider, sitting his horse in the middle of the road. Lady Louise mentally rehearsed what she would say to her forward scouts – then wondered if there were any left to reprimand. She wondered if she should have made the scouting group bigger, but immediately abandoned concern over spilt milk in favour of wondering what this fellow was actually doing there – or thought he was.

The moonlight was very bright, and she could see now that he was riding a truly huge warhorse and wearing plate armour under a surcoat of some dark colour with shiny areas. Silver?

When they got within ten feet of him – he hadn't moved at all – she raised her hand and the Red Death halted, exactly in position. He nodded politely and she nodded back. "I don't know whether you'd noticed, but I'm bringing a somewhat large military force through here. You're rather in the way."

"I wanted a word. First the manners. I am Carlo Meuse, Knight Hierophant of the Temple, Order of Myndarit. I have the honour to be Knight Master of the Long Astley Task Force. Now the word. We found it necessary to take your forward scouts into custody, and so I felt I should warn you that I have a large force of knights on the reverse of that rise just behind me."

"I see." Lady Louise was just managing to contain her amusement. "And what does this large force of knights plan to do?"

She could feel her riders changing formation behind her – her officers didn't need to be told what to do. "Well, in a few seconds…" A deep rumble swelled, somewhere behind him and the ground started to vibrate. "…in fact now, we will have the honour of charging you, madam."

"So … an encounter with the notorious Myndarits. Excellent, I've been looking forward to this."

"So have we, ma'am. Now, if you will excuse me…"

"Certainly. I expect we shall meet again shortly."

Meuse saluted with a friendly smile, turned his horse and cantered back over the crown of the slope. The thunder got louder, was suddenly joined by a clamour of horns and wild shouts, and the Myndarits came over the rise – three hundred Heavies.

The Heavies are the darlings of every chapter, and in each chapter they total a thousand men and women; the best, the biggest or fastest, generally the nastiest of the chapter's fighters. Heavies wear full plate armour – often enchanted for lightness - even more thorough protection than the light plate the rest of the chapter wear. They ride the largest horses – often twenty-four or more hands and all over nineteen – and they spearhead every charge.

The three hundred Heavies in this force were now at full gallop and thundered down on the much lighter KRQ formation with their heavy lances lowered. The Red riders, clad in red leather and mounted on swift and agile thoroughbred horses, split in two and flowed away from in front of the Heavies on either side, swinging around to take them in the flanks.

Which is when they saw the rest of the Myndarits. Two hundred and fifty knights in each of two blocks behind and to either side of the Heavies and aligned so that if the Red Death swung into the Heavies, they themselves would in turn be taken in the flank. Though lighter than the Heavies, the Core, from the point of view of the Red Death, were very heavy cavalry – full light plate or sometimes plate mail suits with breastplates, lozenge shields, huge heavily-barded horses, and broadswords or morning stars.

Too good to get caught in the flank like that, the KRQ officers swung their two flows straight and charged the Core, following their usual doctrine for encounters with heavy cavalry, which was to close, kill a few, use their speed to swing away, and strike again at flank or rear – always using their higher speed and rapid command response to prevent the heavier horse coming to grips and making their weight and equipment tell.

The Heavies carried straight on, and ploughed into and over the infantry formed up behind the cavalry. The infantry had had time to get into a full defensive posture – and it made no difference at all. The Heavies – whose horses wore steel head-plates and steel chest guards, both shaped like the bow of a ship to deflect pikes and spears – rolled straight over the defensive crust – three rows of pikes – and into the closely arrayed infantry behind.

That was the moment at which Garrett sent Jeff's light cavalry swinging in two horns around the outside of the battle between the Myndarits and the KRQ, and into the infantry flanks as they recoiled from the Heavies' pile-driver blow into their centre.

The infantry formation dissolved completely, and as Jeff's riders did what light cavalry have done to broken infantry since time immemorial, the Heavies halted, reformed, wheeled, and swept back into the rear of the KRQ – in about half the time any Red Death officer had expected, or even believed possible. As a result, they caught the light cavalry in the process of disengaging and ground them up against the Core.

A few minutes later, Lady Louise looked around. Her cavalry were outnumbered, surrounded, and inextricably tangled in static, close combat with far more heavily armed and protected warriors on much bigger, massively barded horses. She could that see they were being chewed up rapidly and had no chance at all – light cavalry, however superb, cannot be used like this. Her wing was all about rapid manoeuvre, slash-and-run; this sort of thing was Order of Night territory and her people could not survive more than a very few minutes in this situation. She cursed, cursed again even more foully, and then made the most painful decision of her life.

As soon as she dropped her weapon and crossed her wrists above her head in the universal signal of surrender, the knight she had been fighting saluted her and pulled in close so that his horse and armour covered her from the melee around her. Within seconds, her remaining KRQ had seen her yield and had stopped fighting.

A few minutes later Louise noticed that the young woman with long, lustrous dark hair who had led the Heavies was now approaching her. The woman saluted. "Lady. Your people fought very well. Your cavalry, anyway."

Louise nodded, knowing it was true. "That wasn't enough today, however. Are you...? You are. You will be Countess Caroline ap Gryffudd."

"At your service, ma'am."

A huge half-orc on a massive horse approached behind the countess, who turned and smiled at him. "Lady Louise, please allow me to introduce John Garrett. Captain-General Garrett, Lady Louise Megiddo of the Knights of the Red Queen."

Louise nodded politely. "Captain-General. Excellent strategy, sir."

"It needed to be good, ma'am. We were fighting the Red Death."

"Talking of which, do you have the butcher's bill?"

"Yes. You won't like it. You have forty whole KRQ, and another hundred and thirty-one who are wounded but will recover; we have plenty of Healers. Your infantry…" He looked at a piece of paper. "I'm sorry, I hadn't looked at this. Your infantry have been wiped out. There are some wounded – less than a hundred.

Lady Louise hadn't really had much interest in the fate of the infantry. She hadn't expected many to survive that charge of knights – let alone the swarm of light cavalry that had followed. However, she was able to look suitably solemn by considering what her superiors' reaction would be to her losing a whole wing. Fortunately, she probably hadn't done much wrong. On the other hand, that wasn't necessarily going to save her – though it might. As might her cousin Sarah. Maybe…

In the meantime, the problem would lie in actually getting back to her own side at all. "May I ask what will happen now?"

"You have some choices. If you wish, you may give your parole on Baraani to be obedient and not to attempt to escape or act in any way that is inimical to us and our cause. If you do that, we will take you to the Green Deep, where you will stay rather comfortably at the University of the Woods until this unpleasantness is over. You will be required to answer informatively and truthfully any and all questions you are asked, of course. That will undoubtedly be irritating, but can't really be helped."

"I see. And you spoke of choices?"

"Well, the one choice really. You can, of course, choose not to give your parole. We are currently in contact with a pack of Wayfarers, and they would certainly have a use for you."

She turned to Caroline. "Countess? You would permit that?"

Carol shrugged. "I would not permit torture or indignity, but I'm told it's a clean, quick death, such as any warrior is prepared for. Alternatively, I would be honoured to deliver grace myself, if you would prefer. Or, of course, you can choose to give your parole."

"I will give my parole."

Garrett nodded. "Good. Please excuse the inconvenience, but you're reputed to be a priest of some power, so you will now be bound and gagged until we enter Long Astley and you can swear before a priest of Baraani."

"Being a priest of Marn, I could make oath before my own God, here and now."

"Um, yes. Thank you. But Marn, being Marn, may well approve the breach of oaths in certain circumstances, of which this could conceivably be one. Baraani does not. I think we'll stick to the original plan."

He signalled some riders, who came forward and expertly secured and gagged Louise so that there was no possibility of her being able to cast. At the same time, her rings – three of which had magical properties – were removed and placed in a silk bag with a couple of rather disturbing glyphs on it.

A receipt was placed in Louise's pocket, before which she was shown that it included the same number as was on a tag attached to the bag. It occurred to her that for an unsanctioned outfit that seemed to be irritating their own government as much as they were embarrassing the Alliance, these people looked organised, efficient and possessed of a keen grasp of detail.

Clearly, they needed to be killed off as soon as possible.

Wanted

The Outlaw Druid

Geraint
ap Gryffudd

His Grace the
Duke of Belmond
offers

10,000 Crowns
for information leading to this
notorious wolfshead's

EXECUTION

Chapter 18

Elaine and Louise both have a thoroughly hard day's night but then they arrange very different nights neither one will ever forget

Elaine had volunteered to go with the Wayfarers as liaison, as she could communicate directly with her colleague Amaré, Pindra's replacement, who was with Geraint. While she wasn't regretting it, she was finding it very, very hard keeping up with the pack as they moved into position.

She was also embarrassed that she seemed to be making more noise by herself than the whole of the pack. It wasn't just that they were eerily silent, it was that when somebody did make a sound, that sound *fitted*. It was part of the overall forest background and offered no clue that it had been made by a human, or indeed a living being, most of the time.

The other thing that amazed her was that she still had no clue as to how many there were. They moved through the forest like wraiths, one or two fleetingly visible here, then one over there, then another few somewhere else – all appearing and vanishing in this uncanny silence.

Rory and McLachan, the priest, had told her that there were 'around a hundred and eighty, give or take' in this group. She took their word for it; herself, she'd never seen more than eleven or twelve at any one time since they'd started, although she perfectly well believed they were all around her. She doubted they were even particularly concealing themselves from her – well, not more than they always did.

She was extremely relieved when Rory materialised in front of her, and she could stop the fast jog-trot she'd been maintaining for the last hundred years or so. She doubled up, breathing hard and feeling every bruise to her shins, every thorn prick, and every branch that had struck her in the face. McLachan had told her that packs sometimes hunted deer and other herbivores by simply running them down over however many miles it took to exhaust the beast. At that second, she felt she knew exactly how such a creature might feel.

Rory made a facial expression as near to a smile as he ever seemed to get. "You're a fit young girl. Most people collapse in the first hour."

"I'll just die on the spot now, instead, shall I?"

"Well, do it quietly; we're moving into position. The trees end about two hundred yards ahead."

Elaine touched the ring on her middle finger and spoke to Amaré. "We're just moving into position"

The answer came back at once. "We'll be ready to go in about five minutes, I'm told."

Elaine turned back to Rory. "They're ready in five."

"Good. We won't be quite that fast, so it'll work perfectly. Come up to the edge of the tree line."

A few minutes later, Elaine was sitting a little precariously in a fork of an oak, maybe twenty feet up. To her left, about a quarter of a mile away, were the walls of the town. She could see a large set of gates, from which a good road snaked along past her position, running for perhaps a mile in the lee of the forest before swinging away to run alongside a stream leaning away from the trees.

Just in front of her, across the road on the far side lay about an acre of grass and packed earth. Beyond that sat the camp and a ditch, perhaps five feet deep and ten wide, buttressed behind by an earthen bank. On the bank stood a square log wall, punctuated by simple wooden towers. The wall was maybe eight feet high, the towers perhaps twelve. As far as she could see, the camp was impressively large – perhaps half a mile from corner to corner, although from her vantage point she could see that many of the structures inside were incomplete.

She heard a piercing whistle somewhere behind her. Perhaps eighty Wayfarers broke from the woods and jogged in open order towards the camp, as though they expected it to be empty.

From her tree, Elaine watched the defenders scrambling from their long wooden barracks buildings into position. Their positioning was surprising. Half of them formed up inside the gates, while the rest lined the walls around the gates, to her right. Very few went to her left.

She heard someone shout an order, and suddenly a storm of arrows flew from the wooden walls. Several Wayfarers fell, and the rest moved forward faster, veering – rather naturally – to the left, where the arrowstorm was far less imposing. Somebody was clearly watching this leftward movement and judging landmarks, for suddenly there was an order shouted, and the gates opened.

The two hundred and fifty defenders who had formed up behind the gates charged out, and now the object of the strange layout of the defence became clear. In their natural desire to avoid the worst of the arrowstorm the attackers had gone too far left, and the rapid advance of the Alliance troops had placed them between the Wayfarers and the forest, out on the open grass.

Which was, of course, when Rebecca Wright's light cavalry made its appearance, cutting between these troops and their own retreat through the gates. At the same time the Wayfarers still in the forest opened an intense arrowstorm at the front wall, suppressing the archery from that quarter almost completely, so that Becca's light horse team could pass almost beneath the walls with very few casualties.

Naturally, the Alliance infantry had been watching this evolution with alarm and it occupied their full atten-tion, so the sound of horns, the shouts and the heavy thunder of hooves as the Myndarits began the serious part of their charge came as a complete – and, for most of them, terminal - surprise.

The Myndarits crashed into the already scattering infantry like the crack of doom, rode over them, paused, turned in a tight, disciplined formation, and thundered back into the shattered remnants, striking at anything that moved.

Elaine Mikoyan
Priest of Alma

As this was going on, the rather forgotten initial attack force of Wayfarers had sprinted for the nearly untenanted left side of the wall, and were now scaling it and disappearing inside.

With the defenders huddled behind the front wall for protection from the bridge of shafts flying from the forest, Becca's cavalry – now officially Wright's Riders, or the Second Regiment of Light Horse – were able to bring straw bales, bought earlier from a nearby farmer, to fill the ditch and pile over the wall. As they did so, the archery left the wall and started to drop on targets of opportunity inside the camp.

Attacked from behind by the Wayfarers and assailed over the wall by Becca's people, the Alliance defenders simply folded up.

Rory did his usual trick and materialised in front of Elaine's tree. "That's it. All formal resistance ended. What are the arrangements for assigning captives?"

Elaine relayed the question and got Geraint's answer almost instantly. She looked down to Rory, "He says anybody who has surrendered to Wright's Riders or to the Myndarits is under our protection absolutely. Anybody who hasn't … isn't. Even if they don't know they should, like all those folks in the administration buildings who may not even know anything's happened, yet."

"Seems fair to me. Very good. We're going to be sweeping through that place like the worst plague they've ever heard of. My experience of you Alma people is that you don't have a problem with violence when business requires it, but the kind of violence we're about to visit on those people won't be what you're used to. I'd go and join your main group, if I were you."

"That's rather piqued my curiosity. May I come? Please?"

"You've heard about the Wayfarers' 'sacrificial frenzy' and all that? It's not wholly false, you know."

"I've heard of it, yes."

"Yet you'd trust us to keep you safe?"

"Yes." She made it flat, undramatic, and unequivocal, keeping her more nervous thoughts to herself.

"Alright, if you really want to. You'll regret it, though."

"But I'll know something important I don't know now."

Rory snorted in disgust. "More than you think. Come on then and get your sweet young arse out of that tree. I can't wait for you – I need to be there." He turned away and started towards the camp at that swift, loping trot she'd come to detest. Elaine cursed luridly and slid painfully down the oak to the ground. Then, with a quick pause to brush herself off and wince over the more painful of the resulting bruises, she hurriedly set off after him.

* * *

Geraint's force joined the rest in Long Astley at about ten thirty. He met his cousin and various others in a back room of the Town Hall, passing a priest of Baraani, who was leaving as he entered.

The first thing he saw as he walked through the door and looked around was a Red priest, sitting at the bar and punishing a flagon of wine as though she needed it. Geraint saw Garrett approach and said, "Hello, John. How did it go?"

"Excellent. That's the commander of the punitive force. She's about all that's left of it, and she's just given her parole."

"That was the priest leaving, I presume. Good. Did she swear to answer all questions truthfully?"

"The oath was to be completely obedient, make no attempt to escape, and take no actions contrary to the interests of the Empire and its citizens, all until released by order of the Lady Caroline – and nobody else. The first instruction she was given was to answer fully, truthfully and honestly all questions put to her. Do you want to begin?"

"She's Lady Louise?"

"Yes"

"Right." Geraint approached her. "Louise?"

The red-robed woman turned and looked him up and down. "You will be Geraint ap Gryffudd?"

"I will. Indeed, I already am. Louise, we found a few rather useful documents in your camp. There were four incriminating the Earl Marshall of the Empire as an out-and-out traitor. There was also reference to the Duke of Belmond. No surprises there. But my main concern is the fact that it is clear from the documentation that there is at least one more traitor in high places. Who was that?"

"I don't know his name. I do know that he's a member of the Privy Council, but that's all I can say for certain. Oh, he's certainly a duke, because he was referred to as 'His Grace the High Councillor,' whereas Sir Roland was always 'The Soldier.'"

"But you knew it was Sir Roland?"

"Yes. I met him twice while preparing for the invasion."

"Excellent." He raised his voice slightly. "Cousin! Do you remember that we were thinking that we needed a high profile event to start our campaign rolling?"

"Indeed, Geraint."

"We now have all the evidence we need against Sir Roland. How do you like the idea of calling him out? In public?"

Caroline smiled like sunshine. "I like it very much indeed. Is it my birthday or something?"

Geraint looked around. "Does anybody see a problem with that?"

The only speaker was Lin Gor, and he shook his head. "None. It's just the sort of event that we need. Something like that will echo around the Empire – and that's even before we take steps to promote it. Except… we need to be sure the Countess will win. Sir Roland's very good."

Geraint smiled at him placidly. "My friend, I can guarantee it. I have every faith in my cousin."

Lin Gor looked at him sideways, a look that said, 'You're up to something, but I won't waste my breath asking.' Geraint smiled even more broadly, especially when he observed that Zeéla was giving him exactly the same look. He turned back to Louise. "Has anybody asked you yet what your side's reaction to today's events is likely to be?"

Louise took another sip of her wine. "Not as yet, no. I expected somebody would, in due course."

Geraint waited, expectant. "And…?"

"And that's a complete and honest answer to your question." She coolly poured more wine into her goblet.

Lin Gor spluttered into his own goblet. Geraint smiled deprecatingly. "Well I walked into that, and I don't blame you for doing what little you can." Then he sobered. "But I can't afford to be satisfied with it. Come with me. Zeéla, have you got a moment?"

Geraint led the two priests out the door and round a couple of corners to a quiet dead-end corridor. "Louise, it's this way. You're usually going to be no more than a nuisance doing that sort of thing, requiring an extra question or two and some careful thought, but your rank and status say that you're a highly intelligent woman so you may think of ways to achieve more than that. So I can't allow it. My cousin is your point of control, yes?" Louise nodded. "And she made it clear that my orders are as hers?" Louise nodded again. "Very well. You have not been forbidden to cast spells for your own comfort and convenience, provided they do not impact us in any way. You are now so forbidden.

You will make no enchantment of any kind, nor will you defend yourself against any enchantment cast upon you. Stand there, still and silent."

Geraint pulled an oak leaf from his cloak, followed by a briar thorn and several other less clearly identifiable items. He gave Zeéla a small silver pot, which she held while he mixed the items within, then generated a succession of small dweomers. The contents of the pot smoked, then turned to ash. Zeéla gave it back, then sucked her fingers.

Geraint turned back to Louise. "Sorry about this, it's not very pleasant, but I need your wholehearted co-operation. Or rather I *might* need it, and I can't risk the possibility that you might manage to be clever.

"You will find that you are permanently infested with both fleas and lice. Nothing will remove them. If you persuade someone else to cast on you to rid you of them, they will return promptly. You will find that you are developing arthritis of the hips and spine. Also warts, mainly facial. When you reach the University of the Woods, you will work the morning shift – seven hours – mucking out the stables, and the afternoon shift as a scullery maid. Leaves you ten hours to yourself, I imagine you will choose to shave your head to reduce the irritation from the lice, though of course that will detract from your appearance,

"Now, all these things are already in force, or will be when you get there. I'll rescind some – even all - of it if you show yourself to be outstandingly helpful from now on. But it's up to you to impress me with what you're doing for us. Again, I dislike doing this. However, if it doesn't achieve the desired effect, I will certainly do a lot worse."

Louise looked entirely composed. "Well, well. I'd really come to the conclusion that you people were all terminally soft. I have to say if I were doing it, I'd have done much more and enjoyed it. In fact, I suspect you might be quietly enjoying yourself, whatever you say."

She scratched absently, realised what she was doing, and made a face. "Already?"

"Probably."

'Can I infect other people?"

"No. In fact, any that other people have will transfer to you as soon as they get close enough. You're a magnet. Charms, sigils and medication won't work either."

Louise made a face again. "That truly is disgusting, you know?"

"I rather thought you might see it that way. The warts will become evident in about a week. You should have four or five on your face within fourteen days." He saw Louise shift uncomfortably. "Oh, I forgot.

You have a rather severe rash. Permanently. It's a relative of hives and it happens in all warm, damp areas of the body. I gather it irritates unbearably. It also makes any friction extremely painful. That makes walking profoundly unpleasant because of the areas between the toes, but the main problem has to do with the genital area."

"I don't… Yes I do. That's unkind."

Geraint shrugged. "As it stands, you have a nature priest addressing himself to making your life as trying as possible, and you have no defence against it. That's not a good place to be. I promise you, I've only just begun."

"I think you've made your point, Geraint. If I promise to be as helpful as I can…?"

"When that shows material results, I'll prevent the arthritis and the warts. Impress me with how useful you can be – beyond what I was looking to see – and I'll make your life at the university much more appropriate to your station – maybe allow you to cast for your own convenience and comfort again, with a few constraints."

"In that case I have some suggestions."

"Good. But first an important point. Now this certainly won't have occurred to you, but what I've just done would be seen by some as an abuse of your parole."

"Why? When somebody has sworn what I've sworn, they're yours to enjoy. Actually, the oath was somewhat milder than I'd expected."

"Perfectly orthodox point of view, for a Marnist. But, for instance, Lady Caroline would *not* approve. Hence, the Lady Zeéla is here to support my statement that I have just broken the news to you that I have diagnosed you with a rather nasty – but not fatal – disease. You can guess what some of the symptoms might be. There could be others that might suddenly manifest. Very, very unpleasant symptoms. Do we understand each other?"

Louise smiled with what appeared to be genuine amusement. "Perfectly. Don't concern yourself. I pick my fights and you currently have far too much of the high ground. I presume that you are expecting to be safely dead by the time we've won?"

"Yes. Confidently."

"Pity. But I'll see who I can find."

"You'll need to be lucky. I don't see any of us surviving. Now, your suggestions…"

"Hmm? Oh, yes. Why don't you take me with you to wherever you're going to flush out Sir Roland? I can offer startled recognition, or at least first-hand evidence. And I might see another face I recognise."

"You've seen the other traitor?"

"Not that I'm aware of. But the point is, I *wouldn't* have been aware of it. And I'm almost bound to have seen him at some point, having been in all the right places. So if I recognise a face…"

"Good point. Alright, we'll do that."

"Fine. Any chance of…?"

She gestured at the area between her legs and grimaced.

"Yes, you have been fidgeting rather, haven't you? Well, you get to keep it until we actually see practical benefit. But here." He produced a small vial of oily dark green fluid.

"Find a dunny and apply that - gently, or it'll hurt rather a lot. You'll find that relieves it for about six to eight hours. Apply all of it, though, all over the affected areas. Won't have any benefit otherwise. We'll see you back with the others. And don't be long."

"Thank you. This really is a sod." She snatched the vial and fled in search of a restroom.

Zeéla watched her go with a mildly puzzled expression. "She folded up very easily. Or has she?"

"I think she probably has. It's about knowing who you're dealing with. Marnists are into power, of course, which means they are probably a bit on the insecure side. But whatever the reason, you only have to look at what they do to each other. If a Marn priest gets another one in her power, she plays dominance games with her, taking the woman's dignity and inventing lots of complicated humiliations for her. They play these games with each other all the time. So being a loser is in the culture – as is turning the tables, by the way.

"It wasn't really what I did. It was that it gave her some clues as to what I *might* do, and made her realise that I would. She's not stupid, nor is she made of self-sacrificing stuff. Marnists aren't. She's not going to let herself be turned into a warty, smelly arthritic host for half the parasites in the known world just to advance the cause some tiny bit that nobody would ever know of. If she were willing to do that, she wouldn't be a Marnist. The essence of Marnism is to look after number one and be completely pragmatic.

"Take her behaviour in combat. I'm told she fought very well, and bravely, while she had something to gain from it; and as soon as there wasn't she surrendered. Pragmatic, you see. She is perfectly willing to be heroic while there's sufficient reward for heroism, and some clear way of receiving it. As soon as it becomes pointless, she loses any interest.

"I think she'll be alright now. Practicality says that she serves her interests best by giving us what we want, so that's what she'll do. If she ever got the tables turned, of course…"

"That wouldn't be nice."

"No. The energy Goreb people devote to selfless bravery, Marnists reserve for revenge, served hot, cold or sideways. It's an area where they and Brandur folk appear to meet, though actually it's a bit different. Let's get back."

On their way back to the meeting room they were accosted by a very large man with a lot of thoroughly functional-looking muscles. "Do you know where the Countess Beauclerc and her party are? I need to talk to her."

"Good question, sir. Answer one of mine, first. How did you get through our security to reach this point?"

"Because everybody here knows me. I'm Brutus, Baron of Lark Valley. You've been beating up on the Alliance on my turf."

"*That's* where I've heard the name Lark Valley before. You're the Arena Warrior."

"Three times Imperial Open Classification Champion."

"Well you certainly look the part. Can you prove it?"

"Short of killing you with one stroke, you mean? Well you've got JG with your party haven't you? And Becca Wright, as well. They both know me. I've known John for a decade."

Geraint nodded to Zeéla, who headed for the meeting room. Brutus looked surprised. "Aren't you a bit foolhardy? Doing this on your own? If I were one of the bad guys I'd have taken you down already."

Geraint smiled and said nothing. He was willing to bet a small fortune that Uggò was at that second within six feet of them, protected by Alyssana's gift. A stranger wandering around claiming to be somebody special? There was no possibility Uggò wouldn't be checking on that in person.

Just over a minute later, Zeéla came back with John Garrett. That worthy took one look and strode forward, smiling. "I wondered if you'd make an appearance."

"All this excitement in my own backyard. Why didn't you ask me for help? Not that you needed it."

"We're a bit cautious about putting local people at risk when we've gone. We haven't the force to occupy."

"See your point. What actually do you do in this outfit?"

"Well I've been setting up and organising the strike groups, but there's not a lot more of that to do. They're ready now and they're operating more and more independently, which was always the plan. In the next phase, I want to just concentrate on close protection for our countess. The more I see, the more important she seems – and the enemy isn't going to have missed that."

Geraint frowned. "You're aware that our last friend who made that his speciality lasted a matter of a few tens of hours past the decision?"

"I was there. But she's still alive and he's dead, which is the way round that we'd want it." Garrett looked again at Brutus. "Protection and subject both stand a better chance if there are two in the team."

Brutus nodded. "It's the job I was coming to apply for. I was going to argue that I'm uniquely qualified, but with you here that becomes an interesting question."

Geraint looked at Garrett. "Would you trust him that close to her?"

"I'd trust this man with my li… hold on. It's much more important than my life." Garrett stopped and stared into space for a second. "Alright. I trust him. This is one of the few men I've known for a long, long time who I'd still trust absolutely. Except with my girl. And my women he's welcome to, if they want."

"I'd have to be. You've laid a raft of mine. Including Lady Anne of Lark Valley, as I recall."

"Just one of those things that happened in the heat of the moment."

"Eleven different moments?"

"Ah … well I couldn't just leave it at once, could I? It would have insulted the lady."

"So how come your excess of courtesy stopped at eleven?"

"She fell pregnant with your son. That changed things. A bit of casual fun was no longer appropriate."

"I suppose...?"

"Don't be silly. You can't mistake my kids. Anyway, she was visiting the witch. No risk at all. Do you want to go and meet the Lady?"

They returned to the main room. Geraint noticed that Louise was already there, talking easily with Elaine. It turned out that Caroline already knew of Brutus of Lark Valley and was immediately impressed. "I've seen you in the Arena three times, My Lord. Once at the last championships - the National Finals in Cromreth. You beat Dalla Riora, Marach Ben Goran, Ross van Horn – that was a classic – and Benjani nà Gallachò in the Championship Bout."

"You're an aficionada then, Countess?"

"I went whenever there were top quality bouts in my area – and that one visit to Cromreth. If you are learning to fight, watch experts fighting. Before all this, I'd always hoped I might make a career in the arena myself."

"You certainly have the look of a sword fighter. Lady, do you understand that it's the bodyguards' job to fight if we are attacked? It's yours to remain safe."

"I understand the theory well enough. But I have a task that requires me to drive into the enemy as and when they are encountered." She smiled, deprecatingly. "I should explain. It is not that I am so heroic or foolhardy, but those around us now will guide me in planning our course and making this enterprise a success. The deep and subtle thinking is their part in this. It is mine to be the banner, the standard of our cause. And the standard flies nobly into the face of the enemy to inspire or shame others to follow. That is its purpose, its reason for being. Thus I cannot and will not hold back from a fight."

Geraint smiled at his cousin affectionately. "And the sheer coincidence that this fits your own inclinations so well…"

"Merely shows, cousin, that I am in my proper role – and that Varan is a kindly God and helps His people generously in their endeavours. Though that we already knew."

Geraint turned back to Brutus. 'We know, my lord, how much more difficult and dangerous this makes your own task. If you would like to withdraw from it at this point, none would think the worse."

"That's not sensible. It means she needs me that much more, surely."

"Which is beside the point I was making."

"Possibly, but not irrelevant to any decision I might make. Lady, there are some rules. John and I need to know what you plan to do before you do it, and wherever possible we need you to allow for our cover in your movements. Sometimes that will not be possible, but just be aware of us, at least."

Garrett added "And when we are working, we are not present. That is, we are not companions to talk to, to introduce to passers-by or to engage in discussion. This is applicable whenever there are people even potentially present who represent a possible threat. It interferes with our concentration and pulls our attention from where it should be."

Caroline frowned. "These are very serious precautions, gentlemen. Why are we suddenly so concerned?"

Geraint answered that one. "Because we are starting to make an impression. Our depredations in the rear areas have more or less brought the advance to a standstill. Belmond Duchy, which is at the heart of the invasion, is effectively frozen solid. Our message is reaching and energising the population as a whole. On top of that, we have now challenged the enemy militarily, way behind their own forward areas, and dealt them a double blow. We've destroyed an important control centre before they could get it up and running, and we've prevented the attack on one of our towns. Three blows, actually, because we've also made a dent in the reputation of the Red Death."

"All that I understand, not being simple. Now answer my question."

Iorweth picked up. "With apologies, Lady, it did - we're now a much bigger problem than we had been, as they now know that we can hurt them rather than simply be a nuisance. Now that's bound to result in steps being taken to deal with us promptly. I would expect them to work on more than one level, of course, but one will certainly be an attempt to take out our key people. Now, we really have only one key player."

"But that is simply not true, sir. The loss of Geraint or the Lady Zeéla would be an enormous blow. A fatal blow, I would imagine."

"However, they are unlikely to know that, Lady. They will be aware that these people are important to us, surely, but they'll be looking to kill our movement in the classic way: by cutting off its head."

Geraint turned to Louise. "What do you think your people will do about the assault on their forces and the camp?"

"Two things. They'll sweep a lot – a *lot* – of forces through here. That's one. The other will be a serious reprisal. They won't want to destroy the two towns – these are their towns, now, producing revenue for them – but they will be killing a lot of people, just to make the point.

"Of course, apart from direct response, they will already have plans for taking out the Countess – probably two or three others, as well – but you've already looked at that."

Geraint grimaced. "Yes. And there's very little we can do for the towns, as well. We won't have the force to face down what'll be coming through here."

Louise shrugged. "Why would you try? You've got what you came for. More, because the sort of force they're going to have to allocate to this will probably halt the advance altogether."

"Think of it as a religious foible. But what we do need to do – promptly – is warn the two towns so that anybody who wants to can leave before the storm hits. How long, Louise?"

"At least a week, even if they can set up a portal. Maybe two."

"But surely they know we'll be long gone by then."

Louise shook her head firmly. "No. You might be trying to establish large areas of control on their lines of communication. That would be a real problem for them and require them to bring the whole army back to clear you out, if you were in enough force. That's the problem. The Empire's so big. Until they've wiped out all significant opposition, they've got to keep a big field army. While they do that, they haven't got enough troops to occupy the ground behind them properly – so you can do the kind of thing you're doing – which in turn slows them in bringing to battle the forces that remain in front of them.

Zeéla's eyebrows rose. "But surely the Alliance aren't frightened of Sir Roland?"

Louise Megiddo, Countess Amondir
Priest of Marn
Senior Wing Commander, Sword Sisters

"Clearly not, but what if he's replaced? Then there's the Faerie Royal Levy. That wouldn't be a problem for the field army as it stands, but they wouldn't need to detach all that many regiments for occupation duties before suddenly FRL would look like a very serious proposition. And if it joined with the remains of the Imperial Army, under a commander that intended to fight…" Louise pursed her lips.

"Quite. So they go forward steadily, as quickly as they can, looking to find and wipe out the Imperial Army. It would be helpful if Sir Roland could bring them into action - actually, that was the original plan - but he says that his junior commanders don't trust him and so won't commit to battle. Aother possibility is that he and the traitors in the High Council are simply keeping a force in being until we offer them a deal they like.

"Either way, eventually we'll bring the Imperial Army to battle. Once we do that, the high command can detach much larger forces to occupy. But until they can do that, their supply position is causing them real headaches and slowing them down enormously. Which is where we come to blocks. If you started to establish blocks – say whole baronies, or even shires, defended by serious numbers of troops, they might end up with their communications with Belmond completely cut. Then they'd have to come back - all of them - and clear the blocks."

"But we don't have anything like the troops for that. Not until…"

"…you've got the dukes onside. Yes, I know. But what our high command cannot know, because your High Council no longer meets, is how close you are to achieving that. So you will see a very significant presence come through here in about ten days' time, razing anything that looks remotely like a military installation, and laying waste to a calculated proportion of the land."

Geraint nodded grimly. "And that will more or less stall the advance of your front line?"

"Yes. Completely, I would imagine."

"Worth the price, then."

Carol turned; "Cousin, that is a horrible calculation."

"Did you imagine we could do this without cost?"

"No, never. Did *you* imagine that I could accept that without pain?"

"Not really, no. But it won't be the last time people die as a direct result of our actions."

"And it won't be the last time I lose a night's sleep. It doesn't matter, does it? I get away with weeping a little. *They* lose friends and family. They lose their lives, their homes. Hundreds of years' heritage, sometimes, in one place. Everything that ever mattered to them. And all because we are here and doing what we do. And do you know the worst of it? If the Alliance were to wipe out the whole population of both towns, it would make no difference – we'll just go and do it somewhere else tomorrow, just the same."

"Cousin, are you saying you don't wish to do this any more?"

"I couldn't say that, for I have never wished to do this. Am I saying I *will* not do it any more? That's what tears my heart open. It's my duty to do this, and I have not the slightest intention of stopping until they cut me down, regardless of the cost. The *Stranger's Blessing* is quite clear on the matter. But does that make me immune to grief for that cost, Geraint? No. How could it?"

That wound down the conversation with Louise for the present. Geraint left Carol with Zeéla while he buttonholed Garrett and Lin Gor. "I've organised a conference of Myndarit Knights Commander for tomorrow evening. We need to ensure there are no more Sir Rolands. There are some things we need to set up."

They talked for about half an hour, then Geraint headed for the bar at one end of the room. Louise went with him. "Your countess – is she depressive or something? I would worry about clinical insanity if I were you. I didn't understand one word in ten."

Geraint glanced at her, his eyes dark and hostile. "You keep your clever mouth off her, Louise. In the religion of Varan, that's not called insanity, it's called compassion … decency." He shook his head. "I know, I know, you're Marnist. Those are just words to you, meaning nothing."

"Meaning hypocrisy, usually."

"I can't argue. But did you see hypocrisy tonight?"

"That's my point. No sane person actually means stuff like that."

Geraint stopped and held her eye. "If I were you, I'd leave it exactly there, while you still have your health."

Louise shrugged. "Geraint, you've got the high cards, just now. You speak and I obey. I'll have a red wine, please. Large. Hmm... Actually, do you want to take me to bed?"

Geraint considered as they moved to the bar. Louise leaned her back against it as he stood facing it. Her hand inconspicuously slipped down his front and briefly caressed him with thrilling skill. He felt himself stir. "Why not? Your fleas will stay with you. You don't have to."

"I do if you tell me to."

"I know that, which is why I'm making the point."

"That might have been more of a thrill. I didn't like being low girl in the temple, back as a new priest in my mid-teens, but it was wildly erotic sometimes. And the senior women's punishments for juniors who didn't try hard enough to please were *very* much worse than you're doing.

"But yes, why not? You'll have to give me more of that balm – or at least, I'll beg as prettily as you like until you do – and I think you're likely to be a good deal more fun than spending the night alone with the rash. That rash is acquiring a big, very ugly personality all its own."

Chapter 19

Out of the mouths...

In the morning, Becca's riders went through the town announcing a speech at the Town Hall. When Carol stood on the bed of a wagon to begin her speech, the square was full, and people overflowed into the side streets.

As she got onto the wagon, Zeéla stood beside her and said quietly "You just talk in a normal voice as though you were talking to one of them. I'll make sure everybody hears."

So, with Lin Gor playing a hammered dulcimer gently behind her, Carol began conversationally. "Good morning. Thank you for coming. Those of you I didn't meet last time I was here won't know me, I imagine. My name is Caroline ap Gryffudd…"

She had to stop, for a thunderous roar of approval rolled around the square for a good three quarters of a minute. Carol stood, nodding, trying to smile, to hold back tears.

When they were quiet again, she began once more. "My friends, I doubt that I have earned such an opinion from you, for I have surely brought great trouble on your heads by coming here. You will all know by now that the Alliance sent a thousand troops and a wing of the Red Death to kill many of you because of my previous visit. We know and you know that we cannot as yet protect you from the full strength of the Alliance – with the help of the Gods that will come with time – but such a force as *that* we can show the error of their ways. Perhaps next time around the Wheel, many of them will be wiser."

There was a rumble of fierce laughter. Carol smiled, breathed deeply and resumed "Next time they come, they will be in such force as we cannot repel. But you must choose. We have brought this trouble on you. If you wish, we will stay and aid those of you who would flee; if we do we will probably be caught up in the attack. Or we can go on, continue to oppose the Alliance, and one day be strong enough to throw them out of the Empire altogether – though perhaps more towns will suffer the fate of Long Astley first. What is your wish? I swear to be bound by it. First, who would have us stay?"

Silence stretched across the square. "Who then would have us go?"

There was a low rumble across the square. It washed from side to side and down the packed access streets.

"Very well. I assure you of this, that we will use every means and all our strength to sweep these invaders out of our nation. With your help and that of all the people of the Empire, we will make them regret they ever began this sorry enterprise. Or we will all die in the attempt. On this I am resolved and will not be moved."

She got down off the wagon to an even louder thunder of cheering. Geraint pulled Lin Gor aside. "How did you do it?"

The Elf smiled modestly. "It was just a matter of emphasis, really. Nearly all of them were with her anyway. Uggò accentuated the cheering at the beginning, then damped down any sound when she asked about staying. I just emphasised moods a little. People don't detect it because it creeps into their minds with the music. The cheering at the end was completely spontaneous, though."

"Uggò's getting a grip on sounds, then?"

"Yes, it's coming along nicely, now. He seems to have passed a watershed, and he's getting better every day."

Caroline, having got down from the wagon, approached a group of people at the front of the crowd. "Goodmen, mistresses. I saw you cheering, and I need to ask you a thing. Please don't misunderstand, your support is precious to me, and without it we could do nothing. But how have I earned it? I've brought you nothing but woe."

A man at the front of the group looked startled. "That's stupid!" Then as the woman next to him rammed her elbow into his ribs, he looked appalled. "I'm sorry, Countess, I didn't mean to be rude. But, see, my family've lived in this town for at least fifteen generations, and the Empire's been a good place to live for all that time.

"When your ancestor created it, that made him the greatest man … well anyways, the Empire's a good place to live. Always was. But now look. The Alliance comes, and what does the Empire do? It does fu–" The woman beside him rammed her elbow in his ribs again. "Sorry. I mean, it does nothin'. The dukes sit about, the High Council falls apart, the army loses once and then runs away. We was resigned to the fact that we was goin' to lose the Empire without anyone even tryin' to save it.

Chad Hemmingway
Shopkeeper & Baker
Long Astley

"Then what'll it be? Human sacrifices to Goreb – and that'll be us. Marn's filth – and that'll be our wives, sisters and daughters. Great lords ownin' what used to be our own land and businesses, and you takes what they give you to work on and you tugs your forelock and pays your rent.

"All that, and nobody to say no. It made me want to hit somethin'. Anythin'. I know my neighbours felt the same. Then you comes along and at least you're goin' to *try*. And you're ap Gryffudd. They've never let us down yet. Not like some others. Look, nobody here's fool enough to think we can fight back without consequences. The war will come here, and people will die. Most of us, likely. But at least somebody's tryin' to do somethin'. Somebody we can trust. I'll take that – and I'll cheer you all day if it'll help."

He stopped, breathing hard, and the woman beside him – surely his wife – squeezed his hand, looking proud. Carol looked around the group. "Is this how you all feel? Is this brave man speaking for all of you?"

More people had crowded around while the man was talking, and a woman in the midst of the growing knot of people put her hand up, then bobbed a curtsy when Carol looked at her. "'Tis how it is, your ladyship. That's my brother Chad. He's always had a way with words, and he's right. We can't give it all up without even *trying*. Without makin' the bast– Without makin' 'em *pay*. We can't!"

Carol struggled to speak around a rapidly closing throat. "Well, I cannot promise to stop these thieves – though we will all give our lives trying – but I *can* promise that at the very least they will, indeed, pay in blood for this. I can absolutely promise that."

As they crowded around, just seeming to want to touch her, or merely to have been near her, Lin Gor moved away, talking to Geraint. "I think I've more or less memorised that bloke's speech. I'll feed it to the Scouts and Salesmen. They've been spreading that sort of message wherever they go; it'll be useful for them to know they're hitting the right note."

Geraint nodded. "Whoever came through here did a good job, anyway. Who was it?"

Lin Gor shook his head. "No, that's the point. There's been nobody through here in weeks. I'd say that was his own thoughts. Humbling, eh?"

"Yah. Elaine! Got a minute? Can you have a chat with Borgia for me? Brutus' wife and son need to be got away from here in the next few days and set up comfortably somewhere safe. Can you deal with that?"

"Surely. As soon as you can give me your definition of 'somewhere safe.'"

"Good question. A quiet country house somewhere near the Hams, maybe? False identity of course."

"Right. I'll talk to her."

Geraint went to rescue his cousin from the people flocking around her, to the obvious relief of Brutus and Garrett. He couldn't see Uggò, but had no doubt he was in the crowd, somewhere nearby.

"Cousin, we will need to go to the chapter house nearest. We must visit the University of the Woods before we get to Sir Roland."

"Oh? I thought we weren't taking Louise there, yet?"

"Not leaving her there, no. None the less, we must go there. The Faith of Brandur has a gift for you."

Chapter 20

Uggò sharply points out a traitor...

They reached the Pollock Castle Chapter House early that afternoon and used its portal to travel through to the Elfstone Chapter House at Man Hanging, where there was a conference with all chapter knights-commander scheduled for the evening.

The conference was set up in the dining room of the Temple Guild at Man Hanging, a large, rather beautiful room that had been equipped as a lecture theatre for the session, with a dais at one end and rows of comfortable chairs facing it. The knights assembled in the Bar of the Guild, who had decamped to join the Blue Guild for the night, and moved into the dining room once all fifty knights-commander and their various aides had arrived, so that there were around two hundred and fifty men and women in the hall when the meeting started.

As had become her habit, Caroline opened the meeting and thanked the knights for attending, then handed over to Geraint to chair the proceedings. She felt that it gave her more leisure to consider the issues and people involved, without the distraction of managing the meeting - and yet did not prevent her from intervening when there was something she should address personally. Also, of course, such things were an essential part of a druid's training, while her only experience of managing meetings, before all this, had been charitable committees within Beauclerc.

Geraint, entirely comfortable chairing meetings of any size, regardless of the eminence of those involved, immediately swung into a swift review of progress. "We have now established and developed tactical doctrine for a number of groups of light cavalry, each between eight hundred and fifteen hundred strong.

"These units are associated with Arms of Mannan-Dar who can manage their arrival close to a suitable target, protect them from magical attack during the action, then facilitate their return to a safe location. They are led by able and experienced officers and are operating under instruction from Captain-General Garrett, of whom many of you will know. He has more or less made himself redundant in that role, because the unit leaders and their subordinates – all of whom are personally sworn to the Lady – are now able to operate the plan he has laid down independently of central control.

"Each unit has a base including one or more training septs, and each is supplied by … a large organisation with no overt connection to our activities. Recruits come via a different channel. In addition, the supply organisation is able to furnish mercenaries as required, who never see the training base, but who can be used as the unit commander sees fit. In other words, there is no reason why these units should not operate independently and effectively without limit of time – at least for the foreseeable future." A knight raised his hand. "Ah, yes, sir?"

"Phil Arran, Maisie's. Are these base camps subject to magical disclosure?"

"No, Sir Philip, or at least only with extreme difficulty. Each camp is in … let us say a rural location, and entered and left only via portal to varying points, all some considerable distance away. Goods and supplies are delivered via these portals, so the supply organisation has no knowledge of any camp's location. Further, each camp is protected by a full coven, plus a number of members of the Arm of Mannan-Dar, all of whom have no other responsibility at present than to protect their allotted camp from any magical search – and also to, let us say, *discourage* such searchers. There have already been a number of casualties amongst enemy casters in this respect."

"Oh dear. Nothing, ah … *trivial*, I trust?"

Geraint smiled briefly. "Quite the reverse, in fact."

The big warrior sat back contentedly. "Jolly good."

Geraint moved on. "These units are tasked to disrupt enemy organisation and communications in their back areas, and in particular to make Belmond Duchy sheer chaos at all times.

"It is to our advantage that many packs of Wayfarers have come east – apparently following the legions, for some reason – and are engaged in similar activities. It appears that their God has decided to throw in Her lot with the rest of Her Family in this emergency. We occasionally liaise with these packs where, as co-belligerents, we can be of assistance to each other."

Another knight raised a hand. "Anne Drummond, Unicorn. How close is this liaison?"

"As required by the tactical situation, ah, Countess is it not?"

Drummond nodded, and Geraint continued. "It is always an arms' length arrangement, my lady. At most we might place a communications operative with them for a short time. Normally, there is just a brief conference."

"So it could not be said that we were in any way endorsing these people?"

"No, ma'am. It is strictly business, relating to co-ordination of activities we had severally determined on anyway."

"I'm pleased about that."

"I believe a number of people feel the same way. Now on to the main business of the meeting. Brace yourselves, ladies and gentlemen. We now have incontrovertible proof that Sir Roland, Baron Abbeville, a guild knight commander in this order and the Earl Marshal of the Empire, is in fact an agent of the Great Alliance, recruited not less than two years ago. We don't know by what means that recruitment was effected. My Lady of Beauclerc will be going on from here to call him out and kill him."

He paused as the assembled knights reacted to this news. When the hubbub had died down a little, he resumed. "Documentary proof and the testimony of witnesses are both available and will be presented shortly. In the meantime, there is another issue. Can anybody here suggest what that might be?"

Sir Philip Arran stirred in his seat. "Well that's obvious enough. If we had one traitor in the Order, do we have another – or others?"

"Indeed, sir. And do you have a suggestion as to how this traitor – or these traitors – might be uncovered?"

"Well, I'm not really in the mood for playing games with you, my son. You clearly have such an idea. Share, boy. Share."

"Yes, I'm sorry, you're probably right." Geraint didn't look noticeably sorry. "It occurred to us that an oath of loyalty, to the God, before a Priest, would be good. But of course, Varan followers do not swear oaths. It specifically forbids it in the Book of the Stranger… '*Say I will, or I will not, and so do,*' I believe it says. However there is no reason why each person should not affirm their loyalty to their God and their Order. If this were done in the presence of the God and with one hand upon Myndarit, it would be fairly conclusive, don't you think?"

Arran nodded briskly. "Yes. Excellent. I trust you've got troops outside the door in case anybody feels a sudden, irresistible urge to get some fresh air?"

"Well, some sanctuary knights, but mainly Captain-General Garrett and Brutus, Baron Lark Hill. You may recall his name from the Arena lists. I think it fair to say that venturing to leave this room at present would simply be a rather brief suicide attempt. An undoubtedly successful one.

"Oh, there is also a senior priest of Varan here, until recently a leading Knight of the Temple in the Cromreth Chapter. No doubt many of you know Lady Jolyonne. She has established a Spirit Gate at the door. Anybody passing that will be revealed in their true light.

"If you will open the door, Lin Gor, Lady Jolyonne will come and administer the oaths – that is, the affirmations. To be honest I greatly doubt that there is another traitor in the Order – we were astonished to find even one – but let's be sure."

Lady Jolyonne was a blonde woman in her late thirties, still with the body of a warrior, but carrying with her that indefinable sense of power and authority to be found accompanying all very senior priests. She strode in a business-like way to the dais and looked around at the assembled Myndarits.

"Gentles, I expect and very much hope that this whole process will prove unnecessary. However, we will carry it out in the following way. I will invoke our God. My Lady Caroline, Countess Beauclerc will then stand here, with Myndarit in her hand. Each of you will in turn approach, lay one hand on the blade, and affirm before Varan your fealty to Him and to the order. Any forsworn wretch will of course be instantly revealed. I have agreed to undertake this task on the clear understanding that I will then have the privilege and pleasure of killing the miscreant myself. Lady Caroline was understandably irritated at this, but she gets to kill Sir Roland.

"Very well, we will do this in chapter order. The knight commander and any officers of First Chapter will advance immediately after I have finished my invocation, please."

Jolyonne raised her arms and intoned the invocation, longer and more complex than that required to summon the attention of Baraani, but still less than three minutes long. By the end of that time, the room was almost crackling with the Presence of the God, and Myndarit, bare in Carol's hand, was shining with a pure golden radiance.

Then the procession began, each Chapter's officers in turn coming forward and and announcing their loyalty in firm voices. There was a certain amount of tension, as any traitor's choices were only to avoid the event or affirm and die – for the God would certainly take immediate steps at being defied in that fashion.

Thus Jolyonne stood close by with drawn sword, ready – perhaps hoping - to engage anybody who deviated from a direct route from the dais steps to Myndarit. However, the ritual proceeded with complete lack of event as knight after knight advanced to lay a hand upon the blade of the sacred Sword and affirm his or her loyalty.

Finally, the officers of the Fiftieth Chapter returned to their seats. Geraint apparently addressed fresh air. "Was there anybody? Please point him out."

A man near the middle of the hall screamed and fell writhing with a knife wound in his kidneys. Uggò was suddenly visible behind him.

Geraint tutted. "I hadn't actually meant you to point him in quite that sense, but no matter. Can someone say who that is? Was?"

A large knight was on his feet, hand on hilt. "I am Hal ap Rhys, Cromreth Chapter. This is my adjutant."

Uggò bowed gracefully. "He did be a traitor, Sir Knight. He did pass inconspicuously from the line of people approaching the dais to the line of people leaving it, without ever getting up there himself. Lin Gor and I were present in the body of the hall to watch for just such a trick – it did seem the obvious way to avoid the situation without penalty."

Geraint nodded in satisfaction. "No others?"

Uggò shook his head. "We did be very careful. No others."

Caroline sheathed Myndarit. "Very well, my brothers and sisters, we will now present the evidence which convicts Sir Roland."

They first showed the documents found in the alliance camp, then Elaine told of the information her corporation had uncovered about Sir

Roland's visits to the Marn priest Julia, then finally Louise told of her meetings with Sir Roland before the invasion.

At the end, Hal ap Rhys arose. "In the circumstances, the man should have the opportunity to answer the charges – though I must say I can conceive of no possible answer to this very conclusive presentation. Still, he should have his say."

Caroline nodded. "It is my intention, as Knight Commander of the Order, to offer him the choice of a formal trial – or an immediate combat with me. The evidence being what it is, he is unlikely to opt for trial, and I hope and expect he will choose to fight me. Then I will kill him."

"Good."

Hal ap Rhys sat down. Lady Anne Drummond promptly rose. "This leaves another point. You have cut loose your light cavalry to do what they're good at – but you yourself will be travelling extensively around the Empire. It is surely time we arranged that you have an escort of Myndarits at all times. Do you agree that this is so, Lady?"

Carol nodded. "Aye. And it is all the better that I should be with Myndarits now, for now we know that Myndarits can be relied upon with certainty."

A brief discussion resulted in a simple scheme whereby escorts would change out as Caroline's party passed through the various chapter house portals in the course of their travels, the details being co-ordinated by a small committee of chapter knights-commander. It was also resolved that the escort would always include knights from at least two different chapters, changed out at different times in order to ensure continuity of organisation within the escort itself. It was further agreed that the escort would consist of a hundred and fifty knights, all Heavies, of whom about one third would be Temple Knights. There would also be between half a dozen and a dozen scouts.

Finally, because Cromreth Chapter had brought the traitor, it was decided that they would be one of the chapters providing the initial escort team, so that it could not be thought they were under any kind of cloud. It was felt appropriate that the Gryffudd Mawr Chapter should find the other half of the escort, Gryffudd being Carol's most famous ancestor.

That concluded the meeting, so – these being Myndarits – there was a boisterous and somewhat alcohol-rich celebration. It was held in the Great Hall of the Chapter House and attended by, it seemed, half the chapter, plus all those from the meeting who had no immediate duties with their own chapters.

A couple of hours into the party, Elaine found Geraint discussing with several senior Myndarits and three or four even more senior Varan priests how the government of the Empire should be handled, assuming this invasion were somehow beaten off.

"Geraint, that young Alma priest, Hendricks' friend, will be at the Chapter House gate in about ten minutes. She urgently needs to talk to you."

Geraint raised his eyebrows, excused himself and hurried to the gate, where Borgia and the visible part of her cover team were just crossing the drawbridge. He arranged for her to be admitted with two bodyguards – one of whom, he noticed, was Hendricks – into one of the outer bailey reception rooms.

As soon as the chapter servants had seen to her needs and withdrawn she got to the point. "I sent a team to handle collection of that Baron's wife and son as soon as I got the message from Elaine. But we were too late. His manor's been burned, his servants killed. I'm afraid his son's dead and his wife's missing. I'd infer, fairly conclusively, that she's been taken. Likely it was done early this morning – the bastards were probably just finishing up there as you passed your message to Elaine."

She grimaced, and shook her head frustratedly. "I'm sorry. There was nothing we could do, though I've got people digging into it. If we can find out where she's been taken we might manage a rescue – but you know how rarely that happens. Usually people who are lifted by professionals stay gone unless someone decides to send 'em back. And that doesn't often happen, to be truthful."

"This was a professional job, then?"

"For sure. It was a large team with at least two elements. One was corporate – there are still spell traces – and the other … we're not sure. My feeling is Marn, but it's instinct more than evidence."

"Corporate?"

Borgia jabbed a thumb at her own chest. "Alma corporate. Our main spell specialist there – Angelo, bloody good man – thinks it's one of the two Mallow-based corporations, because of the traces of physical spell components he found there. His guess is Great North-Western General, but I don't have any freakin' idea why he's saying that. If it's not GNWG then it's Amber Amalgamated Trading, but it's rare he's wrong about things like this.

There was a knock at the door. One of the chapter servants came in. "Excuse me, Lord Druid, one of this lady's escort needs to speak with her. May we tell the Guard Commander it would be alright to bring her in here?"

Geraint nodded, and a few minutes later another Alma priest was escorted in. She almost ran to Borgia and bent to whisper in her ear, but her boss waved her away. "Just say it. We don't want secrets here – might give the wrong idea."

The woman – much older than Borgia – nodded. "Your choice. The dead son has just animated, apparently. It's sophisticated stuff, Angelo says, not the sort of enchantment your average necromancer could deal with.

"So, he animated, stood and approached the nearest priest – who was one of our people, as it happened, but Angelo is certain that was coincidence. Don't know why, but he is. Anyway, the kid's corpse said, 'Tell Brutus if he wants her back, he's got to get us Louise. The Greyhound, Dwarf's Bay, ten days' time. If Louise isn't in there by midnight, end of negotiation.' Then he collapsed again."

Borgia cursed obscenely. "I presume that's knackered any chance of resurrection?"

"Angelo had Emma check at once. No chance at all."

Borgia nodded thanks and waved her away, but Geraint touched the priest's arm. "Excuse me – and what is your name?"

She glanced at Borgia, apparently got a signal, and turned to face him. "I'm Rayanna. You are...?"

"Geraint ap Gryffudd. On your way out, would you be so kind as to ask a chapter servant to find us Baron Lark Valley please?"

The woman nodded and left.

"Geraint? You going to leave it up to him?" Borgia looked startled.

"Certainly not. But I'm going to ask his opinion."

"Why?"

"Thirdly, because he's entitled. Secondly, because he'll probably give the right answer anyway, and then we win a bit of kudos with him, that we asked. But firstly, it'll tell us about his commitment."

"A bit cold and calculating, maybe?"

"This from you."

Borgia shrugged expressively. "Well you do all try to pass yourselves off as the good guys. I would have thought that involved some kind of obligation to be, you know, *good* occasionally. Seems not."

Geraint chuckled drily, without much humour. "Well, I try to be. But I've only got room for one set of objectives and loyalties, and Brutus doesn't figure in them except as a means to an end. I don't necessarily like being this way, but we've got a near impossible job to do and I can't be any other way and still get it done. If you want cuddly, go and see my cousin. She has no idea how to be anything *but* good. Or Iorweth, for that matter. He's a really nice bloke. I'm not. I'll try to get the knack of that again when this is all over and I can get properly into the swing of it."

Borgia smiled. "Just winding you up. Anyway, methinks the druid doth protest too much."

"And what–"

At that point Brutus was ushered in. Geraint gestured to a chair. "Park it, my lord. This is Borgia, whose organisation does jobs for us occasionally. They're the ones we asked to collect your wife and son. I'm sorry. Borgia, tell him. All of it."

Borgia outlined what they found at Lark Valley Manor in a few sentences, then went on to tell of the message. Brutus turned to Geraint. "Does that mean he can't be...?"

"Yes. I gather so. I'm very sorry. We were as quick as we could be."

"You must have been, to have the news already. I'd thought there'd be days to spare."

"So did I. Apparently we're getting further under their skins than we thought."

"Hooray for us." Brutus took a deep breath. "Well. Of course there's nothing we can do about the exchange they want. It's just not a starter."

Geraint breathed out a long sigh and then shook his head. "No, sadly, not at all. If they thought we were open to that kind of leverage, there'd be wholesale kidnappings starting tomorrow. But two can play that game. Borgia, can you noise it around please that there's an open contract on all those involved in the attack on the manor, in whatever capacity. Say thirty thousand a head. And the head is what we'd need, together with evidence that it really is the head of someone we want. Also, I'd like to offer a specific commission to your top in-house assassin, whom I know to be unusually good. I want the caster who made the boy's resurrection impossible with that foul message. Alive, I'll pay a hundred thousand crowns for. Dead, I'll pay sixty-five. But I want him or her."

Borgia nodded. "I'll make sure our star assassin knows of your offer." Then she glanced briefly at an apparently impassive Hendricks. "I'm in a position to assure you that he *will* take on the commission, however."

"Good. On an entirely different subject, how is your colleague Magda Leona?"

Borgia smiled very briefly. "Well, as it goes, Magda's mysteriously disappeared too. Obviously, people are looking for her but I just have the feeling that she won't be seen again. Not alive, anyway. My guess is that in a few weeks she's really very likely to turn up recently dead and horribly mutilated, somewhere our Head Office executives hang out.

"But the situation's different in the case of my lord of Lark Valley's lady wife. I've no doubt she's currently alive and she'll probably stay that way – she'd be too profitable to sell, is the brutal truth. And as I said before, we're doing everything we can to get a lead on who's taken her and where. But…" She shrugged frustratedly, "It almost never turns out well."

"Might you pick up a lead in Dwarf's Bay?" asked Geraint.

"It's probably our best chance. We might mount a little charade, see who bites."

"That seems to be it, then. Do you want to join the party?"

"Thanks but no. We've got loads to do tonight. If these buggers *have* left any sign, now's the time to find it." She got up and led her people to the door, then turned to Brutus. "I'm sorry, my lord Baron. We got there as soon as we could. I don't think anybody expected that freakin' swift a move."

Brutus shook his head, face bitter. "I certainly didn't. I don't see how anybody could blame you for that. But if you could manage to find her - or find where I could buy her back, for that matter…"

"We'll give it our best." And they were gone.

Geraint stood up. "What do you want to do? Go and be on your own for a while, or get drunk with us? I haven't really got anything else to offer but sympathy and company – unless a few hours unconsciousness might help. I can arrange that."

Brutus hesitated, then shook his head. "What I really want are some obliging enemies to hack to pieces. But failing that, I think I'll take you up on the drink, if you don't mind a grim companion."

"Come on, then. If ever there was a good place to get legless amongst friends, a Myndarit party has to be top of the list."

Chapter 21

First step in deciding your future is to make sure you have one

Pindra opened her eyes to see a well-lit expanse of living rock, some twenty or thirty feet above her. She was lying on a camp cot, and covered by a sheet and several warm, fluffy blankets. She was warm and comfortable and - she screamed, then again.

An old woman's voice with a kind of... vibrancy... in it said "You're in a comfortable bed and in no danger. Well, no immediate danger anyway. That's quite an unusual reaction to such circumstances..."

Pindra stopped. Swallowed. Looked around again - couldn't see the woman, but she definitely *could* see! "I...I was blind, agony in my face... Wolves were tearing at my legs and stomach, they'd been doing it for... I don't know. Long time. But I've got legs, eyes... What *is* this?

The voice sounded less than patient. "Well, girl, if you want to know things listen and don't interrupt! You'll maybe learn something. This is about time. Time is ... well there isn't just one path; reality flows down just one but there are others it could have taken, equally valid... Reality chooses the path richest in probability mostly... well that's an over-simplification but it will do.

"The wolves, your eyes and so on... that's one possible path. There's another in which one of my priests is watching for you using one of the ravens, cuts you down before the birds harm you, heals your feet and your shoulders, your arms. Brings you here.

"You see, I amend the flow of probability. That's one of the things I do. I rarely travel counter to time, but I can amend probability in arrears, so to speak, so that reality *"retracts from"* the path it was on, and is attracted to the probability I've created in another path.

"If you understood any of that I'll be surprised, but here you are on the cusp, two days after that event. A decision must be made. Either reality comes down this path and you are here, waiting to see what life might bring you next, or it goes back down the other, and you are safely on the Wheel, all pain done with, and waiting patiently for another try at the Realms."

Pindra lay still, let it drift into her, examined it... maybe for a long time, she wasn't sure. Might have been minutes... felt like days - and also like just a fleeting moment. The old woman must be more patient than she sounded, because she made no comment, no attempt to hurry her.

"So... how is it decided, this path or that?"

"With you, at this time, I decide. But in turn that depends on *your* choice. I have a set number of priests, never more nor less. But the one who found you wants to rest for a while. Death isn't all one place - just the Wheel. There are options, at least for some.

"But to go to her rest she must be replaced. None of my priests officially exist in the world. Just as you will not. They are all... *rescues*... like yourself. It gives powers and abilities, but of course there are drawbacks. One of the drawbacks is that once you take the job, you have to keep doing it until a replacement is found. A very long time, sometimes. The rest is pleasant, afterwards, in many ways - and then one day you will be back for another tour of duty."

Pindra thought about it, calmly, with no fuss, for another strangely long fragment of time. "So who are you, then, whose priest I might be?"

"Indeed, Pindra. Who? I deal in probability and use it to warp reality. I bend and shape people's futures. I am in the Realms and not. I am Myself sometimes and sometimes ... another, greater self.

"A deal of turbulence is coming. Some gods, for their own ends, and in alliance with the Spirit Planes - an abomination in itself - have chosen to seek to change the nature of things.

"These changes are for the worse in the case of mortals, but that isn't the worst of it, for they will also very significantly increase the possibility of a calamity even these foolish gods would nor desire - though the denizens of the Spirit Planes would be delighted. Neither of these outcomes is acceptable to Me, nor to My other selves, nor to my... well the nearest is to say My Son. So I will stop them. Alone, if I must, though I seem likely to have help.

"Now, there are enough clues in all that for a sharp young woman like you. Who am I?"

Pindra considered the matter. For how long, she had no notion. An old woman who deals in futures... who would stand against the gods themselves, or some of them... She is part of a greater self - that has to mean one of the Three Sisters, the Faces of Rhiannon.

But then..."Caillach. You are Caillach." Another unknown time passed as certainty crept into her. "I will serve, if you'll have me. I behaved badly and might have done a lot of harm... I deserved what I got. Well not what I got, that was necessary just to show people - but I deserved to get offed."

She paused, waited for however long it took for the certainty to take root and become part of her. "If I can put something up against that in the balance, something of use... will you have me?"

"I know what you did and why, and Borgia wasn't the only one who wanted you to have another chance. She couldn't do it; however I... use your head, girl! If I didn't want you, why would I have spent these very many weeks talking to you? Who do you think it was who sent the raven for my priest to use? Come, my Pindra."

And Pindra was standing, wearing a large black cloak with a big, deep hood. Caillach pointed toward the cave entrance, and the sea beyond. "Now it's time for your lessons to begin."

Chapter 22

Carol makes a friend but Louise... definitely doesn't

The next morning they took the chapter portal to the Elfstone Chapter's Mother House, which was close to the edge of the Green Deep, the vast and ancient forest which contained in its depths the University of the Woods. From the chapter house they travelled the few miles to a large and ancient Sacred Grove, an unusually holy place where even the followers of other religions could feel the slightly ominous tingling of power several hundred yards before they arrived.

The druid holding the post of Grove Father there was expecting them and guided them straight to the portal in his grove – an innocent-looking gap between two venerable, overarching trees – an oak and a holly, in a circle of equally ancient rowan.

That portal in turn came out at the dead end of a short path which led to the junction of that and four other paths, one leading alongside a broad, almost still stream. Geraint walked in front, unerringly leading the way through fairly open forest, having known this part of the Green Deep for years.

John Garrett had been here before as well, engaged in some research at the University, and walked very close to Louise. Brutus stayed equally near on the other side. Eventually, it irritated her enough to cause her to comment. "I'm not going to run off, you know. The oath prevents it - and even if not, long rustic hikes are really not my big thing."

JG shook his head. "I know. I'm not afraid of you getting away. It's the reverse. Marnists are not popular here, to put it mildly, and I don't want anybody getting excited and doing something they wouldn't particularly regret."

"Someone? What someone? You people aren't really the sort for that kind of thing."

"Us? No, not us."

"Who, then? There's nobody within a hundred miles, at a guess."

"You'd be guessing wrongly, then. The Guardians are here, all around us."

"Guardians?"

"You'll see. In the meantime, stay very close to my side. Let's not have any accidents."

It was only ten or fifteen minutes later that Louise saw her first Guardian. They came into a bigger clearing than the previous path junctions had been and Louise saw that the path opposite was blocked by a vast white horse. It stood all of twenty-two hands – perhaps more - at the shoulder. Its long, silky mane was pale grey, as was its equally magnificent tail, but the rest of the beast was white, pure white, from its hocks to its ears. And then Louise stopped dead, seeing in the middle of the beast's forehead a white, spiral fluted horn, looking very solid and distinctly like a formidable weapon, over two feet long.

It was only then that she noticed somebody actually sitting on the animal's back, causing her another double-take. The very fit and attractive young woman, perhaps in her late teens or early twenties, wore nothing but a sword belt. In her hand was a bow, the associated quiver hanging from the saddle. The bow had an arrow nocked and was half pulled, the arrow not *quite* pointing at Louise.

"Are you bringing pets home now, Geraint?" The voice was cold, and somehow older than the body – not in years but in experience and maturity.

The girl met Louise's eyes and her gaze was shocking. Much, *much* older than twenty. "Is it house trained?"

Geraint shook his head and smiled drily. "Why would it matter, Ràel? This is a forest. If you have to be abusive, at least make it vaguely pointed – and no, please *don't* say something obvious about your arrow."

"Did anybody ever tell you you've got a clever mouth, Geraint?"

"Only daily, Ràel. You're going to talk wistfully about bricking it up, next, no doubt."

"If only."

Geraint turned back to the group. "I'm sorry, people. Ràel's spent the last thousand years or so patrolling these woods, and she's sort of lost the knack of talking to people."

"I can talk when I want to." She looked at Caroline. "You'll be the one, then. Welcome. We have a gift for you." She whistled shrilly, and there was a pause.

Louise muttered to JG, "I wouldn't have thought one ratty nude rider would be much protection, even on that beast."

The half-orc smiled. "You can only *see* one. There are … well, a lot of them. I know the Church of Marn as a whole is aware they exist, but you may not be aware of the number. She's unclad because she doesn't need clothes. She's covered by a globe of *Gwyn's Protection* and the unicorn keeps her warm.

"*Gwyn's Protection*. I've heard about that. But isn't there a green shimmering globe?"

"On occasion. I'm not going to tell you everything, am I?"

The conversation was interrupted by the arrival of a second unicorn, even larger than the first. It was saddled and equipped, but had no rider. The huge beast stopped at the edge if the clearing and looked at the group. Then it saw Carol and seemed to nod to itself as it came forward. As the entirety of the unicorn left the thick forest, it seemed to be even bigger. It also became very obvious that 'it' was in fact a 'he.'

He moved through the people in front of him in a straight line, leaving it up to them to get out of his way or be barged aside, until he reached Caroline. He nickered, and nuzzled her very gently.

Ràel nodded in satisfaction. "He's yours, Countess. Well, not exactly yours, they belong only to themselves, but he'll stay with you until you have no more need of him. You'll find him useful."

Carol caressed the soft, pure white face in wonder, but then her face twisted in something like grief. "But there are rules about who may ride these, are there not? I may not. I don't qualify."

Ràel shook her head. "Three things wrong with that, Countess. Thirdly, individual unicorns make their own choices, and they don't always follow that rule anyway – though I've never known one to choose a mother. Secondly, you have never performed the act of your own choice. In this as in so many things, intent is all.

"But firstly – and this is the only consideration that matters – Brandur Himself has asked Léanàré to consider you, and if Brandur says you qualify then you qualify, whatever the rules *seem* to say. So Léanàré has considered you and is clearly content with you. Look at the beast, woman. You don't think you could touch him if he didn't want you to, do you? He could turn the lot of you into bloody gruel in seconds."

Carol gazed up into the flawless white face above her with something very like love. "He's Léanàré? A beautiful name for a beautiful friend."

Louise muttered to John Garrett "She sees a beautiful friend, I see a homicidal maniac. That critter's sheer coiled violence."

JG nodded. "You each see what's there – for you."

The Unicorn looked up at Louise, and she could see the eyes change from a sort of limpid dark blue to a red so fiery she could almost smell smoke. The soft, flexible lips pulled back to reveal tombstone teeth. There was no trace of a peaceful grazing animal here. This was a warrior and a killer.

Louise shuddered and looked up at Ràel. "I'd heard of them, of course. But I'd imagined them as sort of ten hands and friendly."

"Everybody does."

"How did this happen? How does a creature like this exist?"

Ràel snorted and looked away. Geraint smiled, shook his head in mock despair and explained. "They were bred. Long ago, the elves began the breeding program which eventually resulted in the elven horses that we see today – if we're lucky. As their horses got better, they became more and more attractive prey for the woodland predators – for of course, they live wild in the woods and meadows. And there are lions here, and Dire-wolves and Rocs and – well, a lot of predators than can take a full-grown, healthy horse with ease. So the elves sought Brandur's help. He started things off, and with that start, over time, they bred a protector – a sort of horse sheepdog. The start Brandur gave them was in fact very much smaller and rather timid, but the breeding program was extremely effective, and now we have the likes of Léanàré. And they breed true.

"Their original task was to run with the herds and protect them from any danger – they are far, far brighter than even an elven horse. But they are such wonderful warriors – and such fine friends to have – that they soon came to be asked to do other things as well. And, of course, as Creations of Brandur they're magical. That helps, too."

Louise realised that he wasn't talking as much for her benefit as for Caroline's, and the young countess was drinking it in at the same time as she caressed and muttered gentle nonsense to her new friend.

Ràel shifted in her saddle. "Geraint, when you've finished lecturing, I'd like to get on."

"Yes, dear. Sorry."

"Don't call me 'dear'. You know it irritates me."

"Alright, already. Shall we go?"

"Well if you're *sure* you don't want to spend another hour or two dropping pearls of wisdom?"

"Now who's holding us up?"

To Louise's surprise, she realised that Ràel was actually having a problem keeping her face straight. The girl – not a girl, a woman – composed herself and looked over at Caroline. "Countess, if someone can give you a boost, you mount just like any heavy warhorse. Once aboard, remember that the reins aren't control, they're communication. Unicorns' mouths are a little differently structured, and they always have the bit between their teeth – there's nowhere else for it to be. He'll go where you indicate, either with the reins or your legs, and he'll respond equally well to verbal communication. In combat situations, he won't do anything surprising that might unseat you, but on the other hand he thinks for himself and takes his own steps to deal with attackers. You probably won't have a problem, because you'll find him behaving very similarly to a Myndarit warhorse. They have ancestry in common, and no doubt you're used to them."

Caroline nodded. "Yes. Thank you, Ràel. John, could you give me a leg up, here?"

The half-orc bent, put one large, hard palm under her right foot and straightened effortlessly. Carol rose as though being hoisted by a rope and pulley with a large weight on the other end. She slipped her left foot into her stirrup, swung her right leg over the beautiful, dark green leather saddle and looked back down. "Thank you, John. If I didn't do two hours' combat practice with you every day I would have trouble believing how strong you are."

JG shrugged. "Heredity and lifestyle combined, Lady."

With Ràel leading the way, Caroline coming next, and the rest of the group following, they proceeded up another path and then suddenly found themselves in an open space looking down on Wonderland. It was very, very large – three hundred acres at least – and, since they were on a high ridge and the ground sloped gently away from them, they could see a good deal of it.

It was easily the most extraordinary space Louise had ever seen.

Most of it was open to the sky. However, large swathes were shaded by groups of very large trees – oak, ash, rowan, elm, mixed with a range of warmer-weather varieties, particularly olive and orange – whose heavily-leaved branches created shady, protected areas. Some of these had wooden structures amongst and leading off them – sometimes just a wall, sometimes more structure overgrown with vine, ivy and mistletoe. In other places were more substantial buildings, some extremely large, and all prominently featuring courtyards, verandas, and cloisters.

Some of the buildings had rooms with only three walls, and some of these rooms appeared to be carpeted with grass or moss. These were definitely outdoor places, while others were clearly indoors, but in general the one state seemed to flow into the other in such a seamless way that it was difficult to decide the exact point of difference.

Where structures had been built, natural materials predominated to a large degree. All buildings were stone and wood. There was no brick, even for decoration – though assorted decorative effects abounded. Often windows and door openings were framed silk rather than glass or wood, though a great deal of glass was in evidence. All the buildings had more, and far larger, windows than would usually be found.

In combination with streams broad and narrow and at least two significant rivers, cultivated lawns and complex gardens, meadows, banked-earth partitions often planted with riots of flowers or moss or complicated patterns of bushes, as well as shaded dells, and hilltop cupolas, the overall effect was astounding. Louise stared, transfixed, almost intoxicated by the beauty of the scene spread in front of her.

Geraint noticed her wonder. "It's not much, but we call it home."

She shook her head. "It's one of the wonders of the world."

"I wouldn't have thought a Marnist would appreciate it."

"Because it's natural? But it isn't. It's art and artifice of utterly compelling quality. Of *course* I love it."

"Also functional. Guess how many live here."

"I couldn't."

"I'm not sure myself, but it certainly includes over a hundred trainee druids, maybe six or seven hundred would-be witches, more than a hundred in the teaching faculty, maybe another two hundred doing research or other study, a support staff of over five hundred -

ranging from librarians of some wildly abstruse varieties to cooks and cleaners - five hundred Rangers of the Green Deep, two hundred and fifty Guardians, assorted visitors, plus the families of many of the above.

"I would certainly think three thousand – and it could be many more than that. There is a huge amount of underground space, as well. Most of those hills and slopes you see are hollow, with light wells and windows opening under assorted foliage."

He cocked his head. "And, of course, I was forgetting the Brothers' Conclave. When they meet here, that's another ninety-six druids plus staff, consultant experts, interested observers, and whatnot. Probably another five hundred in all. But the place never seems crowded."

"That's your governing body, isn't it? No witches?"

"Sort of. The actual ruling assembly of the Faith is the Convocation of Brandur, which meets a week after every Summer Solstice. That has witches and druids both, and priests of any other Nature God, if they want to come. They can't vote, but they can speak in debates; they have the same speaking rights as the Brandur priests. It's so that the rest of the Family know what we're up to – and can tell us what they think about it."

"Not all priests of Nature Gods."

"Yup."

"Well I can think of two you wouldn't admit."

"Are you thinking of Marn's Children, Jebel and Caeval? Because any such priests would certainly be admitted. They're not strictly part of the same Family as the rest – different Mother – but they're indubitably Nature Gods."

"Good grief! Has anybody ever told them that?"

"I've told you who is entitled to admission. I haven't told you who actually comes, at all."

"Do you mean that they do send representatives? Why doesn't anybody know?"

"I don't mean any more than I said. I've told you who would be admitted and free to speak. I've told you nothing about attendance."

"Well, do they? Wait a minute! Cariseg priests! What about them?"

"Well, that one you should be able to work out on your own."

"They're Nature priests and part of the same Family – She's Thorn's Sister for all the Gods' sake! You can't keep them out!"

"What gave you the idea anybody tries?"

"What? But nobody associates with those disgusting… That's unbelievable."

"I've told you the rules. By the rules they're allowed. I don't say they come, mind."

"Ah. And by the same quiet understanding, the Jebel and Caeval people keep away."

"You said that. I've not said anything at all about attendance."

"What's the big secret about that?"

"There isn't one, really. We'll talk freely about our rules and systems, but our events are our own business. It's no big thing. Anyway, we will require you neither to speak of what you have learned while with us nor allow or arrange for anybody to gain that information, so there's little to be gained from hiding things."

"Hmm. Then why do I get the impression that you're hiding things? Never mind. Who is the reception committee?"

They had been moving easily into the outskirts of the university grounds, and their path turned a corner to reveal an exquisite little clearing, including a stream crossed by a wooden bridge. On the other side of the bridge was a group of people led by a man perhaps in his fifties, bearing a tall wooden staff, heavily carved and topped and shod in silver.

"That is Granedd, the head of our order. He's here to meet Caroline and thus make a point – if anybody could miss the point made by Léanàré."

Ràel held back and allowed Caroline to cross the bridge first. When she nudged Léanàré across the bridge Granedd took a step forward and with clear deliberation dropped to one knee. "Highness."

Louise gasped, then muttered "I see what you mean."

"Yes. And note the language. He's not giving anyone a chance to whinge. She's not been crowned yet, so he's not calling her 'Majesty.' However, 'Highness' is the correct mode of address to the heir substantive. It is inappropriate to anybody but royalty, so it's pretty unequivocal."

Carol had dismounted and now reached a hand to raise the druid to his feet. "Holy Granedd, I appreciate your kindness in coming to meet us."

"Highness, I will hope to do you greater and far more useful service than this small courtesy. But that's for later. I see that you and Léanàré have made friends."

"And there is another cause for thanks. Such a gift was beyond my imagining."

"No thanks to me, Highness. That initiative came from my God Himself. And Léanàré made his own decision."

"Then you must advise me. How do I suitably express my thanks to a God such as Brandur?"

"This is very easy, Highness, and not easy at all. Achieve what you have set out to do, and my God will be as delighted as your own. He doesn't consider you owe Him thanks – He is merely contributing as He can to a joint enterprise."

Caroline stood still, then took a deep breath. "That is responsibility beyond the normal, Holy Granedd."

Granedd bowed assent. "Yes, Highness. Yes it is. All I can say is that whatever we can do to be of use to you, we will do."

"The Faith of Brandur has done a great deal already. We would not have come even this far without the extraordinary skills and talents of my cousin."

Granedd smiled. "If he weren't the best we have, Highness, he would not be here. But it is kind of you to think beyond the weight of your own responsibility to speak of him. We have some refreshment prepared, shall we go in?"

One Misty Moisty Morning...

Chapter 23

Counting the cost once more

A fter five days of intensive discussion, Ràel arrived again, this time guiding a column of a hundred and fifty Myndarits, led by the familiar figure of Carlo Meuse. As his troops saw to the care of their vast horses, Meuse came into the conference room where a discussion of the personalities of the Alliance leaders sought to clarify what their reactions might be to various possible situations.

He immediately sought attention. "Gentles, holy priests, I need to make you aware of some events. I can give you some details on the Alliance's reaction to our action around Long Astley, which inter alia is perhaps pertinent to your current discussion."

Granedd nodded politely. "You have our full attention, sir knight."

"Thank you. There was a very quick reaction. Presumably by dint of magical means, the Alliance sent two whole legions of the Order of Night, supported by a large force of Alma free riders from Gentleman's Corporation, which made it impossible for our light cavalry to get at them. I have to tell you that Jeff tried, none the less. He lost sixty riders and his own life, though the enemy paid in blood for the success.

"However, the Alma light cavalry – excellently led, I must say – saw the Order of Night through to the town. There they met fierce resistance from the citizens, including archery and hand-to-hand defence on barricades.

"The sad fact is, of course, that over the centuries some of the best armies in the world have totally failed to hold well-prepared positions against the Order of Night. The citizens of Long Astley had no chance at all. Their brave defence lasted much less than an hour before the Black Knights were into the town. I have to tell you that Long Astley no longer exists. Very many of the population are dead, the rest have been taken away, presumably for sacrifice or slavery."

"Now, since I knew you would need this information, I have consulted some of our friends in the Faith of Alyssana, and they tell me the Players have already told this tale all over the Empire, though it was only four days ago. Obviously the concern was that people might now be reluctant to have us visit them, for fear of the consequences. However, the Players have shown brilliance in their presentation of the news. They have made the citizens of Long Astley heroes, as indeed they are - or were. But today they are heroes all over the Empire and an inspiration to millions. In short, the Players have ensured that the initial reaction has been not fear but rage and pride – rage that this has been done and pride that ordinary citizens had the sand to stand up for themselves and take a few of the Black Knights with them to the Wheel.

"Lady, I bring invitations to visit twenty towns, with more coming, so I understand. There is very little more that can be said, other than that we believe there were around thirty-five thousand corpses in Long Astley, with maybe twenty-one or twenty-two thousand shipped out to whatever fate it will be."

Caroline stood. "Holy priests, gentles all, before we consider this news and what steps we should take in consequence, we must acknowledge the people of Long Astley. How do we do that?"

Lin Gor put up a hand. "Well here's one thing that occurs to me. We've been invited to lots of towns. Fine. I suggest that every town we go to you start by talking about Long Astley – what the people there said to you and what sort of people they were. That commemorates and honours them and gives the locals a clear idea of what they're getting into at the same time.

"Also, of course, it gives you a start on telling them what this is all about. There's the Alliance – who do things such as that. And there's you – and you do … well, what you're going to tell them about. This way, the people of Long Astley are going to be fighting the Alliance from the grave for a long, long, time to come. Remembering how they were, I think they'd like that."

John Garrett stirred from his standard slouch. "And when it's over, we can do something for the Empire, something important, and name it for them. Something that's going to keep their name and their contribution in front of everybody for a long time."

Geraint nodded. "But they won't be the last; this will happen again and again. We just have to make it costly whenever we can. And also remember the score for when we can repay it." He nodded once, sharply. "Definitely that part."

* * *

They left the University of the Woods the next morning. Rain Hill and the Imperial Army were barely a hundred miles away as the crow flies, but they moved instead to the nearest Myndarit Chapter House and travelled through the portal there to another chapter house near Ryton, a town a thousand miles away.

They entered with a certain amount of ceremony and to much cheering and the local band playing patriotic tunes – quite well, in fact. Nobody stared at Léanàré because Uggò had laid a minor illusion on him that simply made the horn invisible.

There was the usual flatbed wagon in the town square, and Carol dismounted directly onto it. As soon as she stood ready to speak, an echoing silence fell upon the square. "People of Ryton. You and I both grew up in a safe world. A world where crime never amounted to much more than petty theft, and the town magistrate needed to have an honest job as well to make ends meet." That got the chuckle it was aimed at.

"But this is a different world, and we need to be aware of that. I know how I found out. I found out the day my brother was tortured to death in his own garden and his wife was foully abused for hours. But like many of us in this land, she was no easy victim. She stole a rapist's sword and killed him and two others with it before she took her own life.

"She refused to be a victim. That seems to be a habit, here. Take the people of Long Astley. They committed a crime. Dreadful it was, this crime. They assembled to hear me speak. Yes, that's all. So the Alliance sent a wing of the Red Death and a thousand infantry to kill some of them to make the point that such crimes are not allowed.

"Sadly for them, instead of untrained civilian victims, this force met Becca Wright's Riders, Jeff's Light Horse and several hundred Myndarits along the way." Caroline chuckled, briefly. "Now those people are not good at being victims at all. They truly don't have the knack. The jackal went out for rabbit and met a tiger, so you can guess who got eaten. None came home."

A dark rumble filled the square; anger, amusement, satisfaction. "But we could not stay forever there, as the people of Long Astley knew, and we went to see them again to warn them that worse would follow. We thought perhaps they would choose to flee and stood ready to help as we could. They did not flee - but chose not to live as victims and when the Black Knights came they fought them until they could fight no more. Tradespeople, business people, home makers though they were, and confronted with one of the most feared fighting units in the world, they fought until their streets ran with blood. And, of course, they died. I mourn them. We all mourn them. But also we should be proud for them. Truly they've earned it.

"I wish I could tell you their names, every one of them, but I cannot. I do know one name, though, and I must let that stand for all. When I spoke there, I asked a man why he cheered me when I had brought him and his fine town nothing but woe. He said it is because we are willing to fight for that life the old Empire offered and not let it be stolen from him without a whimper as the old powers of the Empire had done. He thought for this reason, and because I am ap Gryffudd, that it was an honour to talk to me. He was quite mistaken. As we all now know, it is my honour to be able to say that I once met Chad of Long Astley, and he was kind to me."

Her voice had gone ragged on that last few words, and she had difficulty finishing the sentence. Then she paused and swallowed, clearly hard pressed to speak around the emotion clogging her throat. "Good people, I shall never forget him. And I shall carry his memory into battle with me whenever I face the Alliance. Chad of Long Astley will be with me the day we claim the final victory and I hope – and trust, for my God is good – that on that day he will know it.

"It would be easy to say we will fight for the people of Long Astley when we go into battle. Easy, but untrue, for they are dead and nothing we do can profit them. We fight for ourselves and for the life we wish to live, rather than the life these thieves of our nation would impose on us."

She paused, looked around, and picked people in the crowd, meeting their eyes. "People of Ryton, may we fight for you as well? Do you wish to stand up against this scourge that infests our land? Will you be like the people of Long Astley and say 'We shall not be victims, even if it means our death?' Or will you quietly submit to the theft of your lands, the sacrifice of your sons on the altars of Goreb, and your daughters in the temples of Marn?

"We cannot make that decision for you. You must make your own. Will you submit, or will you be like the people of Long Astley – and very possibly suffer the same fate?"

There was a pause, then a few voices scattered around the huge crowd began shouting "Fight! Fight!" The voices were slowly joined by a trickle of others, then a rush, then the whole crowd was baying the same one-word answer.

Standing behind the wagon, Louise turned a puzzled smile to Geraint. Having to shout over the thunder in the square, although he was within a foot of her, she said "You're going to get a lot of people killed this way. They can't stand against Black Knights any more than Long Astley could."

Geraint smiled tightly. "We think not. It means that they cannot punish the town by killing ten percent of the population, or whatever. They come here, the town will fight them, and then they'll have to kill them all. That's not economically viable. They are here for many reasons, but an important one is that the Empire is wealthy, and they want that wealth. Now, if you wipe a big and prosperous town out, you immediately shrink your revenue for decades at the least. So they won't. They'll think of some other thing to do, of course, but at least it won't involve murder on a large scale."

Louise nodded thoughtfully. "I like the reasoning. It might work at that, though there may be a few more towns wiped out before my people decide it's too costly."

"Yes. And she's given them fair warning of that. It's their choice."

"Really?" She gestured at the crowd. "How much of that is real?"

Geraint smiled and shrugged. "Fair point, but all Uggò and Lin Gor did was start it off. What you hear now is all real and honest."

"Do you sleep at nights, Geraint?"

"Certainly. We've denied the enemy a key control technique, and thus very likely saved a large number of civilian lives overall. Why would I not feel content with the bargain?"

"You might. But then it's not your town that's been cozened into getting itself wiped out."

"This is a war. People die in wars. And I didn't start it."

"Your delicate cousin might not agree."

"And that's where you're wrong, Louise. She's Varan. Let me quote you the *Book of the Stranger*. This is the full text; there is a briefer version, but it's less clear on matters like this." He paused a second, getting the text he wanted clear in his mind, then stood straighter and spoke more formally.

"The Stranger's Blessing, Stanza the Second, Verse Three.

'Should any seek to compel you to harm the people, or to stand idly by while they do so, that they may serve whatever ends they in their arrogance choose, then you shall bring them low if you can. But mark this and keep it in your heart; never shall you take one step in their service, never the first, though the cost be what it may to whomsoever it may. Mark this also, that God's mind should be clear unto you; a step not taken to oppose them is a step taken in their service and contrary to all that your God would have of you.' "

Geraint shrugged. "Sums it up in a nutshell."

"Whoo! Well that's clear enough. But doesn't that mean she has to sally forth and fight whenever we attack some town? She won't last long that way."

"Perhaps. And that would always be Carol's first instinct. But Varan requires his people to be intelligent about their service, insofar as they are able, and if it's clear that in the bigger picture her throwing her life away is a step in the service of the enemy, then she must not do it – but might send others to die if that is the best way of opposing the wicked. Varan is a kindly God in many ways, but His requirements can weigh heavily just the same."

"I'm learning a lot, here. We don't really look much at comparative religion in our training. It's all about Marn. Oh, we do some work on Jebel and Caeval, for obvious reasons, and it's necessary to know some very basic stuff about Goreb, Alma and Baraani - no more than two or three lectures on each, as I recall - but that's really it."

Geraint laughed and bowed ornately. "Glad to be of service."

* * *

They visited twelve towns, thousands of miles apart, over the space of the next five days. Leaving the last early on a spring morning, they headed towards a chapter house of the Burglars. They were no more than two miles short of it when something rather strange happened.

They were in rough country, and the lead riders were splashing through a tiny, mist-shrouded stream at the bottom of a miniature winding valley, heading towards some heavily-wooded rising ground. The trees before them offered room for the horses to go single file only on the lower part of the slope, and they were going cautiously - but halted in shock as a cloaked figure stepped from the mist in front of them, seeming to materialise out of it, then moved up the hill towards the more lightly wooded crest, where the ground dropped invisibly away. Part way up the slope, the figure pointed to the ground, then moved on and out of sight among the trees.

Carlo Meuse stopped the column and sent a knight forward to investigate the indicated spot, who found an object and brought it back to Carlo. He paused a moment, then trotted back to where Caroline and Geraint were riding, with their friends close behind them. "Countess, we have a problem. It would be standard procedure for scouts to report back at obstacles such as this rough wooded slope, with ground falling away behind it, and I would have expected them to make themselves visible to us where we now are. There's no sign of them, though, which I chose not to be concerned about as in this heavy country there might be many reasons for that.

"However, it's clear I was wrong." He showed them what the cloaked figure had been pointing at, a bloody piece of cloth, quite likely part of a surcoat from a Blue Guild knight.

Carol grimaced. "So there are hostiles ahead and they've killed all our scouts."

"Yes, Lady. Presumably they'll be just over the crest, in the dead ground. And that being the case, I would infer nearly as confidently that we will have hostiles coming up behind us. Whoever that was in the cloak did us a very great favour and saved me from a failure that would have been down to my own carelessness."

He frowned. "Who it was, I couldn't guess. That sigil on the back of the cloak is not one I have ever encountered as the mark of an order of priesthood, and he or she had the look of a priest."

"Which leaves us with the question of what we do about it."

"Do you have a suggestion, Carlo?"

"Possibly. Goodman Uggò. Could you render a group invisible for a while?"

"It do depend on the size of the group, Sir Knight. Half a dozen - a dozen, maybe, at a stretch. No more. And then not for long."

"Five to ten minutes?"

"I do be thinking so. But ten minutes would be my absolute limit. I have been getting better at these things, but I do have a long way to go yet."

"It is enough. Thank you."

He turned back to Caroline. "This misty little valley runs to the left from here, before the rise. As you see, it takes a broad curve and leads into the trees a good way to the north, maybe half a mile. If you were to detach from the column here and ride invisibly along the edge of the stream until you get to the forest, you will be a good way away from the bulk of the enemy at least, perhaps all of them.

"If we make our way slowly through these trees, then suddenly ride hard over the rise into whatever trap they have prepared, we'd be unlucky if they realised you weren't with us before we were amongst them – and then I can guarantee we will occupy their full attention for some time. You should be able to pass through to the chapter house with little or no opposition. At any rate, it's probably the best we can do."

Caroline frowned. "Carlo-"

He cocked his head and smiled at her. "Yes, my Lady?"

She struggled for words for a few seconds, then sighed, shrugged, and then squared her shoulders. "I remember what Uggò said to me once, about friends. He was right. But I have no choice at all."

"None at all, Countess, no. But please don't be concerned; we are not. Everybody dies, and to die in combat while achieving something that matters this much is really all any warrior can hope for." And he smiled cheerfully, saluted, then cantered to the front of the column and led them forward at pace.

Caroline and her friends turned off to the left, into the bottom of the little vale, and at the same time Uggò cast his enchantment. Geraint also uttered an incantation, and as they rode, their tracks vanished behind them, and the grass and foliage they disturbed or crushed was restored as soon as they had passed.

Looking behind, Louise raised her brows. "Now that, Geraint, is very impressive – and so is this illusion of Uggò's. We can see each other, but I gather nobody sees us."

Geraint smiled. "Yes, he's getting very good. It's not *invisibility* such as a mage would cast. With that we wouldn't see each other at all. This is more that people don't notice us, even if we're exactly what they're looking for. But once somebody *knows* we're there, it doesn't work on them – hence we can see each other. It's a very useful dweomer."

"Indeed it is. And that's why you're doing whatever it is with the signs of our passage."

"Yes. So that there's no obvious clue to tell people we're there and spoil Uggò's trick."

At that moment the Myndarits, having cleared the heavily-wooded lower slope, moved walk to canter and from canter to all-out gallop, crashing over the ridge onto the down slope with a concerted cry of "Caroline!" that echoed through the tries.

Carol stiffened, "Oh! Oh, that's horrible."

Geraint, riding alongside, touched her arm gently. "You're the Knight Commander of the Order. Of course your name is one of their war cries."

"Yes. I knew that in theory. But – oh, dear." Then she clenched her fists and closed her eyes, tears seeping out of the sides. "I *will* be worthy of it! I *will*!"

As they dashed along the floor of the little valley towards the rapidly approaching trees, the sound of violent combat came from the road. Clearly, Carlo Meuse's appreciation of the situation had been accurate. Whatever force had been waiting was finding a hundred and fifty Myndarits something of a handful.

They dashed in amongst the trees and rode hell for leather along the narrow path between the heavier woods on either side, weaving between large areas of heavy undergrowth that reduced visibility to a few tens of yards, and sometimes a few feet. Without warning, they came on a little group of riders in brown leather. They were amongst them before anybody could say or do anything, and the heavy Myndarit warhorses they were riding just barged the much smaller light cavalry mounts out of their way without even slowing down.

As they thundered on, Uggò visibly relaxed. "No more I can do. It was reaching the end of my capabilities anyway."

"Well done, anyway." JG patted the gnome on the shoulder, then he and Brutus moved in front of Caroline and Geraint. Zeéla, producing a light morning star that glowed blue with enchantment, dropped to the back of the group and rode with her head almost permanently turned to watch behind them, trusting her horse to keep with the others.

With only a few seconds' warning, they burst out of the trees and saw the curtain wall of the chapter house five hundred yards away, across open fields. They reduced speed to an easy canter and rode on, the sounds of continuing battle receding and vanishing behind them, while ahead of them the drawbridge dropped and the portcullis rose.

They'd gone about two hundred yards when a force of light cavalry, numbering perhaps a hundred, burst from the trees some way to their south and rode at a flat-out run diagonally towards them. The party moved back to full gallop, and at the same time JG and Brutus moved to the right-hand side of the group, riding line ahead, with Zeéla moving up behind them.

While the Myndarit warhorses were fast for their huge size, and carrying far less weight than their usual fully armed knights in field plate, they were not nearly as fast as the light cavalry thoroughbreds racing to cut them off, and the distance closed rapidly. Caroline, looking around for the fifth time in the last twenty seconds, drew her Sword again. "They're going to catch us. We'll do better turning to charge them head on than being taken in the flank."

Geraint shrugged. "Better is a relative term. But they will certainly catch us, so why not?"

The party turned, changing formation so that Caroline was at the front between Brutus and JG, Zeéla and Geraint were directly behind, with Iorweth and Elaine, then Lin Gor, Amaré and Louise following, and Uggò bringing up the rear. As they rode, Lin Gor looped some cord around Louise's wrists. "Just so they don't mistake you for one of us. You should be fine."

Louise smiled at him, then said, "But you would be better to kill me, you know. Don't rely on my gratitude. I haven't got one."

"I wasn't. You won't have anything but corpses to be grateful to anyway."

"True. Good luck all the same."

"Thanks." And the cavalry were on them. Geraint and Zeéla cast simultaneously. The horses in the front few ranks just to the right of the party suddenly had a collective fit of hysteria, rearing and screaming, while a fireball materialised just to the left of the group and blasted into the leading cavalry on that side with a thunderous roar.

Their flanks clear – at least for the moment – the party crashed their huge horses into the opposition directly ahead of them, JG and Brutus clubbing attackers aside with their heavy swords. The unicorn was in his element and clearly enjoying himself. He shouldered the first horse aside, speared the rider of the second on his horn and threw her, screaming, ten yards behind Iorweth with a single toss of his head. A gap started to open in front of him.

With the riders to either side still neutralised for the moment, the party forged ahead into the brown-clad opposition before them, killing or unhorsing the lightly armed and armoured mercenaries as they went. Iorweth was reminded of the man falling off a hundred-foot high cliff and thinking, after the first twenty feet, 'So far, so good.'

Suddenly there was a flurry of orders, and the enemy horses turned and withdrew rapidly towards the trees, where a much larger force of mixed light and heavy cavalry could be seen forming up. Looking over her shoulder, Caroline saw the reason for the sudden retreat.

At least two hundred Myndarits had managed to get outside the chapter house in that short time and were now charging in a solid phalanx across the open ground. Geraint was looking startled, then glanced sharply at Uggò, who was sweating. He touched Carol's arm. 'We need to make for the chapter house. Now, cousin."

Caroline also glanced at Uggò and smiled. "Aye."

In a tight group the party thundered towards the approaching, impressively detailed, Myndarit phalanx, then through them. At that point, of course, they vanished, and through the illusion appeared a large number of real Myndarits, armed with heavy lances, who were starting to form up outside the chapter house. The force at the edge of the wood surged forward, then seeing that they were now never going to catch the party before they got within the chapter house walls, they withdrew again to the trees.

As they dismounted in the outer bailey, Carol spoke urgently to the commander of the chapter house, who had come to meet her. Within ten minutes, that worthy rode out at the head of about four hundred riders – who had been arming ever since the party first appeared from the trees – and the whole force hurried to the woods. They rode more slowly back about an hour later, with a considerable number of horses and very many bodies.

The commander, Yuriko Sahita, was grim when she dismounted. Carol had hurried across to her, but slowed as she saw the knight's expression. "I'm sorry, Countess. There were no survivors. We don't know how many they took to the Wheel with them, for those bodies are gone, but by the look of it there are a *lot* of dead no longer there. I knew Carlo slightly and I'm entirely confident he wouldn't have gone unescorted."

"As am I. But it is a sad loss, both to the Order and to me, personally."

"That it is, Lady. I suspect he would have led his chapter within a few years."

"You will have perhaps heard about Sir Roland?"

"Yes, Lady."

"I find I cannot for one more day than is necessary abide the idea that he is honoured within the Empire while proper men, men like Carlo Meuse, lie dead. Tomorrow we will confront him, and he will die."

"Countess, at least Carlo has done me a favour. For now I get to see it. I will have a hundred and fifty riders ready whenever you wish to depart.

"There is a chapter house at Rain Hill, is there not?"

"Yes, City Reivers. It's on the same portal chain as we are."

"At about dawn tomorrow, then."

Chapter 24

Watch out for the ugly boy...

Having completed his stock presentation on the size, composition, equipment and state of readiness of the Imperial Army, Baron Roland of Abbeville resumed his seat with a frosty glance at his distinguished, though unexpected, visitor. "Have you any questions, your Grace?"

"Well, a large number actually." Martin, Duke of Ninian, regarded Sir Roland with unconcealed hostility. "Let's begin with the obvious. Why are our troops just sitting here while independent forces are able to contrive to hamstring the Alliance advance and cripple their supply effort? Surely, surely, this is the time to jump on them."

"It's too big a risk, Your Grace. At present, we have a force in being they have to consider and be wary of. If we lost that…" He spread his hands expressively.

"But if it continues to sit around much longer, the enemy will surely *stop* considering it. And it must be very damaging to the troops' morale to be sat doing nothing while the enemy is in possession of nearly half the Empire."

"That is an issue, certainly."

"How gratifying to have your agreement. Now another question. If troops loyal to this Countess Beauclerc can cause the enemy so much inconvenience and difficulty, why cannot the Imperial Army do a great deal better still?"

"She has numerous and excellent light cavalry forces, led by a first-class man, and she has the full co-operation of a whole sheaf of bodies

– not least the Arm of Mannan-Dar, the Faith of Brandur, and above all the Order of Myndarit."

"And why does the Council not have these assets itself?"

"You would know the answer to that better than I, your Grace."

The duke looked sour. "Yes. Indeed I would."

At that point a young officer knocked on the door and came in swiftly. He saluted Duke Martin, then turned to Sir Roland. "My lord, the Countess Beauclerc has just entered the camp with around a couple of hundred Myndarits and sundry other persons. We would have stopped her at the gate but the gate guard could do nothing against that size of force without calling the troops to arms. That seemed a bit over the top, considering who she is."

"I see. I presume she has some purpose in this incursion."

"She's come to see *you*, sir. She requests your presence on Parade Square immediately."

"I am otherwise engaged."

"By no means, my lord." Ninian rose and gathered up his papers, his staff rising with him. "I'm all agog to meet this lady who can achieve so much while the official forces have achieved so little. I meant to seek her out when my business with you was concluded, so it's more than fortunate. Lead on, sir."

Following Sir Roland onto the Parade Square, Ninian was a little startled to see that the fabled Countess Beauclerc seemed to be a girl barely out of her teens, if indeed she was. He'd been told she was young, but this was absurd. In addition, she seemed to be supported by a truly motley collection of people. A number of them had signs of breeding but there was also a truly immense half-orc, a rather disreputable-looking gnome – and if he was not mistaken in that symbol around her neck, a priest of Marn.

Sir Roland performed the introductions. "Your Grace, I have the honour to present Lady Caroline, Countess Beauclerc and the Knight Commander of the Order of Myndarit. With her are her cousin Geraint ap Gryffudd - who I believe has been outlawed, so an arrest may be in order - the Lady Zeéla, Countess Néaness, Uggò gà Nachàn, His Royal Highness Lin Gor, second son of the Queen of Faerie and Brutus, Baron Lark Valley. I believe you, sir, would be Captain Garrett, lately of the White Company, yes? Thank you. And this lady I, er, don't know."

"Yes you do, Roland." The Marn priestess – Ninian was certain now that was what she was – had that air of serene superiority so many senior Marn priests affected. She tapped Sir Roland on the chest. "We met on at least two occasions in Mallow while we were planning this adventure."

She turned to Ninian. "Excuse me, I am Louise Megiddo, Countess Amondir and Priest of Marn. I am Senior Wing Commander in the Sword Sisters. Or I was until I was captured by these people when my wing was defeated at Long Astley. I expect there is a new Senior Wing Commander now."

Ninian inclined his head, politely. "Ah, yes I heard about that. I'm sorry, I'm forgetting my manners. I'm Martin, Duke of Ninian. I was a High Councillor when such things had any value. But what were you saying about knowing Sir Roland? That sounded quite odd."

"Yes. It seemed odd at the time. I have never before planned a military engagement in concert with the commander of the opposing side. I have to say it did make things a lot simpler."

Sir Roland reached for his sword with an oath, but JG and Brutus, who had been ready for just that sort of thing, held him firmly. Even a man of Sir Roland's considerable strength couldn't make any impression at all on John Garrett's grip on his sword arm, while Brutus used his own considerable bulk and strength to hold him in place.

Ninian smiled. "Holy Priestess, I am impressed at your devotion to your cause in sowing dissent amongst us."

Geraint shook his head. "Your Grace, the Lady Louise has, of course given her parole before Baraani. As you would expect, that included a requirement for absolute truthfulness. Also, perhaps you would care to examine these documents? We found them in the Sword Sisters' camp at Lark Valley when we sacked it."

Geraint suddenly paused and cocked an eyebrow towards the Marn priest. "Louise, a thought occurs. Do you in fact recognise this man?"

"No, Geraint. This isn't anybody I've seen before. And as I said, I'm sure I would have at least seen the other one, even if I didn't know who he was at that time."

"Good. Then please examine these papers, Your Grace. You will see that they clearly name my Lord of Abbeville as being in attendance at a number of meetings. Rather peculiar behaviour for the Earl Marshal of the Empire, do you think?"

Ninian leafed through the documents, at first quickly but then far more slowly as he grasped the nature of their contents, his face darkening steadily. "Distinctly peculiar. Sir Roland, at first glance it seems that these documents are indeed incriminating. Gravely incriminating. Do you have an immediate answer, or would you prefer to reserve it for your trial?"

Caroline stepped forward. "Your Grace, I am Knight Commander of the Order of Myndarit, as you have heard. My lord of Abbeville is – or was – a member of that honourable order. That being the case, he has dishonoured us, and as the order's principal representative I demand satisfaction. At once. Sir Roland, will you fight me? Or do you prefer to be arrested and held for trial?"

Ninian raised a hand. "We won't do that, I think. Sir Roland is due his trial – whatever his own wishes – and I become persuaded that we probably would not want to risk someone who has been so effective so young in a duel with one of the great solo fighters of recent history."

Brutus snorted. "Well as to that, your Grace, you may be aware that I, too, have some small reputation as a solo fighter. And having faced the Lady Caroline on the training ground every day for the last few weeks, I have to say that personally I'm not much concerned for her welfare, against Sir Roland or anybody else. She'll be just fine."

Ninian inclined his head to Brutus. "My lord, I am aware of your reputation. But the fact remains that Sir Roland must stand trial."

Caroline shook her head. "No. Far too many strange things have happened. And we know for a fact that there is at least one more traitor high in the government. I will have my satisfaction here and now."

"Lady, you will not."

"Well, your Grace, there are two issues. First, my cousin Geraint declining the claim, I am the eldest surviving member of the senior branch of the ap Gryffudd family, and I have claimed the throne. Thus, it is purely my decision. Secondly, there are here a hundred and fifty Myndarits, and they are at my command. So please stand back, your Grace, if you would be so kind."

"I had not heard that you had claimed the throne. I cannot speak to that without some thought and research. However, I do feel that you would be subject to the rule of law, here. Myndarits are not bandits."

"You suggest that my cousin is."

"Well, it was Sir Roland who mentioned that. But he has indeed been outlawed."

"For taking ill-gotten gains from the disgraced so-called Duke of Belmond."

"Yes, but it is clearly improper for someone to appropriate duchy money for his own use."

"He didn't. How do you think we have funded our actions against the Alliance? After all, you know the High Council haven't helped us."

"But still, duchy funds…"

"Which were in the hands of the Alliance, but by our action have since been used against them. Your Grace, I am the sword-fighter of the family. It's my cousin who is the politician. If even I can destroy each of your points at a stroke, how weak must they be?"

"Yes, well I don't know the details of the case. It was dealt with by Executive Order of the Lord President."

Geraint stepped forward. "We're wasting time. Sir Roland, will you fight my Lady? I warn you, she's not what she was when last you saw her."

Sir Roland lifted his chin. "I'll take my chances on that. Yes, I'll fight her."

Ninian made to speak - then sighed, shrugged and stepped back. Twenty Myndarit Knights of the Temple stepped forward and formed a circle, perhaps fifty feet across. The rest of the Myndarits, mounted, formed a much larger circle outside this, just to ensure that nobody left suddenly.

Outside that cordon, a very large crowd of curious soldiery had gathered, those that had been present from the beginning relating to their colleagues how the business had gone down. It was noticeable that none of these appeared to be considering mounting any kind of rescue for their commander.

When everything was ready Geraint looked around, but was unable to find Uggò. He smiled, humourlessly. "Right. My lord, My Lady, are you ready?"

Sir Roland also looked around. "Was Uggò gà Nachàn not here? I saw him…" Then he shrugged and walked to a point about five feet short of the centre of the circle and waited. Carol came to the equivalent spot facing him. They drew their weapons together and saluted, and Sir Roland paled. "That's Myndarit! How…"

Caroline shrugged, almost imperceptibly. "Does it matter? Do you wish to withdraw?"

"I have never withdrawn from a fight. I never…"

"Good. Let's get it done, then."

Sir Roland sighed and swung. Caroline stepped out of reach and moved to her right. Sir Roland stepped to follow her, and she bounced off her far foot, rolled forward under his blade, and struck upwards, all in one motion.

Sir Roland, however, hadn't gained his reputation by accident. He stepped back and to the side at a speed that belied his age, bringing his blade down on Carol's unprotected back – only to find that she had rolled and parried with Myndarit. Then she rolled again and was on her feet facing him.

Sir Roland nodded, curtly. "Fast. Very, very fast. Strong, too."

She smiled, though her eyes never left him. "John has me working with weights every day. I am very much stronger than I was."

"On the word 'was' she speared forward, no backlift, no warning. Sir Roland just barely parried, but it put him badly off balance. However, since he was falling anyway, he ignored attempts at balance and rapidly fired a foot forward to catch and trip Caroline. She measured her length and instantly rolled, but the older knight had caught himself on his left hand and used it to bounce to his feet – though his cry of pain suggested that it might have been at the cost of damage to his hand.

Nonetheless, it meant that he hadn't fallen and was rushing in while she was still recovering. He would not be in time to strike at the body, she was simply too fast, but he was already aiming his point to run through her leg, crippling her, when his left heel caught his right ankle, causing him to stumble. He recovered like a cat, but by the time he'd gained his balance the chance was gone and Carol was on her feet again.

Without pause she rolled forward again, but this time instead of coming out of the roll with a stroke, she threw herself to the left as she exited the roll, thus just avoiding the blow he'd swung in anticipation of her repeating her previous move.

The miss would have unbalanced a normal fighter, but Sir Roland regained his equilibrium almost instantly – but that 'almost' meant that Carol was already striking before he could completely do so.

Clearly startled at her sheer speed, he nonetheless brilliantly managed to parry in low line, to his right. But she had pulled the stroke, which would have been impossible with any sword but this one, and the parry, without the balancing effect of meeting her sword, accentuated his slight loss of balance just enough that he was flatfooted for nearly a second – far too long – and could not quite get his sword back in position in time to stop her running him through the stomach.

His counterstroke would have taken the head off anybody not quite so fast – though the very tip of his sword did just slice her cheek over the cheekbone – and then the effects of her strike took him. He doubled over, dropped his weapon, then fell, rolling awkwardly onto his back.

Caroline saluted, then dropped to one knee beside him. "What happened? How did you come to change sides?"

A twisted smile. "Pray you never find out."

"Why did you stand as my sponsor for the Sanctuary? Wouldn't that be the last thing you'd want?"

He chuckled, wheezing as he shook his head. "I thought you might kill yourself if you didn't gain the Sanctuary. We knew what the Faiths of Brandur and Alyssana were planning from High Council sources, and your death would have left Geraint ap Gryffudd bidding for the Crown whether he wanted it or not. There'd be nobody else.

"I'd seen his tutors' reports from the University and they were frightening – so it was either the most talented young genius they'd had there since Owain a millennium ago, or the callow, stiff-necked daughter of an Inner Brethren prig. Which would you have wanted if you were me? How could I know how you'd develop? And how fast you'd do it? Nobody could have predicted..."

"Who is-"

Suddenly Sir Roland twisted in the most extreme agony. He extended a palm shaken by agonized tremors. "No more. She'll rip me apart before She will let me betray anybody, and I'm too far gone. Grace." His body convulsed repeatedly in spasms of what was clearly the most intense agony.

With no way even to ask who or what "She" might be, Carol decided she would not permit any person to continue in such pain if she could prevent it, nodded, stood, set herself and thrust. Sir Roland died.

The Duke of Ninian came forward. "If necessary I'll attest that he admitted the charge before he died. Not that it *is* likely to be necessary, I think. Now, I think we should adjourn to what used to be this traitor's office." He stared malevolently down at the corpse. "Half a million died at Cole Valley, did you know that? Half a million! And this… this… this walking piece of faecal matter stage-managed it." With something close to a sob, he kicked the body and turned sharply away.

As they walked across the Parade Square, passed through the crowded soldiery by a double line of Myndarits, Geraint noticed Uggò walking just behind Caroline. He came alongside, took his arm and slowed down so that they were out of earshot of his cousin. "Did you happen to notice that convenient trip that spoiled Sir Roland's strike at Caroline's leg?"

"Aye. I did happen to see it."

"Well done."

"Thank you."

"And it never happened."

"What did never happen?"

"Precisely. But we all owe you one."

They sat around the conference table in the Commander's Office, Ninian at the head of the table.

He opened proceedings. "First, Countess, congratulations on your victory. That was extraordinarily impressive."

"Thank you, your Grace."

"No more than you deserve, not at all. Now tell me, what are you trying to achieve?"

"The death of a traitor."

"And bravo for that, but I was thinking more generally."

Carol gestured to Geraint, who picked up. "The eviction of the Alliance. So far, we have crippled their supply lines. They're getting food locally, but weapons and other warlike supplies are causing them real problems. If we could take whatever units of the Imperial Army are still worth anything – not many, most probably – and add the dukes' forces, then put that together with the Arm, the Myndarits and the Foresters of the Deep, we might have something. If we then add the forces of Faerie…"

"Holy druid, Countess, it's just purely a pleasure to hear people talking possibilities instead of problems.

"Look, Countess, I recall a question the Lord President of the Council asked me. I didn't have an answer for him then, but I'm rapidly coming around to the view that I have one now. The dukes have been pulling their forces back, away from the Alliance. What if I were to get some of the best of them together for a meeting? A quiet, informal meeting, somewhere. Could you address them, see if something could be done even at this late stage?"

Carol nodded. "I could. Certainly I would. Where would we do this? It should probably not be anywhere where we will attract notice."

"Hmm… There's a village where I met my wife. Nice place out in the country, in a cup of hills. Cloiston, it's called, not far from the head of the Golombek Gap. Say four weeks, to give me time to get the news quietly to some of the more useful dukes. Can you get there?"

Carol looked at her cousin. He nodded. "Yes. There is a lot of forest nearby. We'll choose a place, maybe get some … *woodsmen* to host our party. We could do with a show of force for that, cousin. Do you think you could arrange for a couple of chapters to turn up?"

"Yes, I think that would be a good idea. We can bring…" She turned back to Ninian. "Can I get in touch with you between now and then, so as to be sure that we don't have a silly accident? Dukes may not be very happy with the appearance of large numbers of troops – even Myndarits – in their territory just now."

"Yes, you can deal with my Head of Military Forces, Sir John Bentley, here. You will know where to find him, while I'll be round and about, talking to dukes. If you think there's another traitor near the top, I'll tell nobody anything but the meeting place." His mouth twisted slightly. "Ah. Except the Lord President of the Council, the Grand Duke of Quem. He will no doubt insist on knowing everything and I can't really refuse – he *is* the Lord President, at the end of the day."

He held out his hand, and Caroline slapped palms and gripped it. Then he paused for a second, snorted, and held his hand out to Geraint, who also slapped palms and gripped.

"Let's be about it, then. I need to find a lot of dukes. See how many I can get there."

He nodded politely, turned, strode briskly out at the head of his staff.

Caroline and Geraint looked at each other. "Have we just got somewhere at last, Geraint?"

"I do believe we have, Highness."

"Highness?"

"You're in touching distance now, Caroline. Touching distance. Let's see what we can achieve."

And they turned for the door.

Appendices

University of the Woods
600 acres (240 hectares), extends downwards 250 feet (76 metres)
Normal resident population 3000 :: Maximum poulation 5500+

Appendix 1
A Brief Glossary &
A Pronunciation Guide

Glossary

Alma – God of business, trade, organised crime, corruption, police of all kinds, time and its manipulation. Alma never thinks in terms of Good or Evil – She thinks in terms of Useful or Harmful to the Faith and its followers.

Alma Corporations – Vast combinations of temples. These are the largest and most powerful business organisations on Rigantona. Every temple collects a tithe from its members and these funds are devoted by the temple priests to operating businesses (of wildly varying legality) in which members of the Faith may find employment. Followers of other faiths or none are welcome also, if they wish and have useful skills or talents to offer, provided they tithe their income to the founding temple. Some temples succeed better than others, and they will take over the less successful ones for their resources and members. Thus huge and (through survival of the fittest) well and aggressively-managed corporations have arisen, many multi-national in their scope and some inter-continental.

Alyssana – God of gamblers, thieves, tricksters, shysters, con artists, performers, actors, players, singers and also everybody who hates externally imposed rules on general principles. Known for the assertion that anybody who wanted to be a priest of her religion would by definition be too boring for her to bother with. Is reputed in popular myth to have two sisters, called Ceredwen and Caillach, both rather shadowy and a touch ominous in popular myth. Most scholars doubt or deny their existence

Amelyn Abbey – The largest Abbey and the largest University anywhere on Rigantona. Mother House of the Arm of Mannan-Dar and Seat of the Lord Abbott/Lady Abbess of that Order (who is also, thereby the Abbott/Abbess of Amelyn).

Arm (the, an) – The Arm of Mannan-Dar. Mother House: Amelyn Abbey (qv), towards the Eastern end of the North coast of the Amelyn Sea. An Order of Priests in the Faith of Mannan-Dar. These Priests are all trained in at least two disciplines, so that in addition to their priestly roles each will be a warrior or a sorcerer, a necromancer, a wizard etc.

Amelyn Abbey offers research and educational facilities and funds second to none on the planet, recruits only the brightest and most talented candidates and charges them nothing for teaching or accommodation. Thus, it attracts very many supremely talented students, the best of whom go on to join the Arm of Mannan-Dar. This being so, there are many such priests who, rather than just one additional skill, have mastered several. The famous polymath the Countess of Néaness is an extreme example.

The Order is quite large (more than 20,000) and very wealthy. Its function, apart from pure research, is to protect Mannan-Dar's Preaching Order (The Voice of Mannan-Dar) and the Pastoral Order in their work - and to advance the Faith in general.

Like all MD clerics, the Arm are researchers and academics by inclination and, apart from its protective role, Amelyn Abbey houses one of the great Universities of Rigantona. Amelyn is particularly known for its ongoing research projects in the fields of Sorcery and Necromancy and as an institute for the study of Undead.

Because of its function as the primary Arcane research centre in the Empire Amelyn is set up to be defended from all arcane and mundane attack from without, and also to protect the rest of the Abbey (and the world) from sudden emergencies in the Research Laboratories –hence its design, which is in the form of nested pentacles and pentagrams.

The Abbey is central within, and is the major employer in, the City of Amelyn (Pop 597,000). It will not surprise the reader to learn that Amelyn City is also laid out as a Pentacle, whose functional centre contains the Abbey and whose arms hold the city.

Beliar – Beliar, the Great White Dragon, and Tiamat (qv), the Great Chromatic Dragon, are brother and sister, the two children of the originating great deities, Typhon(qv) and Rhiannon(qv). Their own children were the Elder Gods, most notably including Brandur and Ravenne amongst others. It was Beliar's role to dream the Universes and Tiamat's to realise that dream and give it form. It was Beliar and Tiamat's rebellion and patricide that moved Brandur and the Elder Gods, aided by Rhiannon, to deny them entry to the Universes they had made – an entry they have sought ever since.

Beliar's Gate – A separate Creation, quite small, which touches every Prime Material Plane where one might transfer from one Creation to the other. Originally created by Beliar and **Realised** by Tiamat to facilitate His re-entry into the Realm of the Nine Universes when the Elder Gods, at Brandur's urging, closed it to Him. However under the control of Brandur's child Lucifer, the Shining One, the Great Gold Dragon, Beliar's

Gate, also, has been closed to Him. It has, however, periodically provided a channel by which people and creatures could ascend from the Lower Planes – particularly Plane One – to reach the Higher Planes.

On Plane One, Beliar's Gate touches the planet Earth. On Plane Nine, it touches the planet Rigantona. Thus many humans (with a wide range of other Earth creatures and flora) have over the centuries made their way from Earth to Rigantona, bringing their cultures, music – even quite a lot of literature, latterly – with them. Thus also, Rigantona and Earth have become a particular area of interest and concern to the Gods of Creation.

Why this path opens only (or at least predominantly) in one direction, and why it opens only periodically, is presumably known to at least some gods – but not to anybody else.

Brandur – God of nature and of life. Senior of the Elder Gods and Conqueror of Tiamat. The Creator of all mortal life in the universes. His Priests are Witches (predominantly female) and Druids (largely male). In any part of the Empire with 12,000 people or more there will be at least one coven formed of twelve witches and one Druid. The Witches are effectively the Pastoral Order and tend to the daily needs of the people in their area. The Druid handles politics, issues of fertility and fecundity and conservation. He is also the first point of contact for protection and combat. Should the situation be beyond any member acting alone, the Coven will act in unison. In unison it is far more than 13 times more effective than any one member.

Cariseg – God of destruction, chaos, terror, sacrifice and the Death of Gods. Cariseg is hated and feared throughout most of the known world. Her followers, 'Packs' of Wayfarers, have for millennia descended without warning on villages, small towns or caravans of travellers. Nobody survives to tell of what happened on these occasions, except that it is known that everybody – everybody – taken in such a raid is sacrificed to the God Cariseg. How this is done is unknown, for the remains are always burned to ash.

Cromreth – The City of Cromreth, also known as 'The High Towers', lies in Cromreth Bay at the far eastern end of the Amelyn Sea. Its population is slightly over four million and it is the cultural, political and administrative heart of the Empire. It vies with Son of God, Méharé, Néaness, and Elf Haven for the title of the second greatest city on Rigantona. Mallow, of course, is generally acknowledged to be the greatest.

Demon Planes & Hell Planes – When Beliar Dreamed the Universe, His intention was that the principal inhabitants should be a range of beings of spirit. These were established on two sets of nine planes of their own, and the nine Prime Material Planes were established to contain mortal beings to act as food and game for these entities. When Brandur took control of the Universes, he changed this scheme so that Life was its central purpose, which marginalised the spirit beings – and, obviously, annoyed them.

There are two general kinds of these beings – and a plethora of varieties within these general kinds. They have become known by the names that humans have given them, and thus the Demons reside on the Demon Planes and the Devils reside on the Hell Planes (qv).

Empire of the Holy League - Gryffudd Mawr (Known in the early years as "Gryffudd Goch" because of his dark red hair and beard) was king of a commercially and militarily powerful - though not particularly large - kingdom called Cwm Reddan, which covered roughly the same geographical area as the Grand duchy of Cromreth today.

He noticed that feudal and other absolutist systems operated far more efficiently than democracies, but that this effectiveness rarely served their populations because there was no way - by definition - to ensure that the rulers and aristocrats considered the interests of their subjects as their prime motivation.

Gryffudd was quite clearly a brilliant man, and while still in his teens he developed an idea for making a very efficient system work for the benefit of its populace. On his accession to the throne, aged just nineteen, he set about putting this novel scheme into practice. He arranged a conference with the chief priests - or in one case a 'chosen representative' - of what he considered to be the "good gods" (Alyssana, Brandur, Mannan-Dar, Thorn and Varan) whereat he proposed that, in return for the good offices of these gods and their priests in the deities' various fields, he would undertake to...

Establish these religions throughout his lands - and furthermore, would grant them in perpetuity the right and absolute duty, acting in unison, to supervise the behaviour of all civil office holders and to require the removal - or failing this to effect the execution - of all those officials whose rule did not seek to serve the population for which they were responsible as its principal aim.

Alyssana's representative declined the offer, saying her god declared She was nobody's policeman and never would be, though she brought the good wishes of her god and Her Sisters for the venture in general - and she made it clear that her god would assist wherever She felt She could help. The other representatives, however, were able to establish that their deities approved the idea warmly, provided that their participation was always voluntarily confirmed by every sucessive ruler. It always has been

- even the worst of the Reis Emperors have had more sense than to mess with the arrangement. Of course the High Council, not technically being "a ruler", is not in a position to dissent.

Gryffudd then established the system of rule by aristocrats who were (amply) salaried rather than owning the land they ruled, and who were answerable both to the major religions and to their superiors for their conduct. The pool of candidates for these roles, since everybody was aware that peculation would lead to dismissal or death, tended not to be people seeking their own enrichment, but folk who saw a very well-paid opportunity to help build something astonishing.

The result was that this marriage of the effectiveness of (very nearly) unlimited authority with absolute guarantees that such authority would be used only for the benefit of the populace fruited as triumphantly as he had hoped, and the standard of living within Cwm Reddan rose dramatically over the first decade, during which time the present network of covens was first established and the Faith of Mannan-Dar established many schools, universities and hospitals, all wholly free of charge to the patient or student.

The climax of this first growth came in the eleventh year. First the ap Rhys family, close allies who ruled the neighbouring Kingdom of Amelyn, joined their nation with Cwm Reddan under Gryffudd's command. Then, only a few months later, came an even bigger gain. Under pressure from Varan's priests (pugnaciously supported by the Knights of Quem - see below), the large and powerful Kingdom of Quem, whose somewhat venal royal family had been weakened to the point of futility by a succession of inter-familial wars, proposed a merger of the two kingdoms under Gryffudd's rulership.

[It has since often been suggested by usually-reliable historians that a succession of assassins, apparently all Alyssana people, had played a significant part in the neutering of the Quem royal house, but there is no conclusive evidence of this].

However it came about, this merger transformed the situation of the newly-named "Empire of the Holy League". Quem's army was large and well-equipped, and also it had been battle-hardened in all those internecine wars. When added to Cwm Reddan/Amelyn's highly efficient army and substantial naval strength (on the Amelyn Sea), the result was that the new-born "Empire" was in a position to dominate all the Amelyn Sea's coasts, plus the entire large swathe of territory that lay between Quem and Cwm Reddan.

Even more important in some historians' view was that this brought into the Empire the Knights of Quem, an independent and fanatical order of warriors dedicated to Varan. This was the body which, much later, became the Order of Myndarit.

From then forward, the expansion of the Empire to occupy almost the whole of the continent (other than the Kingdom of Faerie, with whom relations have aways been exceedingly cordial) was simply a matter of time, hard-nosed carrot-and-stick diplomacy and sticking firmly to a successful formula.

Foresters of the Green Deep – A collection (organisation is too strong a word) of 5,000 woodsmen/warriors with some limited priestly powers who patrol and protect the Green Deep.

Gryffudd's Palace – Also known as Cromreth Palace, this is the historic and exquisite Palace of Gryffudd Mawr. Often quoted as the most beautiful building anywhere, though the University of the Woods, (q.v.) and the Main Temple at Red Queen (q.v.) have competing claims, the Palace is nearly impossible for most people to see as it lies in the centre of many acres of ornamental gardens including numerous trees – and these lie behind massive, sixty-foot-high curtain walls supported by many eighty-foot-high round towers and fronted by a moat and large barbican. Security in Imperial times is under the control of the Cromreth Chapter of the Order of Myndarit. When the High Council rules, it is under the control of the Lord President's Guard – an elite brigade of the Imperial Army. Protection against magical or other arcane attack is provided by the Arm of Mannan-Dar.

Guardians of Brandur – A force of Elven and Half-Elven women, riding Unicorns and packing a range of dweomers and magic items. Their purpose – to which each has been appointed by Brandur, personally – is to protect the University of the Woods and most particularly the Library of Brandur. Nobody coming without prior permission is allowed to cross the border of University territory – or indeed to go away, usually. These ladies are not known for their kindly and generous nature and they are very good indeed at what they do.

Mage – Any practioner of the crafts of Mind Magic – Illusion/Mind-Magic, Death-Magic, Summoning and Manipulation - or any who study Mind Magic as an abstract subject. Heart Magic is the preserve of priests.

Mannan-Dar – One of the two Gods of Magic and a founder-member of the Holy League. Mannan-Dar is principally concerned with the acquisition and dissemination of knowledge, both for its own sake and for use in improving the lot of the ordinary person.

His followers believe that people tend to know what is right without the need for a lot of rules and regulations, and that red tape just gets in the way. They very strongly believe in defending themselves and their own if attacked. There is a Temple of Mannan-Dar in every town of any kind of size in the Empire – and many other places on Manifòra – and every single such temple contains or funds externally a large free school of excellent quality.

Outside the Empire, the main activity of the Pastoral & Preaching Orders of Mannan-Dar Priests is teaching at, building, managing or funding schools and universities, all of which establishments are always free to all students. The Arm deals with protection of priests, patients and students at these establishments.

Marn – The other of the two Gods of Magic. Marn is also the God of Art, Creativity, Inventiveness, and above all Pleasure. Marn's view, however, is that pleasure's most intense moments come from the winner's triumph and the loser's pain. One of Her best-known tenets is that if you kill a defeated enemy, then their knowledge of defeat, and yours of triumph, die with them and so are brief – whereas if you keep them alive in your power, then you can taste your triumph and they can be made to taste their subjection every day thereafter.

Marn's other main teaching is that laws, morals and social rules of conduct are excellent – for the flock. Those who prey on the flock, however, should know all such rules for what they are: a device by which the flock may be subjected, managed, culled and fleeced - and no more than that.

Necromancer – One who uses the arts of Mind Magic to summon, arrange, manipulate and deal with death, the dead and the never born.

Orcs – Actually, these creatures know themselves as the Ghazhakha'kha'Gi-rach or "Warriors of the Fells" - a name which is more or less entirely unpronounceable by any Human or Elven voice. Thus they have always been known by their Elven name Hobhr Gofalin, which directly translates as "Ugly Stinkers." However, over the last couple of hundred years, the new name "Orc" has gained currency, both amongst humans and elves.

Interestingly, this name shows unmistakeable signs of having been imported from Earth via Beliar's Gate – which is more than odd, because there are no Orcs native to the planet Earth or indeed any other planet in any system in Plane 1.

There have been (very) occasional migrations to Earth via Beliar's Gate, but the most recent is at least eight hundred years ago, whilw the name "Orc" appears to have appeared on Plane 1 many centuries later. A satisfactory answer to this puzzle has yet to be found.

Orcs are humanoid, to the degree that they can interbreed with both Humans and Elves – though rarely in the latter case, because Elven women cannot usually carry an Orc child to term.

This interbreeding is an essential part of Orc culture, for their own women will become pregnant on first insemination and will then become entirely unattractive to Orc males until they are delivered and again ready to conceive. Thus most adult Orc females are unavailable for sex most of the time, and orcs are not subject to the perversion of sexual interest in females too young to conceive.

This issue is exacerbated by the fact that Orc males' sex drive is particularly strong, and the additional consideration that the vast majority of Orc males prefer intercourse with Human and Elven females anyway. Rather sadly for them, this preference is absolutely not reciprocated. Very emphatically not.

Since they know this, Orcs generally resort to the simple remedy of not waiting to be asked. And indeed, in many tribes a young Orc male is required to take a Human or Elven female slave as part of his initiation into adulthood. Thus Orcs are universally despised by both Humans and Elves, which bothers the Orcs not at all.

Orcs range only between 5'6" and 5'11" (167-180cm) tall. They are muscular and heavily built, sacrificing agility and flexibility for strength and sturdiness. Their skin is thick, tough and leathery, and gives off a slightly unpleasant exudate which protects it from the rays of the sun, as they were originally nocturnal.

Their faces lack individuality, of shape by the nature of their skin. However, this is laid out in a woodland camouflage pattern of blotches of brown, dark green, black, pale green and light brown. Thus, individuals may be identified by this pattern. Bone structure is *very* heavy, and leg and arm bones curve slightly. Front teeth are large and sharp, with grinding ridges behind. There are two fang-like incisors, in approximately the position of eye teeth, which usually prevent the mouth ever entirely closing.

Orc intelligence is often traduced. Few Orcs are actually stupid, though on the other hand none are very intelligent. It has been estimated that Orc IQ runs from about 95 to around 108, and very rarely leaves that narrow range. These numbers should be treated with caution, but do indicate that Orcs are not deep thinkers.

Order of Myndarit – An order of knights, under the authority of the Faith of Varan. The Order consists of fifty Chapters, each having a nominal establishment of 5,000 warriors. This order has a very well-earned reputation for great effectiveness and professionalism in battle and is noted for the astonishing – many would say insane – courage routinely displayed by its members. To maintain this reputation, the Order will gently – but swiftly – ease out candidates who cannot manage to attain the necessary standards of professionalism, discipline, courage, combat skill, ferocity and encyclopaedic knowledge of the Order's remarkably thick Evolution Manual.

However, the only rule for membership outside these very demanding professional requirements is that the applicant should be a worshipper of Varan and should absorb and follow the laws and traditions of the Order. Race, gender and sexual preference are disregarded by the Order in its recruitment and subsequent management of members. There are in fact no Orc Myndarits – though a number of Half-Orcs – but only because no Orc has ever been found who is willing to follow the Order's laws and traditions.

The Order of Myndarit is considered one of the world's three elite battle-field forces – all three are religious orders.

Order of Night – A military order under the aegis of the Church of Goreb. The Order of Night recruits its troopers - and thus also its NCOs - from the unemployed, the starving and the peasantry, while its officers are drawn from the lower and middle aristocracy and its senior commanders from the very best families. Nonetheless, the Order is extremely selective in recruiting at all ranks, and its obligatory training regime for senior officers, officers and men alike is long and harsh.

The Order is organised into 180 legions, each with a standard establishment of about 2,500 troops. These break down, in the ordinary fighting legions, into 1,200 mounted heavy infantry - very heavy dragoons - 500 light cavalry and 800 very heavy cavalry.

The dragoons are fine horse soldiers but, once dismounted, are undoubtedly the most effective heavy infantry anywhere. Or at least, anywhere outside the Faerie Royal Levy, who do not ride. The heavy cavalry, on the other hand, are entirely beyond compare with any but a Myndarit Heavy Echelon. The Myndarits have greater panache, more creativity and those wonderful horses, but the Black Knights are arguably even fitter and even more tightly disciplined.

Principalities of the Sea - a long archipelago of islands, some large and some small, extending in a huge southward curve from not far from the South-Eastern coast of Scythéa to approach the Southern coast of Manifòra. Each island is a nation - or several - in its own right and they are fiercely independent. They do, however, participate in a customs union, a common legal framework and a set of trade agreements, all collectively known as the "Common Market" This carefully measured "collaboration within independence" has made the Principalities wealthy and therefore of interest to predators, but they also have a mutual defence pact which, together with the very large naval force their wealth affords, has kept them safe from the ambitions of Scythéan kings and Reis emperors alike.

Oddly the Common Market is not particularly popular in many states of the Principalities, as it's an easy target for those looking for something to blame their ills on, and people who don't understand its often complex benefits often agitate to leave - quite frequently on grounds of patriotism (always the last refuge of scoundrels and also their means of selling the terminally stupid any idea, however ludicrous) but of course no state in the Principalities is crazy enough to actually consider doing it.

Ravens - Ravens are the totem bird of Cariseg, but they, and the corvids in general, are closely involved in all the Nature religions. All Nature Priests have the **Borrow** dweomer, for instance, which allows them to see through the eyes of, and influence the behaviour of, a bird or small animal - but 90% of iterations of this dwomer are related to corvids, and usually ravens.

Examples abound: for instance the druids' groves of Brandur always have flocks of corvids associated with them, acting as lookouts and protectors, but also used as the "eyes" of the coven. Priests of both Marn's Children are traditionally associated with corvids, too, though in their case there is typically just an individual bird.

Interestingly, legend maintains that Alyssana's two mythical Sisters are also closely associated with corvids, though of course the "Three Sisters" are not strictly Nature Gods.

Rigantona – The world on which most of the events in the Realms of Beliar take place. It is made up as follows:

Manifòra – The eastern continent of Rigantona, Manifòra is some 7,300 miles east to west and 3,800 miles north to south. The eastern 5,200 miles is taken up by the vast Empire of the Holy League.

Of the remaining western area, the northern 2,100 miles is held by the Empire of Mallow, while the remainder is a complex of small kingdoms, large grand duchies, variegated duchies and other polities, known collectively within the Empire as 'The Badlands,' though in fact many areas here are well-governed and civilised. A number of others, however, emphatically are not.

Scythéa: The western continent of Rigantona. It is about 5,500 miles from north to south, and around 2,800 miles from east to west at its widest point. It contains the following kingdoms:

Anderel: The southeastern kingdom of the continent and one of the two wealthiest. It's a massive clamshell shape, straight edge to the southern coast, approx. 1,800 miles wide by 1,500 miles high. It is Goreb heartland, and Marn is the only other God with political influence. Alma is present, but considered somewhat subversive.

Clovelin: Centre of the worship of Marn, Clovelin is a long slice of the western side of the continent. It is around 2,000 miles long, and while its lower half is only about 600 miles wide, its northern half stretches well over 1,500 hundred miles from east to west. Clovelin is an extraordinarily wealthy nation, exceeding even Anderel, and was once the heart of the Empire of Marn.

Sadrich: A land of huge variety. Around the Sea of Jewels (the inland sea on its southeastern border, 500 miles north to south, 150 miles east to west), it is as wealthy as Clovelin and Anderel to the South. As one goes north, however, the country becomes rougher and poorer. Sadrich is around 1,500 miles north to south. It's southern parts stretch 1,000 miles east to west, but it tapers to just over 100 miles at the northern coast. Sadrich is not dominated by any one deity, though Marn and her children Jebel and Caeval have much influence here. But then, so does Alma.

Melniren: A wild and mainly poor land, filled with tundra, nomads and pureblood Vampires (who in fact bring in considerable wealth from outside Melniren, but rarely spend much). Perhaps 800 miles north to south, and a little less east to west. The major deities here are Alma, Caeval and, amongst the purebloods, Goreb.

Kasáván: Another poor northern kingdom, larger and better organised than Melniren, and somewhat wealthier. It's another Goreb stronghold, home of that strange and deeply contentious Goreb sect, The Pure. It has a huge northern coastline, extending some 2,800 miles – though that includes the Noregatt or "Dragon's Neck" Peninsula on the northeast point of the continent, which is some 600 miles long, tapering from 500 to less than 100 miles wide. Excluding the peninsula, Kasáván is around 1,100 miles wide by 800 high.

Rohlich: Rohlich is a huge contrast to the kingdoms to its north. Its wealth is exceeded only by Clovelin and Anderel – narrowly - and it's both a centre of trade and a huge food producer, boasting hundreds of thousands of acres of farmland, both arable and mixed, while its southern forests are extensive and rich in every kind of product from rare woods to venison and truffles. Shaped like an isosceles triangle standing on one point, Rohlich stretches at its most extreme points nearly 2,000 miles north to south and around 1,500 miles east to west. There is no one dominant deity; Marn, Goreb and Alma are all prominent.

Ritual Magic - As may be seen from perusal of Appendix II, Brandur split magic's power into two parts, Heart Magic, which the Gods package for use of their Priests, and Mind Magic, which involves manipulation by mages of the magical forces tailored for this end in a small Realm created by Brandur for this purpose.

However, Brandur left a channel by which the full power of raw magic might be accessed. It is possible to raise arbitrarily large amounts of energy - far more than is involved in casting dweomers - by "tuning" the mentral processes appropriately. This gives access to magical power directly, via the Lens of Alyssana.

See elsewhere for a more detailed description; suffice it here to say that certain electrical patterns need to be generated by sentient brains and meshed together, typically those of a number of people. There are various ways of generating these patterns, but all participants in a particular rite must use the same set of techniques. These involve sounds, actions and other things, the performance or observation of which generates the appropriate electrical patterns in the mind.

To achieve any significant results usually requires lengthy and precise activity to connect to the Lens, then "program" it to raise, focus, control and target the energy available - and this is a complex and wildly dangerous undertaking. However, it has the advantage that - in theory - there is nothing that cannot be achieved by such a means, provided those involved have the necessary knowledge, focus and strength of mind.

Ritual magic is - as might be expected - discouraged by the Priests of many religions and most civil authorities, both because it dwarfs their own power and because it can easily endanger anybody within many miles radius of a failed exercise. None the less, Brandur covens sometimes resort to it, and so do specially talented and knowledgeable practitioners of the faiths of Marn and Mannan-dar. Alectis' priest were also known to engage in ritual magic, when She had any.

Sorcerer – One who uses the arts of Mind Magic to summon, deal with and (where possible) control the spirit and energy beings that exist within the Universes, including the assorted denizens of the Demon and Hell Planes. Such attempts range from very challenging at the lower levels, to horrific at intermediate levels. Beyond there, only the most talented and knowledgeable have any hope of success at all.

It should be noted that of all the various branches of Mind Magic, this particular specialism has the most serious consequences for the insufficiently competent or the unfortunate.

Thorn – God of Music, musicians, lovers, scientists, composers, the lonely and the oppressed. His priests walk the lonely places of the world, looking for those in need of help. They are excellent fighters as well as being casters of great power. It is said that the God Himself will sometimes take on the role of one of His priests and will walk the world seeking those in need.

Undead – a creature the force of whose sentience and awareness sustains its existence, rather than this being done by its body (if it has one). Most necromancers wish to "penetrate the Veil" and become undead. There are various kinds of undead, ranging from ghosts and zombies through assorted flavours of vampire, spectre, etc, to the truly horrific and vastly powerful Lich and the almost godlike demi-lich. There is one higher level of undead, but there is only one known example, the being "Khadesh".

Vampire – The only "naturally" occurring form of undead. There are 3 kinds:

Pure Blood Vampires: Pure Blood Vampires breed (almost) in the same way as mortals. They consider themselves superior to every other kind of undead - and everybody else, too, for that matter. **Half Blood Vampires:** Half Bloods are those mortals who have become vampires via the infection of a bite. A half blood vampire is the absolute slave of its creator until that creator is destroyed, at which point it both becomes free and becomes able to create half blood slaves of its own. **"Veil" Vampires:** These are necromancers who have successfully passed through the veil to become undead.

Varan – God of battle, warriors, honour, justice (ideally achieved by the wise creation and application of law, but if the law systematically fails to produce justice then justice achieved however it may be done). Also courage, duty, personal honour and all those who seek to display, teach or promote any of these things.

Varan also maintains that people should always try to enjoy all life's aspects, including enjoying duty whenever its nature makes that remotely possible. Varan folk assert that it follows, therefore, that enjoyment is itself a duty – as is making duty enjoyable, for those in authority.

While this precise statement doesn't appear in ***The Book of the Stranger*** - Varan's holy writ - the God has never found it appropriate to discourage the idea in any way, and indeed at every Varan temple "Enjoy Life!" is always displayed prominently over all entrances - and the main altar as well - so it must be reasonable to assume that Varan is at least comfortable with the notion even if He has not actually promulgated it formally.

Wizard – One who uses Mind Magic to cause effects directly within the physical world, usually by manipulation of physical objects or energy flows, as opposed to summoning or persuading some spirit of the dead/undead or else some spirit or energy being to create the effect required.

Pronunciation Guide

The common tongue of Rigantona is near universal amongst humans and is also spoken by most elves, dwarves and gnomes, as well as many orcs. It is based upon English as carried across the Gate from Plane 1, with three notable sources for pronunciation. These are the Old Tongue of Goreb, also known as the Lateen, the Elven tongue and the ancient tongue of the druids, the Cymraeg. These various tongues are discussed elsewhere, but a few pointers as to variations in pronunciation they produce might be helpful. It should be noted that, in the Cymraeg in particular, not all pronunciation carries over exactly from Earth. This is occasionally also true in the Lateen.

Elven Diacriticals & Cymraeg Letter Pronunciation

There are several diacritical marks which affect the pronunciation of vowels and have been universally adopted into the common tongue. The most frequently seen are given in the attached table. Stress in the word normally rests on syllables containing diacriticals – hence 'Ugg**ò**'.

Similarly, some letters in the Cymraeg are treated quite differently from their English usage – and slightly differently from Welsh usage on Earth…

Elven

Letter/diacritical	Pronunciation	Example
é (e acute)	ay	**Zeéla** (prn *Ze-ayla*)
ò (o grave)	oo	**Uggò** (prn *Uggoo*) **Manifòra** (prn *Manifoora*)
á (a acute)	ar (as in part)	**Port Sán** (prn *Port Sarn*)
à (a grave)	or (like paw)	**nà** (prn *nor*)

Cymraeg - as used on Rigantona

Letter/letter pair	Pronunciation	Example
f (solo f)	v	**fách** (prn *varkh*)
ff	soft f	**Gryffudd** (prn *Gruffith*)
u	i(short I, as 'bit')	**Gryffudd** (prn *Gruffith*)
w	oo	**cwm** (prn *coom*)
y	almost always u; (sometimes 'i' occasionally ee)	**Gryffudd** (prn *Gruffith*)
dd	hard th as 'that'	**Gryffudd** (prn *Gruffith*)
ch	as German 'achtung'	**fách** (prn *varkh*)

Appendix II
The Origin of the Gods and of Magic

A view of the Amelyn Sea from the small fishing village of Ely Bridge, just outside Ledingham on the Sea's South Coast. Ely Bridge is known as "The hauntedest place in the Empire", from the number of strange events people have claimed to see.

Book the First

The Origin of the Gods and the Creation of the Universe

This is a presentation in the common tongue of a copy taken from a very ancient manuscript, unearthed in a ruined - but still dangerous – Library dedicated to Khytan, some four thousand years ago.

The original from which that scroll was a copy (or, more likely, a copy of a copy) appears from internal textual and linguistic clues to be the work of a Mannan-Dar Priest of the Devine Voice order. This order became defunct more than five thousand years before that time, having been replaced by the Order of the Voice of Mannan-Dar, which still exists. Thus the original text cannot be less than nine thousand years old, and may easily be twice that.

This text is notable for being the sole document of real authority we have which offers support to that small, though distinguished, band of academics who argue for the literal existence of the mythical 'Rhiannon'

Reproduced under licence from, and by kind permission of, the Lady Abbess, Amelyn

Rhiannon and Typhon came before all. From whence they came we know not. Nor do we know the manner of their coming to be, for the one will not tell us and the other cannot. It may be that they themselves are ignorant of this thing. It is known for certain, however, that their first Creations were the great Dragons Beliar and Tiamat, greater than worlds, fruit of the joining of Typhon with Rhiannon.

In their turn, these Great Ones came together and their children were the Elder Gods – first Brandur, then Ravenne, then Khytan, then Gardoch, Ostari, Ximineth, Dagrellin and finally Abiddonne. But Ravenne was wroth, even then, that He was not the first. He resolved that, though junior to Brandur, yet still should He prove the greater; a project where He has not yet proved successful.

Then Typhon said to Beliar "Bring you forth Creation, for lo, this is the task for which You had Your birth." And Beliar heard Him, and He considered how this thing might be accomplished. After a period of time, limitless and undefined, the Great White Dragon bethought Him of a plan and this plan seemed good.

Then, of another unmeasurable time, Beliar Dreamed, and Creation was his Dream, wide and lovely. But yet was His Dream not whole, and it could not therefore stand. Then did Rhiannon guide Him and He Dreamed again. Long was his Dreaming, though how long cannot be told, for how shall measure of it be taken? But now was His Dream whole and entire. None had Dreamed such a Dream before, though the Gods who saw this thing done might do it again, acting in concert – indeed, the greatest amongst them might accomplish it alone.

And Tiamat, Beliar's sister and lover, saw that His Dream was whole and She Realised it, and gave it form.

Thus began the First Age.

When this had come to pass Typhon looked on Creation, and great was His satisfaction with that which His children had wrought. "Good," He said. "This is well done. You have accomplished that for which you were created. We shall enter upon this creation, this Planar Matrix, and We shall be the Gods of it, to Our glory."

But Beliar and Tiamat said "This thing shall not be. We alone created the Universe. We alone shall be Gods of it." Then They fell upon Typhon and They tore at Him, so that the sound and fury of that conflict echoed across the Places that Were and the Places that Were Not until all were filled with the sounds of conflict, And still to this day does that fell sound echo around every Plane of existence, nor will it ever cease.

Then Brandur said to Ravenne, "How should those who would destroy their own Creator, all for no reason, how should they inherit the Universe as the fruits of their crime? They must not. We shall enter on it and close it against them."

Ravenne answered and said "So be it, but We are not sufficient, all of Us together. Tiamat and Beliar will enter, strive as We may."

So Brandur said to Rhiannon, "Will You aid us in this thing? The life that I will grow in this Creation will not ever be safe in the hands of such as They."

But Rhiannon said "Yet, are thy siblings fit for the task? Will the life that gives Creation meaning be safe with them?"

Then did Brandur stand incarnate, and He raised His hands, and before Her He said "With Your guidance, I shall cause the life of the Universe to be. Once it lives and has its being I shall protect it, I myself, and none shall work its destruction – whether My parents, My siblings or any other. This is My Word and this I shall do. I have spoken."

And Rhiannon said "It is good. Let us then enter on this Creation and be its Gods that it prosper, and so what glory we gain we shall earn."

Waging war across the Places that Were Not, Tiamat and Beliar triumphed over Typhon and tore Him into four pieces, but these They could not destroy. But as They did this thing, Rhiannon and the Elder Gods entered upon Creation and closed it to them. Then, to mark and commemorate Brandur's Oath, Rhiannon made for Him the Staff Baraani, and henceforth on that Staff were all Gods' Oaths made.

Now the four parts of Typhon were scattered in the Places That Are Not to the grief of Rhiannon, and She would not have it so. But these parts were still the essence of a God, though the God they had been was no longer present in them.

So Rhiannon and Brandur studied together and decided. And they took the four parts of Typhon, that could not be destroyed, and Brandur breathed the Breath of Life on them, while Rhiannon brought out from their latency the properties that each might show. And lo, each part knew itself and lived. And these were Goreb and His sister Alectis and also Alma and Her brother Varan.

Thus did the First of the Younger Gods come to be.

Then did Brandur and Rhiannon take counsel together once more and Brandur set Life in the Universes in its many forms and varieties, and further, he set mechanisms within this life, such that it might grow and change to meet the dangers of the Universe without need for His aid. And while it had been Beliar's Plan that the Universe should hold abundant life, for else it would be a cold and meaningless thing, yet was Brandur's scheme for life different.

Beliar would have had mortal life be a secondary thing, existing only as food and sport for the immortals of the Demon and Devil Planes.

Yet Brandur overturned this scheme and turned His face from it. At Brandur's decree, mortal life became the central life force of the Universe, and the nine Prime Material Planes which bore it became the Universe's reason for being. The Immortals of the Nonmaterial Planes became peripheral, their power much curtailed, and for this reason they were – and remain - wroth with Brandur and with the mortals He had caused to be. Yet even for those great beings of spirit, to be wroth with Brandur is one thing, to do something meaningful about that wrath is quite another.

Yet all was not well in the worlds and Brandur said "Rhiannon, You are too mighty. Creation cannot hold together in the face of Your glory. Over time, it will shred and dissolve. For a while it can abide You, but not forever."

Rhiannon smiled and said "Then shall I be within it and not, and myself and not, as seems best from time to time." So came the Triple Goddess, the Three Faces of Rhiannon, to be. And few were those who lived in Her Universe that even knew the name Rhiannon. Even two of Her Faces were hidden, both from mortals and, often, from Gods also.

Now did Beliar and Tiamat see the growth of Life in the Universe, and that it prospered independently of them. Then did they strive to enter on Creation to be its Gods, but it was closed against them. So Beliar Dreamed a Gate, whose Planes touched all the Planes of Creation, and His Dream was good. Tiamat saw His Dream, and its worth, and She Realised it and it came to be.

The Elder Gods were amazed that Beliar, unguided, had wrought this thing, and they said "Now are We undone," for They could not enter on the

Gate that Beliar had Dreamed to close it against Him, yet it touched upon every Plane of the Universe and thus gave Him Access thereto.

Yet the Life that Brandur had created and cared for loved Him, and freely gave Him worship – a thing never seen before. This worship and love gave him strength beyond any he had previously possessed. Filled both with this strength and with love for the Life that had so freely responded to Him, Brandur resolved that Gate or no, Dreams or no, the Great Dragons should not wrest the life of the Universe from His protection, let the price be whatsoever it might.

Again, He sought the counsel of Rhiannon, and together they decided, with no joy, what must be done. Blessed by Rhiannon, Brandur took the Staff Baraani and with it He assailed Tiamat and struck Her with the Staff and conquered Her, that She could not resist Him. And Beliar would have come to Her aid, but Rhiannon interposed, and Beliar was not sufficient, alone, to defy Her.

Then Brandur took Tiamat, though She would not have had it so, and at His will She brought forth the Golden Dragon Lucifer, the Shining One. Lucifer was of the stuff of both Brandur and Tiamat, and so could enter both Creation and Beliar's Gate. Thus, at Brandur's wish, Lucifer entered on the Gate and closed it against Beliar.

Beliar was very wroth.

But Brandur said, "This is not enough, of itself. Now we must prevent Beliar from creating another Gate. We cannot reach him at this time without leaving Creation unprotected but we have Tiamat, and She must serve My will, though She would not. We shall take from Her the power to Realise that which Beliar Dreams, and so shall Creation be safe."

Then He coupled with Tiamat again and, sorely against Her will, she obeyed Him and brought forth Her power to Realise. And She brought this forth in the shape of many Dragons, male and female of each kind – Gold, Red, Brown, Silver, Blue, Black and Green. When the Dragons had left Her, She no longer had the power to Realise that which was Dreamed, it was dispersed amongst the Dragons.

Then did Brandur release Her. Ravenne was angered at this, and would have had Brandur keep Her that Her power – which was still very great – might serve them. But Brandur said "This is not right. Those things I did were necessary for the protection of Creation, for that is what I swore to do. But it grieved me sorely, and I will do no more – not for My benefit, not for Yours."

Ravenne's rage knew no bounds, and He would have smote Brandur – but Brandur was He who had conquered Tiamat, and Ravenne dared not essay this thing, rage as He might.

Book the Second

The Origins of Magic and Its Gods

This is a far more recent text, produced at Amelyn Abbey by the notable scholar Jeri ap Clerc [1,524 – 1,610 Imperial Era]. The document has a very different style from the vastly older piece above, displaying the typical lightness of touch that apClerc introduced into the Mannan-Dar academic style, and which is still such a feature of that religion's writing. Being written by ap Clerc, however, its meticulous accuracy is, as ever, unimpeachable.

Reproduced under licence from, and by the kind permission of, the Lady Abbess, Amelyn

The doings of Lucifer and the other Dragons, and their impact on the worlds, make another tale. Here it is enough to know that the Dragons made their Home on the nearest Prime Material Plane to the Centre of the Planar Matrix, Plane Nine, and here they gave off the power to realise in actuality the fruit of imagination. This power is what is commonly called Magic *[except that on Plane One, where in fact it can rarely be performed, some refer to it as 'magick', to distinguish it from the deception of conjurors. Presumably this is to distinguish that which can rarely be performed from that which can be performed whenever desired - by the skilful - but works no change on the world].*

Brandur observed this power and He saw that it was far too potent for mortal creation to use, for its power was too great and too wild, though the Immortals of the non-material Planes drew on it to use in their own ways. So Brandur mused on the problem, then He took this power and divided it into greatly unequal parts. The larger part by far he called Heart Magic – why is a mystery none have plumbed - and he gave it into the keeping of the Gods, so that those in need might receive aid from their Priests, through whom the Gods could exert this Power. Yet – of course - Ravenne refused to pass this Power to the people of the Planes. He would not even exert it through His own Priests, choosing instead to work miracles from His own power, at whim, for those who pleased Him. More, He imposed His will on the other Gods of Creation.

The smaller part of Magic Brandur dubbed Mind Magic – again, for reasons he has not explained - and set up a system whereby Mortals might use it. He recalled what Beliar had done and, once more advised by Rhiannon, he Dreamed new Realms, which he stocked with entities and animate objects made wholly of Mind Magic. Then Rhiannon approved and Realised these Realms.

This is how it all works. The females of the new race of Dragons lay eggs, and these give off a magical effusion called Aether. A mortal Mage might form this, by use of thought, word and gesture, into a pattern of force. Brandur so arranged matters that this pattern would stimulate powers in His new Realms to perform the action required.

These would be small, simple actions. For more complex or powerful enchantments, a linked series of such reactions is required. Often, for complex dweomers, an adept might invoke several simultaneous effects, simply to produce some other effect which in turn stimulates a more powerful reaction from Brandur's Realm. To achieve the result he or she seeks, several such multi-level enchantments might need to be caused to interact in deeply complex ways.

A notation has grown up by which such 'recipes' for dweomer might be recorded. As is well known to all students of this arcane art, however, every mage has his or her own dialect of this language, so that the task of translating another mage's working notes into a functional spell ranges from very difficult – at best - up to suicidally dangerous.

New enchanters are encouraged by the assurance that these high level spells are much less fiendishly difficult and dangerous for the caster than at first they seem, but in reality they are not. Skill, natural talent, focus and precision are required, in addition to compendious knowledge and not a little courage and boldness. For a proper discussion of the workings of this system see elsewhere. For our purposes, the above brief overview will suffice, though some might find that it confuses more than it enlightens.

All that remained after Brandur had arranged all this, was to put in place the connection – 'interface' is the technical term mages use - which would relate the patterns in the Aether to the appropriate magical animatrons in Brandur's Realms.

To this end Brandur selected the 'simple' – He called it - solution of a multi-dimensional lens which would stand outside the Plane Stack, but within the Realms of Beliar, and cast energy patterns formed on a Prime Material Plane into Brandur's Realm.

He taxed His siblings with the comparatively trivial task (for a God) of actually designing and constructing this lens. However – no surprises here – Ravenne pressed his siblings to refuse, and succeeded in getting them to do so. "It is not right" said Ravenne, "that mortals should have access to this power. Let them pray to their Gods. If We see fit, We will grant their prayers." And Ravenne thought long on the design of such a Lens, but would not actually create it.

Now there had already been friction between Brandur and the other Elder Gods. Brandur received Sacrifice and Worship - freely given - from the people, and cared for them. The other Elder Gods demanded Sacrifice to their power, and punished with grotesque severity any and all communities who did not deliver it in sufficient quantity – but they took no systematic care for their people, aiding and harming at whim.

This offended Brandur and distressed Him greatly, but as a God of Creation he was bound by his oath on Baraani not to act against them directly. His people, of course, bereft of either Earth or Mind Magic by the embargoes of Ravenne, could not have any effect against the direct miracles of the Elder Gods' favoured servants.

Brandur spoke, therefore, to Varan, brother of Alma and one of the first four Younger Gods. Varan was at that point neither a God of the Creation of Beliar, nor yet bound by the Oath of Agency, and so could act in His own person. Known only as 'The Stranger', His true identity concealed from even the other Gods by Alyssana, Varan strode the worlds opposing cruelty and injustice wherever He encountered it, regardless of whether the perpetrators of these things might be supported by divine sponsors.

Very soon the Elder Gods found their wishes thwarted at every turn by the activities of The Stranger, so they decided He must fall. To this end, they sent warriors and assassins against Him, but these never returned to report their failure. So the Gods sent their mightiest favourites against Him; but all were overthrown. Exasperated, they sent great armies against Him, and these He routed. Finally, they sent their most puissant miracles against Him and, perhaps, His power might have failed Him (though perhaps not, also) but He was sustained by Brandur and by Alyssana, and thus the Elder Gods could not prevail against Him.

Then Varan said to His sister Alma, and to Goreb and His sister Alectis, "Creation goes ill. These Godlings take sacrifice upon sacrifice and the people of the Worlds suffer greatly for their benefit, but they do not see to the benefit of their followers in return, as Brandur and Rhiannon had planned. Let us oust them and set Creation to rights."

[Author's note. The source from which this quotation was obtained has 'as Brandur and Rhiannon had planned' and there are further references to Rhiannon or to the 'Triple Goddess' in my source material.

All such references appear in this text, for it is my duty to present the information that comes to me honestly and without imposing my own view upon it without good reason, but it seems likely that these surely mythical references are a spurious insertion. I was tempted to remove them but I did not do so as there is insufficient evidence to justify me in distorting such ancient sources, but I most strongly advise readers to regard these passages with great caution.

J. apC]

Now the Younger Gods did not all share Varan's care for the people of Creation, yet they all believed that a God should receive worship and give care in return – all felt that both Gods and mortals gained benefit thereby. So they joined with Varan and strove to oust the Elder Gods from Creation. People yielded them worship; they gained sustenance thereby and supported their worshippers. By this means they became powerful in Creation and forced back the Elder Gods.

Enraged, the Elder Gods sought with the utmost vigour to destroy their opponents' worshippers, but they could not turn Nature and natural forces against them because Brandur refused to allow it. More, whenever the Younger Gods' followers were left without the aid of their own Gods, they could appeal to Brandur or to any of the Three Faces of Rhiannon and would always be supported. Even Alyssana's shadowy sisters, Ceredwen and Caillach, acted in support of the Younger Gods' worshippers, and often in those days did Caillach or Her priests stand at a ford and foretell the future for some hapless servant of Ravenne, while the Holy Assassins of Ceredwen went hither and yon to the Elder Gods' rage and sore loss.

[Whether this be legend or fact, this writer cannot say with certainty, though it should be noted that such times are always fecund sources of legend. It is also said in other ancient texts that Alyssana walked unrecognised in the Councils of the Elder Gods, spreading confusion, alarm and discord, just as her followers did amongst those Gods' mortal servants - and that, on the other hand, has a real ring of truth to it.

J. apC.]

Soon, bereft of alternative, the Elder Gods broke the Oath of Agency and stood out from Creation and confronted the Younger Gods directly. There was strife between them in their own persons, and Ravenne and His siblings fought for Creation – which could not be guaranteed to survive the event. And this breaking of their Oaths cost all the Elder Gods power, for that of themselves which they had invested in the Staff as earnest of their Oaths was lost to them, and became embodied in the Staff. And by this means came the God Baraani to be - God of oaths and of contracts, of true-dealing and record-keeping and of those who honour these things.

As the great conflict waxed in intensity, with Brandur, Alyssana and *[allegedly, J.apC]* Her sisters fully engaged on the Younger Gods' side, it became clear that no single Elder God whatever could stand against Brandur and only Ravenne Himself could resist Varan or Goreb for longer than a brief moment. All the Elder Gods chose to avoid conflict with Alyssana, Ceredwen and Caillach, who operated as a group that - *[again allegedly]* – on occasion reformed into Rhiannon Herself.

With all the Elder Gods but Ravenne retreating, Brandur gave life to His aspect as Thorn. Then the three warrior Gods, Varan, Goreb and Thorn formed a Trinity, using a focus of power created by Alyssana. This juncture of three Warriors confronted Ravenne and utterly overthrew Him. As soon as this was so, Brandur resumed his Thorn aspect, as there was no balancing principle in the universe at that time and Brandur was intensely aware of the need of the Universe for balance in even small things, let alone the attributes of Gods.

Ravenne was not destroyed (for at this time Gods could not be killed), but he was completely subdued for a short timespan. This was sufficient, for they took the power focus Alyssana had made and formed it into a prism of power, This could be done instantly, for Alyssana could make its form and function be whatever She willed, and its power was very great.

So the Gods imbued the Prism with their own essences and said 'As all Gods are creatures of energy, not matter, so their essence may be manipulated in those ways pertinent to energy. We will cast Ravenne through this prism and as with all that passes through a Prism, He will be divided. And the shadows of Ravenne thus produced will be mixed with our essences, three parts Ravenne's essence, plus one of ours. Thus the shadows cast shall not be the shadows of Ravenne alone, but adulterated with our own presence, But where shall we cast?"

Then Goreb said "Let the shadows be cast via the Gate of Beliar, that they fall as distantly as maybe.." So this was done and Ravenne was split into three shadows and these were cast via the Gate of Beliar, which touches all Planes on the Matrix, to alight at the furthest end of Creation on the "bottom" Prime Material Plane, Plane One, the Plane upon which Brandur had brought the race of Man into being..

But Alma betrayed them. She retained some form of Ravenne intact, by use of Her power over time, and this will be told elsewhere. But the Gods knew not of Alma's betrayal and this cast their plans awry, for the essence of Ravenne which entered the Prism was not thus exactly as they thought. In this way the admixture of their own essences with Ravenne's was entirely upset.

The first shadow they cast received three parts from other Gods, not one, forcing out two essences of Ravenne from this shadow into the second one. Thus the first shadow was three parts the Gods of Creation and one part Ravenne. When it fell onto the lowest Plane of Creation a new God of that Plane came to be, and that God was Thoth. And then the second shadow fell on that Plane, and this was now five parts Ravenne, so it was more Ravenne than Ravenne Himself had been, and thus came the God Sett to be, Finally the Third shadow fell, bearing no formal admixture from the Gods of Creation, and so was pure Ravenne. It was changed none the less from what it had been, as it had been touched and altered by passage through Alyssana's Prism itself, and now it had its being as the God Isis.

[It is said that Isis also presented Herself in other divine forms in other places on that poor benighted plane, but my source documents offer no detail.

J. apC]

And when the Gods of Creation saw the new Gods that had formed on the First Plane of Creation, and were the Gods of it, they were dismayed. Brandur said "This is ill done, for these Gods are not what we planned – and two of them are fell indeed."

Goreb said "So be it. We cannot undo that which we have done, so we must mend it. I will undertake this thing, as it will require battle and war without mercy and these things are Aspects of Mine own. We shall cast a shadow of My own Self onto that Plane and I will contend with them there. I shall take the People of the Plane to Myself and they shall have none other Gods but me. It is not needful that they know why this must be so, but it shall be so." And so began the long and blood-soaked tale of the Jealous God of Plane One, a tale told elsewhere.

But Brandur said "Yet more must be done, for we have the other Elder Gods to conquer. We cannot rid ourselves of them in this way, lest all fall awry again, so we must seek a more absolute solution. There must be death for Gods."

Then did the other Gods object, and great was the clamour amongst some - notably Alma, who was not pleased with the consequence of Her schemes – but Brandur was implacable and could not be moved by plea or prayer, reason or threat.

Then did Brandur lie again with Alyssana, and She brought forth twins, for Brandur would ever have all things in balance, that the fabric of the Universe not be stressed. The one of these twins was Thorn, whom He had previously realised as an Aspect of Himself. And Thorn was a warrior God, standing for all that Nature can create through chaos and death, so that He was a Hunter and a Shepherd, Creator of Gods, Shaper of Species and Protector of the Weak. And Thorn and Varan were friends and allies from the first and forever thereafter.

The second twin was Cariseg, and She was very fell, for She was Queen of Sacrifice and Destruction, Scourge of the Worlds, the Death of Gods. So now there was Death for Gods, and they could die. This made the Younger Gods to grieve, and they would not recognise Cariseg by reason of what she was, that they would have not be so.

But Varan embraced Her and gave Her warm welcome, for He would have none excluded from comradeship through fault that was not their own. Then Thorn said "Let those who will not embrace My Sister go their own way, for I will have none of them." And Thorn walked alone ever after, acknowledging brotherhood with only Varan among the Younger Gods. But yet he fought alongside them at Brandur's request for He honoured Brandur, and Alyssana also.

Now did they all fall upon the Elder Gods that remained. Some they killed, and these were no more, and some they drove down. None could stand against them, for though Sacrifice alone gives Gods great power, Worship, Love and Sacrifice together are far greater. And they strove until the Elder Gods were utterly defeated, and most were no more; the survivors joined with Ravenne/Isis/Sett on Plane 1.

Then Brandur said. "Very well. It is done. Now let us forge the Lens of Dreams, the Link between Aether and the Realms that will give mortals magic of their own.

And again they turned to the Prism of Alyssana, and purposed to make of it the Lens of Dreams. But still they could not give mortals magic of their own, for the detail of how this thing might be wrought had been Ravenne's study, and He was gone.

And Alyssana said. "We might regain the knowledge and techniques lost with Ravenne, but yet the problem is deeper, for one or more amongst us must ward this power and be God of it once mortals have gained it, that it never go awry in times to come. How shall we resolve this problem?"

And some said that Alyssana Herself, or Her sisters – particularly Her sister Caillach - might be God of Magic, but Alyssana demurred and said "I will not be Lawmaker for the power of Magic nor yet for any other thing, importune me as you may. And Brandur would not have My Sisters in that role, for they do not love the People of the worlds."

Then Goreb and Varan's sister Alma turned to Brandur and said "Is this thing so, that Alyssana tells us?"

And Brandur laughed, and said "When has Great Alyssana ever been wrong?"

And Goreb laughed in his turn, though wryly, and replied "That She has ever been mistaken, I greatly doubt. Whether She has ever lied, on the other hand, to that I offer no opinion; Alyssana is the God of Deception, so how could I know? I am nevertheless full convinced that She has on occasion told the complete truth - and still led all of us astray - aye, even the Gods.

"This is a part of Her Aspect as a God, and it may well be that therefore it must be so for the good of all – but it does mean that one might do well to seek confirmation of one's understanding of Her words from third parties with knowledge of the facts. So, Brandur, Is this thing so, that Alyssana tells us?"

Then did Brandur smile and incline His head with respect in acknowledgement of Goreb's words, and He said "Indeed, what the Great Lady says is perfectly true. I will have none of Caillach as that God, for She is too harsh and wholly wanting in mercy. Ceredwen I would accept still less, for She is too partial for this person or that. She would never be even-handed.

'Let me be clear that both are great Ladies whom I respect deeply, and love, but still I will not have them for this task."

Then Goreb was filled with wrath. He stood before Brandur and He said "Yet we would accept either one. Why should your will overmaster ours? It shall not be so."

But Alyssana said "Waste no time on useless posturing, Death God. Brandur has said nay and My Sisters have heard. They will not go against the will of the God of living things in any way that touches His Office. Indeed it is in the last degree unlikely that they would go against the Will of Brandur in any matter at all. Some God must needs be pre-eminent amongst us and absolutely it shall not be me. Who then better than Brandur, who has sworn to protect and care for life in the Universes for eternity?"

Goreb remained where He stood. "I, Goreb, might be better."

"Yet you wish for that eminence, while Brandur is wholly unconcerned one way or the other. Thus Brandur is the better qualified for that reason. And some might say there are many other reasons besides, but that is no matter. This reason is sufficient."

At these words, Goreb cast His gaze around the Gods, first His sister Alectis, then Alma, then Varan and Thorn His fellow Warriors, and finally even Cariseg. Yet there was no voice to speak on His behalf. Understanding that none but Varan's sister would have him, and She only were there profit in the matter, He nodded courteously to Brandur. "Matters are as they are and You are paramount amongst us. Yet at last shall the Universes come to death and stillness. Then it is that I shall reign, struggle as You will."

Brandur nodded gravely. "This may be so. Perhaps. But there will be a brief intervening period before then – some tens of billions of years – during which time it would be well if the peoples of the Realms of Beliar had magic to use. Shall we therefore turn our minds to making suitable arrangements?"

So the Gods studied what should be done, that mortals might have magic. And Alectis said "If we seek the God Isis, who is the shadow of Ravenne barely altered, within Her is this knowledge. Yet it is sure that we should not give her power on any plane but that which imprisons Her, for still She is Ravenne, in Her fashion. Can we use Her knowledge without thereby making Her free of the Planes?"

So they considered, and decided how this thing might be done. They used the Lens of Alyssana to cast a shadow of Isis into the Places Which Were Not, wherein the Gods had their being And they cast this shadow upon the seed of Brandur as it entered Alyssana. But they did not do this randomly, for they had planned with great care, and the shadow of Isis fell exactly as they had decided that it should. However, still they knew not of the retention of some essence of Ravenne by Alma, with the intention to profit thereby, and so their plan was flawed and the work went awry.

Alyssana conceived and brought forth two siblings, that there be the Balance that Brandur loved, and these were in truth the new Gods of Magic – part Isis, part Ravenne, part Alyssana, part Brandur and entirely themselves. Of these two, Mannan-Dar was exactly as they had planned, but His sister, Red Marn, was far too much the image of Ravenne. And Marn Herself was unhappy with what had been wrought, for She said "The path that Ravenne took when He was cast out is a path that He might take to return, for where once He has passed, He can pass again."

Then Goreb said "Not so, for there is no longer a vacancy here shaped for Ravenne. Creation, outside that one unlucky plane, does not know Him."

And Marn replied " Foolish God. Creation knows *Me*, and I am too close to that shape. He might snuff Me out and take that place which is mine."

Goreb was wroth at her slighting of Him, and rose up in His might. "Then I shall smite Thee, Godling, and so solve our ills at a blow."

Marn faced Him, unafraid and mocking. "An' you feel sufficient to that task, O mighty Warrior, lay on. For I am Magic – and more, for also I am Creation and Learning and Nature and Death and yet more, all from those who made me, and so shall I be too much for thee." But she frowned, and added "And too much like Ravenne. This must be mended, and at once. Brandur, lie with me."

And Brandur understood Her design and He lay with Her. Then did She bring forth Caeval, God of Death in Nature and of the Hunt, and His brother Jebel, God of Death by Artifice, and of the Harvest. Then she said "Now am I only Marn, God of Creativity and Learning and Magic and Art. God, above all, of Pleasure. Now is Ravenne's Way closed, for His shape is divided into three, and no one exists whom he can snuff out and replace.

And so came all the Younger Gods to be.

Then using the knowledge that Marn and Mannan-Dar brought from Isis, that was Ravenne, as well as the skills and wits that they could call their own, the two Gods of Magic together forged the Lens of Dreams that cast the patterns of Aether, woven by mortal mages, upon the Realms of Brandur. As this thing was being done, the Gods of Creation arranged Heart Magic into packets of tailored Power. These they made available to their Priests that they might work the dweomers which would succour and protect their people.

And now all was as Brandur had wished, and had striven so long to achieve, save that Aether, the key to magic, was unfortunately not equally available on all the Planes of Creation. Aether is the effusion that surrounds dragonlets in the egg, nurturing them as the magical creatures they are. When the dragonlet hatches this Aether, exceeding dense while in the egg, spreads wide.

Now dragons reside almost exclusively on Prime Material Plane Nine. The Aether flows very widely, and nearly as much is found on Plane Eight as on Nine. Slightly less reaches Plane Seven but still an ample sufficiency for all needs, and to spare. So it continues, with more than enough Aether still available on Planes Six, Five and Four. Plane Three, for various reasons, has no life, so no Aether is used there and thus there is a bare sufficiency for most essential purposes on Plane Two. However, almost no Aether reaches Plane One, and that which does is thin and unpredictable. Thus magic is rarely possible on Plane One, and when it is available it is woefully unreliable.

This was most frustrating, for Plane One was the Plane of origin of Humans, who after Elves were the most adept users of Magic in the Universes. Thus Brandur made two provisions. First, He arranged that certain physical characteristics of Plane One be slightly different from other Planes, so that all the peoples thereof might make comfortable environments for themselves. Most particularly, the atomic and subatomic structures of certain substances were slightly changed to make them more useful to humans.

This author has read extensively of the writings of the humans of this plane. A number speak of the 'Anthropomorphic Principle' and gaze in astonishment at a Universe that appears to have been designed for them. Did they but know it, this is exactly what's happened – or rather, if it was not initially designed for them, then at least it has been carefully restructured with them in mind.

However, these changes caused certain difficulties in the fabric of that Universe, and also by their use it was likely that Humans would slowly make their worlds uninhabitable, so Brandur also arranged that Humans might on occasion, by the permission of Lucifer, Lord of the Gate, pass into the Gate of Beliar and use it to reach points in other Universes where they might make a better life. He also arranged for some Humans to be actively collected and brought to the Upper Planes, where their aptitude with magic made them most useful additions to the population. However, Brandur arranged most carefully with Lucifer that nobody should easily be able to descend to the lower Planes by this means, as they are dangerous and not truly fit for people to live in. Particularly Plane One, of course.

These arrangements of Brandur enraged the Gods of Plane One, both those trapped there and those, such as the Shade of Goreb, who had descended there for other reasons.

These deities, bitterly opposed one to another as they were, still were all united in their opposition to their folk being removed, or enabled to escape to better places and they made every attempt to ensure that people would, at least, not willingly take such offers. They painted Brandur and Lucifer as the embodiment of evil and represented them so darkly as to ensure that folk would flee them or their emissaries.

Yet this met only modest and temporary success, and one day, strive as they will, these dark godlings will be left bereft of followers, trapped alone and impotent

Aye, so mote it be.

J. apC.

Books in this series...

The Realms of Beliar Book 1 Volume 1
The Sword Myndarit

The Realms of Beliar Book 1 Volume 2
A Beginning and an End

The Realms of Beliar Book 2
The Enemy of my Enemy...

The Realms of Beliar Book 3
...And Treat Those Two Impostors...

Lightning Source UK Ltd.
Milton Keynes UK
UKHW02n1404280618

324928UK00001B/7/P